LETHBRIDGE-STEWART

MOON BLINK

Based on the BBC television serials by
Mervyn Haisman & Henry Lincoln

Sadie Miller

Foreword by
Gary Russell

CANDY JAR BOOKS · CARDIFF
A Russell & Frankham-Allen Series
2016

The right of Sadie Miller to be identified as the
Author of the Work has been asserted by her in accordance
with the Copyright, Designs and Patents Act 1988.

Copyright © Sadie Miller 2016

Characters and Concepts from 'The Web of Fear'
© Hannah Haisman & Henry Lincoln
HAVOC developed by and © Andy Frankham-Allen & Shaun Russell
The Vault © Gary Russell

Doctor Who is © British Broadcasting Corporation, 1963, 2016.

Editor: Shaun Russell
Deputy Editor: Andy Frankham-Allen
Cover: Adrian Salmon
Editorial: Hayley Cox & Lauren Thomas
Licensed by Hannah Haisman

Published by
Candy Jar Books
Mackintosh House
136 Newport Road, Cardiff, CF24 1DJ
www.candyjarbooks.co.uk

A catalogue record of this book is available
from the British Library

ISBN: 978-0-9935192-0-8

For all my family

The Bump

I've known Sadie Miller all her life. Quite literally.

The first time I met her, she was a bump in her mum's tummy, in America, in November 1984. That was also the first time I met her fabulous mum, Elisabeth Sladen, coincidentally. It was a huuuuge *Doctor Who* convention in Chicago, where I was introduced to Elisabeth, and the 'bump', by the actor Nicholas Courtney, who I'd known for a few years. He was delighted to learn that a couple of chums and I had trekked all the way across 'the pond' to see him. It seemed churlish to point out we'd come to see him *and* a dozen other *Doctor Who* actors of course, especially as we were in the bar at the time and he was buying. Actor Ian Marter was there too, he and Nick having just done a turn in the evening cabaret, reciting a slightly revised version of Hayes' poem, *The Green Eye of the Little Yellow God*. I honestly cannot recall if Elisabeth had done a performance that night; my memory is that she hadn't, wanting a well-deserved rest after a long day conventioning. But she was walking outside the bar when Nick motioned her in and she sat with him and Ian for a few moments. And thus I was introduced to her. 'Call me Lis,' she said very quickly, which I thought was nice and charming for someone she didn't know. I guess being mates with her mates was a good personal reference.

Shortly after this event, Lis dropped out of the *Doctor Who* circuit for a while. She later told me that she found conventions hard, sometimes seeing her fellow actors exaggerating or indeed completely fabricating 'stories' to entertain the fans, and feeling that this was against the spirit of why she was there. 'If my stories aren't entertaining by being the truth, and heaven knows, I'm quite sure they *aren't* entertaining,' she said to me in 1991 in yet another bar, 'I'm certainly not going to try and *be* entertaining by lying to people.'

Lis had very firm morals and was very protective of both her own integrity and also that of her character, Sarah Jane Smith. I admired that. Sometimes, in our professional dealings over the subsequent years, it could also be frustrating, but I never lost my admiration for Lis' determination to remain 'pure and honest to the character' at all times.

A few months later, Lis invited me round to her West London home because I wanted to outline to her an idea I had to devote an entire *Doctor Who Magazine Special* (I was editing the thing by then) to Sarah Jane Smith, the centrepiece of which was to be an interview with her. I wasn't there to do the interview – I was being 'auditioned' to see whether or not she trusted me enough to put her back into the limelight. And that was when I met Sadie for the first time, who would have been seven or eight by then. Sadie wasn't shy about coming forward – in that respect she was absolutely her mother's daughter.

Sadie had been recently given a few VHS tapes of a TV

series I once appeared in and despite the fact that I looked nothing like I had in that show, Sadie was very interested and pretty much ended up interviewing me about it, in her own living room and getting me to sign a tie-in book or two. I think it was the fact I got Sadie's seal of approval that ultimately got me Lis'.

Over the years I saw, periodically, Sadie grow up into a confident, witty and oh-so-smart young lady who was, if I'm honest, the only person I ever saw argue with her mum and win. Concisely and absolutely. I argued with Lis a few times. I lost. Teenaged Sadie never lost.

At one point, I was running a company called Big Finish, purveyors of fine audio drama CDs based upon *Doctor Who*. I had, over nearly a year, convinced Lis to play Sarah Jane Smith once again in a mini-series. Lis wanted some involvement in all aspects – she vetted the storylines and writers, the actors and of course the director, which was me – at the time the only person she said she would allow to direct her. She asked for one favour; could I find a small role for Sadie, a couple of lines in one story? It was clearly a request, and not a demand. Precisely because of that, I created a regular part for Sadie, as Natalie Redfern, a wheelchair-bound reporter who would be Sarah's right-hand lady and researcher. As I said, this wasn't out of feeling I *had* to (Lis had made that clear; if there was no such part available, that was fine), but because I liked and respected Sadie and simply wanted to work with this amazing, funny girl I had seen so many times over the years.

A few years later I quit Big Finish, and began working for BBC Wales who were making *The Sarah Jane Adventures* and I went to the initial read-through for the pilot episode. I sat opposite Lis, and I think (well, okay, I know) she was very grateful to see a familiar face. Lis was always terribly confident on the outside but inside, to those she knew, she would always confess she had problems doing things like this. We talked late into the night once about whether, if this got picked up for a series, she should say yes and expose herself to the world of television again. Of course, I and a dozen of her other friends all told her the same thing. She was brilliant, amazing and a whole new generation would fall in love with Sarah Jane Smith. So I'm sure did Sadie, who would make periodic visits to the set once we were into the eventual series.

And then, five years later, Lis wasn't there anymore. Just like that. She'd kept the seriousness of her illness secret from so many, and so the shock of her passing was huge, and an amazing outpouring of grief from kids and adults all over the country was on TV and in the papers. For a lady who constantly refused to accept people adored her, or exploit her fame or success, Lis would have been amazed, genuinely, to discover just how beloved she was.

At her funeral, her amazing husband Brian read a poem he had read to her on their first date. Sadie read out messages from strangers, from the countless children who had written into the BBC about how sad they were. She read these beautifully, and proudly. Her mum was utterly loved by millions and she wanted those millions represented in some way at what was really a very private service.

I have never been prouder and more in awe of Sadie than I was at that point.

*

And now, here she is, writing a book set within the *Doctor Who* universe, about the Brigadier as played by Nicholas Courtney, the man who indirectly introduced me to her as that 'bump' all those years ago (coincidentally, Sadie discovered she had developed her own 'bump' mid-way through writing the book).

There is nothing Sadie Miller can't do, I reckon. Again, she gets a lot of that from Lis. But most of it comes from within her, because she is so damn talented.

And I'm honoured to have been allowed to call her my friend, since before she was born.

Gary Russell
New South Wales
March 2016

— PROLOGUE—

A new month and new files to read. Colonel Alistair Lethbridge-Stewart hadn't planned on remaining at the Chelsea Barracks so late but time had got away from him and now he was all alone in his office with only a straight whisky and a collection of top secret files for company. He knew he only had just under two months left until Dolerite Base was operational, and until then he had to continue to work out of the Barracks in London, trying his best to maintain his tenuous cover. He was looking forward to visiting Edinburgh, inspecting the base later in the month, but until then...

He eyed the stack of files, wondering where to begin. There was still much work to be done; a *lot* of homework for him to get through before he officially took command of the Home-Army Fifth Operational Corps, a new military taskforce affiliated with the Scots Guards, formed to deal with alien threats to the United Kingdom.

He opened the first manila folder and scanned its contents.

The *Space Race*, as it was euphemistically called by the press. It seemed that the Soviet and American space programmes had developed into something far more advanced than a mere schoolboy rivalry over who would be first to put man on the Moon – they were *already* there!

He sipped his whisky and took a deep breath.

No wonder so few had seen these files. They showed evidence of mining activity on the Moon, specifically with the intention of creating nuclear reactors using the excavated lunar material. He turned the page. The Russians had even gone so far as to install a complex gravity imitation system on their base, making it possible for men to work there just as easily as inside a nuclear control room back on Earth. The Americans, it seemed, had soon copied their technology with nothing staying secret for long, even on the Moon.

As if that wasn't surprising enough, the files continued to explain about the *British* Space Programme run by one Professor Ralph Cornish and the British Rocket Group, which was aiming beyond the Moon – to Mars itself. Only recently they had launched *Mars Probe 5*.

Lethbridge-Stewart looked up from the file. This was incredible. He hadn't even known there was a British Space Programme, never mind that it was arguably more successful than that of the Americans and Soviets. RHIP, he supposed. In this case the privilege was the knowledge of secrets that could get a man killed. Or worse.

He took another sip of his whisky and enjoyed for a moment its warming sensation as he looked out of the window across to the concrete towers that housed some of the Guards Regiments' four companies. The dusky summer light dappled across the desk and he closed the file.

It is already late, he thought. *No need to rush.*

The sun had not quite finished setting but already the Moon had appeared in the sky. Lethbridge-Stewart watched as they shared the horizon for a moment. He found himself calling to mind the words of Sally Wright, his fiancée. She wasn't one for silly sentiment but her last parting words had struck a chord with him.

'Whenever we are apart, know that we are looking at the same Moon.'

That's all very well, Lethbridge-Stewart thought. *The more pertinent question is who on the Moon is looking back?*

He shuddered. Lunar bases, the forthcoming Moon landing… He'd never look at the Moon the same way again.

Demetrius' feet rang out as he walked quickly through the corridor. He didn't dare run; there was no running within *Gagarin Base*. Besides, if he ran someone would know something was amiss and Demetrius knew he couldn't risk anybody finding out something was wrong.

The base had been completed six months ago. Back in the Ukraine he had been one in a long line of builders working at the shipyards at Odessa, and his family had been one of the first to utilise the connection between nuclear power and the propulsion of ships. He had had no idea he was working on a lunar base until he had woken up there several months back, and now he knew he was trapped there until whoever was running the base decided they could return to Earth.

Helium-3 had been mined successfully from the lunar surface and now he was helping to build the fusion reactors. Things had been going to plan until the Soviets had realised that they were not the only people who had discovered the Helium-3 rich crater crusts. Now an American base was stationed just the other side of Plinius, visible but far enough away to not have caused any problems for them – yet. But the Americans were not the only ones on Mare Tranquillitatis.

There had long been rumours of aliens, spacemen living on the Moon too, but it wasn't until the week before that Demetrius had realised that one of those stories was actually true.

It hadn't been hard to lose, Demetrius thought as he continued his pursuit. Why did it have to look exactly the same? Why couldn't it have been green with strange shaped heads and eyes like the stories he had heard as a child? But these aliens were nothing like anything he had ever read about as a little *rebenok*. This one had wanted him to know it was an alien, it had left out the special powder, and ever since then it was all Demetrius could see. Now Demetrius kept his head down as he made his way through the maze of corridors, keeping his eyes low as he watched the alien figure nimbly slip its way past the others on board.

No one seemed to take any notice of it and Demetrius quickened his pace. He could call out, get someone to stop it, but he didn't want to be known as the man who let one of them escape. He needed to be here, his bosses had made sure he knew his family were counting on him to complete the mission, otherwise they would never see a ruble of his salary payment.

The alien came to the exit and Demetrius saw it reaching for the door handle, struggling when it found it locked. Quickly Demetrius reached for his respirator, sliding it over his mouth and breathing in the oxygen, his lungs expanding gratefully as he stepped forward to the pull the alien back from the door, but the figure was too quick for him. The door suddenly gave way and the figure stumbled out onto the rocky, uneven surface.

Once outside the confines of the base, the figure moved nimbly, almost gliding across the otherwise impassable surface. Demetrius closed the door quickly, the warning alarms signalling that a door had been open. Helplessly he watched as the figure climbed over the divide and ducked under the bridge, making his way towards the US base.

'*Chto zdes proishodit?*'

Someone was shouting behind him. Demetrius shrugged his shoulders, casting one last glance across the now deserted Mare Tranquillitatis. The alien was somebody else's problem.

Over in *Horizon Base*, the figure straightened itself, its clothes suddenly matching the uniform of the new base, fading from blood red to a deep royal blue. It was not the first time it had walked between the two sides; it knew exactly how to manipulate its appearance so as to be accepted without question. All at once it became a male with pale eyes and tanned skin, complimented by thick blond hair; the all-American poster boy. He passed through the corridor unnoticed, making his way into the control room.

'Where did you get to, Bobby?' Nick said, turning away from the control panel he was manning, the younger man at his side turning around too, the multiple screens behind them all blinking as one as the machine interface continued to control and monitor the critical operations of the base.

'Just fancied a walk,' Bobby said to his erstwhile colleagues. 'Stretch my legs.'

'Thought you might have cut out on us there,' Nick said,

looking Bobby up and down with an air of suspicion, as he always did. Cabin fever was beginning to set in, and for Nick it was worse than most.

'Not far to walk to,' Jed muttered morosely, no doubt thinking longingly about the long stretches of road and river in his Mid-Western hometown.

'What did I miss?' Bobby asked, taking up his seat beside them.

'Nothing much, just working on the Moon, no big deal.' Nick reached out to punch him playfully in the ribs, but Bobby moved easily out of his reach.

'Freeze dried strawberries?' Bobby asked, dryly.

'Naw, I'm sick of all this rehydrated crap, I want some real food!'

'Cool your chops and listen up,' Nick said. 'I've got something you're going to want to hear. A rumour.'

'What kind of a rumour?' Bobby wondered if he responded a little too quickly.

Nick paused and stretched out his jaw, not seeming to notice. 'One that sounds like maybe we could all be going home soon. Real soon.'

'I don't buy it,' Jed said. 'They don't seem like they're done with us yet.'

'Who aren't?' Bobby asked, a note of suspicion creeping into his voice.

'Whoever it is we're working for.'

'Oh, sure. Them.'

'You thought I was going to say something else, huh?' Nick got to his feet, his hands rising to his thick hips.

Bobby shrugged. 'Possibly. But I don't mind being wrong.'

6

The colour flamed in Nick's cheeks. 'You trying to say something about me? That I always got to be right?'

'Not at all.'

'No, I can take it. Lay it on me.'

'Stop it, Nick,' Jed said, shifting in his seat. 'Ain't no point lip flapping when we all have to be here 'til who knows when.'

'There are others you know,' Nick said darkly. 'And I'm not just talking about guys like us! Others.'

'Don't go saying stuff like that,' Jed said, his eyes bulging with fright. 'There's no one here except us and those guys across the way.'

Nick turned to Bobby. 'Where did you say you came from again?'

Bobby blinked at him. His eyes darted around the room quickly, avoiding Nick's gaze. Nick began to pace around the small, cramped space.

'You see, me and Jed here were working at the same plant in Monroe, Michigan. I was there when the odium cooling system malfunctioned, caused a partial core meltdown. I've seen things you wouldn't believe.'

Bobby said nothing. He was still looking around him, his eyes searching for a name, anything that could give him an alibi, buy himself some time. He should never have tried to fit in with them, he realised. He had only wanted to know who these men were that came to his planet, but it was too late now. Beneath Jed's uniform he could just about see the stamped blue logo of one of his t-shirts from home; *Discotronic Funk Commandoes: Detroit Michigan.*

'Detroit,' he said quickly.

'What nuclear plant you been working at there?' Nick

7

scoffed. 'None that I heard of!'

'I was working in a laboratory,' Bobby said, confident with the word. Nick narrowed his eyes.

'So if you're really a Michigander, what's your team? I'm a Wolverines man myself. Who's yours down in Detroit? Go on,' Nick pressed. 'Who's your team?'

Bobby remained silent; he could see from the pulsing muscle in Nick's cheek that he was about to lose his temper.

'Pistons or Titans; could have gone for either one! So if you're no Flatlander, who are you really?'

Bobby didn't respond.

'I bet your name isn't really even Bobby either, is it?'

Bobby got to his feet, his hands shaking as he grappled in the pockets of his uniform, searching for something.

'What you doing, Bobby?' Jed asked him nervously, but Bobby didn't answer. Jed turned to Nick like a child looking for reassurance. 'What's he doing? Hey, Bobby, what's the matter with you?'

Jed shook him, but Bobby didn't answer. Then all at once his hands stopped shaking; he had found the item in his pocket. He looked across at Nick and Jed in silence.

The whole room seemed to close in on them. Jed's heart pounded in his chest, the sweat on his head trickled down... Slowly, slowly.

'I'm scared,' Jed said, his protruding teeth biting down onto his lower lip. 'Do something, Nick! Make him talk!'

Nick stepped forward, his hand balled into a fist, but Bobby held his hand up, signalling for him to wait. Nick held back, confused for a moment.

'Take this,' Bobby said, stepping forwards suddenly and handing something to Jed. 'It will make you feel better. It will help you see them, then you won't need to be afraid anymore.'

'Don't touch nothing from him,' Nick said, charging over to get between the two of them. 'He's one of them, I know he is! He's going to try and kill you!'

Jed looked up at Bobby, and then down to the small parcel in his hand. It was a rock, purple in colour, a hard centre with a crumbling exterior, leaving a white cast on his palm. The powder of the rock was rising into the air, tickling at his nasal cavities. Behind him Nick started to wheeze.

'What the heck...?' He gasped.

The powder was glistening and sparkling like a biotite. Jed stared at it and then looked back up to Bobby. His mouth hung open in surprise and fear as he saw the eyes in Bobby's head begin to widen.

'Holy–' Nick began, darting across to the wall of the small room, his hand reaching for the emergency lever.

Bobby stood in front of Jed, turning into something that wasn't human. He reached out a hand.

'Don't!' Jed called after Nick. 'It's still just Bobby, he doesn't want to do us no harm!'

But it was too late. The emergency sirens were already going off, the red lights flashing across the whole of the station. Jed looked back at Bobby. There would be no escape for him now.

CHAPTER ONE

The Eagle Has Landed

The location of the Vault was innocuous enough, none of the very infrequent passers-by would ever have dreamed of the terrible secrets that lay beneath the sweeping vista of green and yellow slopes that straddled the Anglo-Scots border. Anne Travers had learned a lot since joining the Vault and seen many things, some of which she wished she hadn't. On reflection she wasn't sure if she would have chosen to be there, but she couldn't resist the opportunity to learn things most of her colleagues in the scientific community would have killed to learn. That she was working there as a kind of spy for the British military only added to the risk, but she'd seen enough in the last few months to know that the risk was worth it. Now she was beginning to feel restless again, longing for the freedom to work under her own steam. She held her handbag close to her, the telegram and its message concealed safely inside. A trip to see her father was a welcome distraction, despite his strangely urgent and cryptic message.

Tim Gambrell, a fellow scientist at the Vault, and possibly the only one she'd consider a friend, had dropped her off at the nearest train station. The traffic moved quickly; it seemed no one wanted to be on the roads tonight. There was a strange calm in the air that Anne couldn't quite put her finger on. By the time they reached the station to catch the last train of the evening, the platforms were empty and there was no one to share her carriage with, for which Anne was grateful.

The train pulled away and she took a moment to look out of the window and watch the station disappear into a cloud of steam before settling down to examine the telegram again. Her father was often sending her odd requests, which usually called for Anne to go and see him in person to fully appreciate their meaning, but something about this one seemed different. She noted he had sent it to her brother, Alun, too, though there was no explanation yet as to why.

The journey didn't take long but Anne was exhausted; she was often kept underground in the darkness of the Vault, only to come out into the night at the end of it. She slept fitfully in the empty carriage; the rocking motions of the train soothing her into a brief dreamless sleep.

It was very late by the time Anne's train had pulled into Kings Cross Station. She hailed a taxi, which took her to the doorstep of her father's house, situated in the borough of Kensington and Chelsea at St James's Gardens. As she opened the door she could already hear her father clattering around inside, the house in total darkness. She sidestepped across a pile of papers and a stack of books, the top volume in Nepalese with a title that Anne roughly translated as *Mountain Man*. She felt along the hallway for the light switch.

'Hello?' Anne called out. There was no reply. She looked around the house. It was so chaotic, not like the order she insisted on at her small bungalow in Kilham. She wondered how her father could think straight living there.

'Hello?' she called out again. 'Is anyone home?'

She made her way into the back of the house. Her father was racing around the living room frenetically, items of clothes and open books strewn about on every side. She wondered what time Alun had arrived and felt annoyed that he hadn't tried to make some kind of order.

As she made her way into the living room she could see her father was hunched over; his hair at odd angles as he busied himself with an object on the side table.

'Father?' she said.

It took a few more moments for him to realise she was there. As soon as he turned and saw her, he stood and ran towards her in one motion. 'Anne!' he said, clasping her close to him. 'You made it!' Childish delight spread across his heavily lined face. Anne looked at him quizzically, wondering what on earth could have come over him. 'I'm so glad to have the opportunity to share this moment with at least one of my children.'

Ah, Anne thought ruefully, *that explains the mess.* So Alun clearly hadn't made it after all. He was never the best at managing his own time, much preferring to stay firmly ensconced in the past.

'Yes,' Anne said. 'I got your message. Your very *urgent* message,' she added pointedly, pulling out the telegram from her handbag.

Her father nodded, his face suddenly serious. 'Indeed,' he said. 'I have a surprise for you.'

He stepped to the side so that Anne could see into the cluttered room behind him.

'Behold!' he said with a flourish.

Anne was nonplussed. 'What am I looking for?' she asked. She really did not enjoy these eccentric games her father liked to play, especially not in the small hours of the morning.

'This!'

Anne eyed the nineteen-inch colour TV on the table behind him.

'I took the liberty of purchasing it for the occasion. What do you think? Oh! I'm forgetting my manners. Would you like something to eat, drink? I suppose it must be getting very late, I must admit I do lose track of time these days, not much of it left for me now so important to make the most of it. How's the Vault treating you? Alun was most put out you wouldn't fill him in. Spending lots of time in that dark inhospitable place I presume?'

'Yes, actually.'

Her father chuckled with delight. *He doesn't know how right he is,* Anne thought. He continued to bustle around her, asking her question after question before she could even think to answer just one of them.

'Sorry, you must forgive me, it's been so long since I saw you and there's so much I want to ask, but take a seat, my dear Anne, you must be tired. Take a seat.'

'Just you and me then, is it, Father?' Anne asked, looking around her to see if any of her father's guests were still in evidence.

'Yes, just us two,' he confirmed, sitting down next to her.

'Alun won't be joining us then? Your telegram mentioned you had invited him also.'

'Well it's a long way for him, isn't it, from Oxford?' her father said. 'I'm sure he's far too busy with teaching work in any case.'

'While Northumberland is just around the corner,' Anne remarked.

'Besides,' her father said, ignoring her comment and reaching out to squeeze her hand conspiratorially. 'Alun will be teaching about today for years to come I shouldn't wonder.'

'I think you'll find I'm the one who looks to the future, Father. Alun is much more interested in what has come before. The real world doesn't sit so well with him.'

'Perhaps not,' her father mused. 'But we make history in every moment, Anne. Besides, history tells us so much about what the future will bring. You just have to look closely enough.'

He got to his feet a little unsteadily and made his way over to the bureau at the edge of the room, squashed into an alcove it shared with a stack of boxes piled up high on each side. He selected one of the half-filled decanters, pouring out a tumbler of the dark liquid for both Anne and himself. He returned to his chair and passed across her the drink. Anne took it and the two of them chinked glasses in an almost silent cheers.

'Good health,' her father said after swallowing down a couple of gulps. 'Ah, I needed that after struggling with that monstrosity over there for half the evening. Who would have thought such a small box could be so much trouble?'

'What time is it?' Anne asked, looking around at the clocks, which all showed different times. She glanced down at her wristwatch for confirmation.

'Almost time!' her father said excitedly, getting to his feet again and smiling at her with delight. 'We're nearly ready,

Anne!'

Anne watched him make his way across to the television and, after a few fumbling moments, switch it on. The screen crackled for a moment, then the blackness lit up with moving pictures.

'What is going on, Father? You didn't make me come all the way down to London to show me a new television set.'

'On the contrary! I called you here to witness tonight's important event with me, a once in our lifetime experience to be shared together.'

The penny dropped loudly in Anne's tired mind. 'The Moon landing,' she said quietly. With spending all her days underground, she had almost forgotten it was happening.

'Can you believe it?' her father was saying over and over, more to himself than to Anne.

'No,' she replied dryly. 'At least, I can't believe they're putting people on the Moon and letting the whole world watch.'

'But of course,' her father replied. 'The Americans are the winners of the *Space Race* as they liked to call it; they want to show the whole world the victory over the Russians!'

Anne sank down further into the plush old armchair, dislodging a stack of papers and a rather angry cat that had been dozing underneath the cushion.

'Careful now,' her father said crossly. 'I didn't bring Sasquatch all the way back from Tibet to have her meet a sticky end now.'

The small black cat glared at her, its amber eyes wide with unconcealed malevolence. Anne made a hissing noise at it under her breath, and the cat jumped down to the floor,

15

still looking at her darkly. Her father reached across to squeeze Anne's hand.

'I had hoped that you of all people could appreciate the joy of this momentous occasion, to see how far we have come as a species, that we may actually one day find ourselves colonising another planet.'

Anne's mouth felt suddenly dry. She sipped at her tumbler of whisky and wondered what turn tonight was going to take. Her father was still lost in his own world, his eyes shining with all the possibilities he was imagining in his mind.

'We are so fortunate,' he began. 'To have experienced first-hand the wonders of alien intelligence, wouldn't you agree, Anne?'

Anne's mind flickered to the darkest corners of the Vault, the unclaimed bodies and the extra-terrestrial secrets she had uncovered. 'Of course, Father,' she said. 'But don't you think that perhaps humanity is safer living within the comfortable and blissful ignorance of Earth?'

Her father nodded but he was only half listening to her now. '*Those seized with fright by the full Moon are visited by a goddess.* Do you know who said that?'

'Hippocrates.'

'Ah! Yes, indeed. Father of modern medicine, and even he could not explain away the allure of the Moon.'

'He also said, *there are in fact two things, science and opinion; the former begets knowledge, the latter ignorance.* These Moon landings may prove more problematic than enlightening. People are not always ready to receive the information science reveals to us,' Anne pointed out.

Her father coughed. 'Yes, well perhaps so but I think

that's enough for now.' He tired quickly of quotes when he was not the one espousing them. 'Get yourself comfortable. Should be almost time now.'

He got up to change the channel, then resumed his seat, sipping at his tumbler of whisky as he watched the screen with unblinking eyes. Anne found her eyes drawn to Sasquatch who was cleaning herself rather theatrically on the carpet. Anne wasn't quite ready yet to see what the Moon had in store for them tonight.

'Oh, Anne, you look so tired and terribly pale – go and take a look in the kitchen. I made some awfully good meatballs with grape jelly for Sasquatch, if I do say so myself. I'm sure there must be some leftover.'

'No, thank you,' Anne said. 'There was a buffet car on the train. Besides I–'

'Sshh!' her father hissed, holding his finger in the air to silence her. 'Look! It's starting!'

Black and white pictures began to form on the television screen. Her father turned to her, his face shining, clearly missing the irony of forking out for a colour television to watch an event transmitted in black and white. Sasquatch eyed them from her position on the floor. Anne looked from her father to the television screen. The picture was grainy, the audio crackling making it hard to hear exactly what was being said between the Eagle lunar module and Mission Control, Huston. Anne watched as Eagle touched down in Mare Tranquillitatis.

'I'm going to step off the LM now.' Astronaut Neil Armstrong was taking his first steps onto the Moon. 'That's one small step for man. One giant leap for mankind.'

It was so unbelievable, it didn't look quite real, though

Anne was in little doubt that it was. There was no way the Americans would risk doing something so dangerous as falsifying a Moon landing; public opinion would never recover. Anne glanced down at her wristwatch. 3.56am, but she felt wide awake.

She watched as Armstrong continued to take his first steps across the lunar surface, which looked to her both hard and soft at once, powdery in texture rather like a desert. He moved slowly, bouncing from side to side, a little like a drunk at closing time. There was plenty of back and forth between Armstrong and Mission Control, most of it seemingly directed at his sample collecting. Anne squinted to try and get a better look, but the picture quality was just too poor. She wondered what discoveries lay in wait in the deep craters, wide as football pitches.

Armstrong was not alone for long. Fellow astronaut Edwin Aldrin soon joined him.

'Beautiful view,' Mission Control commented as Aldrin moved across the surface.

'Isn't that something? Magnificent sight out here,' Aldrin said.

'Beautiful,' Anne found herself echoing in spite of herself. 'Isn't it, Father?' She glanced across at her father, but his eyes were closed, his chin sinking down to meet his chest as his belly rose and fell rhythmically, the air rushing in and out of his nostrils, making a soft, sonorous sound. Anne smiled to herself.

All the preparation and he had tired himself out, falling asleep at the most crucial moment.

She reached across and covered him with the throw, Sasquatch dutifully pottering over and making herself comfortable on the toes of his slippers.

'To bed with you,' Dougie said, ruffling his son's hair.

Jacob, his dressing gown tight around him, pyjama legs poking out, looked up from his position on the floor before the telly. 'Aww, Dad! Can't I stay up a bit longer?'

Dougie turned to his wife, and she shook her head.

Lethbridge-Stewart watched the domestic scene with a half-smile, and noticed Sally glancing his way. He knew what she was thinking; *one day that'll be us, Alistair.* He pretended to not notice. She may have been right, or she may not have. He still wasn't sure.

Jacob approached Lethbridge-Stewart and reached out a hand. 'Goodnight, Uncle Alistair,' the boy said, and they shook hands.

'Goodnight, Private,' Lethbridge-Stewart said, with a smile, and stood himself. He yawned unexpectedly. He'd had a busy day, and a long night. Time for home and sleep.

Dougie waited for Penny to take Jacob out of the living room, before turning to Lethbridge-Stewart and Sally. 'Well, that should put the cat among the pigeons,' he said, referring to the Moon landing.

'Yes,' Lethbridge-Stewart said, and handed his car keys to Sally. 'Can you get the car warmed up? I need a moment with Colonel Douglas.'

'Just one night off, Alistair,' Sally said, shaking her head. 'Is that too much to ask?' She pecked Dougie on the cheek. 'See you soon,' she said, and left the room to say goodbye to Penny and Jacob.

'Yes, well. Sorry about that.'

'Trouble and strife,' Dougie said, with a light smile.

'Hand in hand with marriage.'

'Yes, quite.' Once he was certain they were alone, Lethbridge-Stewart said, 'The Moon landing… You don't know the half of it, Colonel.'

Immediately, Dougie's posture changed and he became Lieutenant Colonel Walter Douglas. 'Was it faked?'

'Oh no. But I don't think the Americans know about *our* space programme.'

'Sir?'

'I'll show you the file tomorrow, now that General Hamilton has approved it, but needless to say that the UK is aiming beyond the Moon.'

Douglas nodded. 'I see. When do we leave for Scotland?' he asked, changing the subject.

'Two days. Just a few things to tie up at the Barracks, hand Bishop over to Hamilton, and then we're off.' Lethbridge-Stewart looked at the television, where the programme about the Moon landing continued. 'We really are drawing attention to ourselves, aren't we?'

'Which is bound to be bad news for Earth,' Douglas agreed.

A few hours later, Anne was awake. She made her way downstairs to find her father still in the living room. He was struggling with the television, which he had nestled on his lap, several cups of tea surrounding him, all of which looked as if they had gone cold.

'Missed it!' he kept muttering to himself. 'Bloody missed it!'

'Everything all right, Father?' He didn't respond, his attention still engrossed in the back of the television. She asked again.

'Why didn't you wake me?' he said, turning to her with the pursed lips of a petulant child.

Anne laid her hand on his arm. 'I didn't realise you had fallen asleep,' she said.

'Asleep? I was just resting my eyes,' he countered gruffly. 'No, it's this blasted television set! Must have tuned it to the wrong channel. Missed it!'

Anne watched him for a moment but said nothing. She didn't want to ruin it for him. 'Well it's been lovely to see you, Father, but I really must be getting back to work now.'

Anne moved to the hallway to collect her things, the single bag she had brought with her resting against the leg of the hall table, Sasquatch sitting on it territorially. Her father appeared beside her, his eyes blinking at her through his spectacles, his hair still wildly clumped on one side as if he had slept in the chair all night.

'Not staying for breakfast? You must take care of yourself, Anne, you never know when someone might come and take you away from all this work you do in that deep dark hole.'

'Yes, Father.' She agreed with him about the Vault, but she wasn't about to give up on her solo scientific endeavours quite yet. 'But I don't want to miss my train.'

'Oh, come now, there will always be another one along shortly. Can't tempt you to a tea? You must have something before you go; it's not good for the mind, working on an empty stomach.'

At the mention of food Anne could feel her insides starting to growl, and after a moment's hesitation she let her father take her back towards the kitchen, where he began hunting through the cupboards, which were filled with jars and specimens that belonged in a laboratory rather than a domestic kitchen.

'Porridge?' he offered finally. 'There's a bag of Scottish raw oats, no milk mind, but it's just as nice with water. Your mother used to make it beautiful with just water, do you remember?'

Anne didn't reply. She didn't often like to think of her mother, it was like a jarring shard of light piercing through the darkness of her memory.

'Let's get the kettle on – oh, I seem to have used all the mugs.'

'Just porridge is fine,' Anne said, distracted as she started to move around the kitchen. She didn't particularly want to get back to the Vault, but an evening with her father was about as much as she could take.

As she made her way around the kitchen island something caught her eye. She walked across to the fridge and then paused to look at a postcard pinned behind a rather gaudy magnet of Mount Everest.

'What's this?' she asked, retrieving the postcard from the fridge.

'Oh, that came for you,' her father said distractedly.

Anne turned it over in her hands. It was from the Kennedy Space Centre Complex, Florida. She sat down at the table and began to read.

Dearest Anne, it began. *Have taken a trip down from Washington to the sunshine of Florida for vacation, heading up to Huston soon. Apollo 11 mission commencing in two weeks. Heading across the pond week after, can't wait to see those Northumberland hills. Fondest love, Patricia.*

'When did you say this arrived?' Anne asked glancing at the postmark.

'Hmm? Oh a fortnight ago perhaps, I forget now,' her father called back, stirring the hot pan full of the thickening oats. 'Nothing important I presume? Nothing important gets sent on a postcard.'

'I'm not sure,' Anne admitted. With all the hub of space activity going on in the States, she couldn't imagine why Patricia would choose now as a time to come and make a trip to England.

— CHAPTER TWO —

The New Moon

The following week, just as her postcard had promised, Anne's friend and former colleague, Doctor Patricia Richards, made her way from Washington DC to England. Patricia had even called her the night before and Anne had dutifully offered to meet her flight at Heathrow Airport. But Patricia had declined, saying that she couldn't possibly ask Anne to come all the way down to London. Barely anybody came to call on Anne now that she was so far out of the way, so she was glad about Patricia coming to see her small place. But something at the back of her mind was telling her that, perhaps, Patricia wasn't being completely honest with her.

Still, Anne found herself sitting patiently in her cosy bungalow living room waiting for the purr of Patricia's taxi. As it pulled up outside, she rushed to open the door and greet her old friend. But Patricia was already out of the car and hurrying forwards to greet her.

'Oh, it's so good to see you, Anne!' Patricia said, as she threw her arms around her old friend, her voice flavoured with an American twang.

'And you!' Anne looked across Patricia's shoulder to the taxi, which was piled high with luggage.

Patricia hugged her tightly, then pulled away saying,

'Enough of all that. Now let me get a good look at you.'

She smiled at Anne who studied her in return. To Anne, Patricia looked just the same, if perhaps a little tired. Her straight black hair was pulled back from her face; her dark eyes shining with delight, faint purple bags concealed beneath a soft layer of make-up. *Yes*, Anne thought, *there was something different about her*, although Anne couldn't quite put her finger on what.

'You look just the same, Anne!' Patricia exclaimed. 'Whenever I see you it is like no time has passed at all.'

The engine of the taxi was still purring in the driveway, the driver half leaning out of the window, puffing out his cheeks to attract their attention.

'Come on, Pat. Let me help you with your bags,' Anne said, making her way towards the waiting taxi, much to the obvious relief of the driver.

'Oh no,' Patricia said quickly. 'Don't worry about that, Anne. I can manage.' She hurriedly left Anne standing alone in the doorway. 'You stay inside,' she called back to Anne, motioning for her to go into the cottage. 'No use standing out here getting cold. I'll only be a moment.'

'All right, if you're sure,' Anne said. She watched her friend suspiciously for a moment, then went back into the hallway and waited.

She peered from the window as Patricia unloaded her bags one by one, but the evening was growing dark and from behind the net curtains it was hard to make out what Patricia had brought. Anne was surprised Patricia seemed to have so much with her in any case. It was almost as if this were more than just a visit, as if she were planning to stay with Anne for some length of time. The prospect made Anne feel nervous. She was very happy to see Patricia, but her life was not one that made entertaining guests an easy task.

'Is that everything?' Anne called out when she heard Patricia step back over the threshold.

'Yes, I think so!' Patricia's head appeared from the front door. 'You couldn't do me one favour though, could you, Annie?'

Here we go, Anne thought. 'What's that?' she asked.

'I don't think I quite got my currency conversion right. Would you mind paying the cab fare for me? I'll pay you back just as soon as I get my bearings.'

'Of course.' Anne gave an inward sigh of relief. 'I'll just go and get my purse.'

She went into the kitchen to retrieve her handbag. By the time she got back to the door Patricia seemed to have disappeared. 'Patricia?' she called. 'Pat?'

There was no reply, but Anne could see the rug had turned over in the corner. *Looks like Patricia has found the guest room.*

She heard the voice of the taxi driver calling to her from outside, accompanied by a very loud honk of his horn. Anne grabbed her purse and rushed outside. When she got there, his puffed up face was looking at her from the open window, his cheeks red.

'Look here, love, I don't want to be rude, but do you think one of you could pay me so I can get back to town?'

'Oh, yes, here,' Anne apologised. 'Sorry to keep you waiting. How much is it?'

The taxi driver answered her gruffly again and Anne paid up. 'Cute,' she heard him say as she headed back towards the house.

'Pardon?' Anne asked, turning back to him in surprise.

'The little fella with her,' the driver said. 'Very good he was. Quiet the whole way from the station.'

Anne looked at him quizzically. 'I think you must be thinking of someone else,' she said. 'Patricia has been travelling alone.'

'I know what I saw. He was with your friend who just went back inside,' the cabby said, thumbing in the direction of the bungalow.

'Right,' Anne said, deciding to ignore him. 'Was there anything else?'

'Nope, the fare is all paid. Anyway, thanks again!' He pulled out of the driveway and disappeared back onto the misty evening roads.

Anne watched him go, wondering to whom he could have been referring. Patricia had been completely alone. Perhaps it was someone dropping her off at the station, or maybe a colleague came in on the flight with her? Anne didn't have much time to ruminate on the matter before she heard Patricia calling out from the open door.

'Was it all right? Not too expensive? I never know how much I should tip on this side of the pond.'

'Everything was fine,' Anne said, raising her hand and making her way back towards the cottage.

'Thanks for that,' Patricia said gratefully, and then she leaned in to embrace Anne again. 'It really is so good to see you. I almost thought I might not make it here at all.'

Anne's ears pricked up. 'Really? Why is that?'

'Oh, nothing important I was just running late for my flight, that's all,' Patricia said dismissively. 'But enough about me. Come on, let's go sit down and catch up properly.'

'So, how long are you visiting for?' Anne asked.

'Oh, I haven't quite decided yet.'

'I see. Was it work that brought you to England?'

'Of sorts.' Patricia was still giving nothing away. 'But let's not talk about that now, Anne; we have so many more interesting things to catch up on.'

'Absolutely. But one more thing, Pat...'

'Yes?'

Anne hesitated. 'Where are you staying?'

There was a pause.

'Actually, I was hoping I might be able to stop with you?' Patricia said, flashing that old cheeky smile of hers. 'There's an urgent situation I desperately need your advice on. I won't be in the way, I promise.'

'Ah.' That strange feeling she had felt at Patricia's postcard returned in an instant. Anne should have known there was something funny going on. But if it was her advice Patricia needed then Anne would do everything she could to help.

'How was your day at work?' Patricia asked, quickly changing the subject. 'I hear you're working for a covert government organisation now.'

'Not covert enough, clearly,' Anne said wryly. 'But I took the afternoon off. It's been a long time since we've seen each other. I didn't want to have to rush away.'

'That was very kind of you,' Patricia said.

Anne smiled and patted Patricia's knee. 'What else was I supposed to do? Now, I'll go and make us some tea.'

Anne watched her friend from across the kitchen. They were

from similar backgrounds, both studying hard to make their way in their chosen scientific fields. They had first met in the arid dryness of the Nevada desert, had become instant firm friends the moment Anne had joined the think-tank there, but Anne couldn't remember her friend being so secretive before.

'Here we are,' Anne said, handing over a cup. 'I think I have some fruit loaf in the cupboard somewhere.'

Patricia examined the teacup as if the leaves inside might somehow tell her future.

'The best family China is still in my apartment back in America,' Anne explained. 'But the Yorkshire tea set should still be just fine.'

'Everything looks good,' Patricia said, sipping nervously at the cup. It was getting dark outside. 'How wild it is here,' she said, looking out from Anne's kitchen window across the fields. 'You could get lost out there forever.'

Anne stirred her cup, not so easily distracted. 'It really is so good to see you, Pat, but I must ask you something.'

'Of course. Ask away.'

'All right. You said you had an urgent matter you needed my advice on, that was why you needed to stay with me?'

'Oh yes,' Patricia said, pushing aside her cup. 'The only problem, Annie, is I don't really know where to begin. This story has many twists and turns and I'm almost a little afraid that you won't believe it all.'

'I have seen my fair share of the strange and peculiar,' Anne said. 'Nothing you can say will seem far-fetched, trust me.'

Patricia took a deep breath and Anne waited expectantly. Then, rather annoyingly, the doorbell rang. Patricia's face paled.

'Are you all right?' Anne asked. 'You've gone positively white.'

'Oh yes, I'm quite well,' Patricia said dismissively, taking another loud sip of tea. 'I suppose it's just a little jet lag. I'm sure I will recover by this evening if I make an early night of it.'

Anne wasn't sure she believed her. 'I'll just go and see who that is.'

Not wanting more guests, Anne reached for the door. *Perhaps it's Patricia's mystery man*, she thought idly. Instead, to her surprise, she found Bill Bishop on her porch. Anne almost didn't recognise him at first, so rare was it that she saw him out of uniform.

'Good afternoon,' Anne said a little too formerly. 'I wasn't expecting you, was I?' She was certain Bill didn't know her home address.

'Ah, no, I'm afraid you weren't,' Bill admitted, his face colouring slightly. 'I hope I'm not disturbing you? I suppose it should really be good evening now.'

'Not at all,' Anne said. 'But I do have someone staying with me.'

'Oh,' Bill said. 'I didn't think Doctor Richards was due to arrive until tomorrow.'

Anne looked at him, startled. 'She arrived this afternoon. How did you know Doctor Richards was coming? More to the point, how do you and Doctor Richards know one another at all?'

'He came because I called him!' Patricia's voice said brightly, appearing around the corner and into the hallway.

Her face lit up as soon as she saw Bill. 'Lance Corporal Bishop, I'm so glad to see you. I presume you got my message?'

'I did, but not sure how you got my personal number.'

Patricia smiled. 'I do know how to use a telephone directory.'

'I must admit, you got here quicker than I expected.'

Anne looked from Bill to Patricia, and then back again. 'If you expected her tomorrow, why are you here now?'

'I've been in the area carrying out some liaison work for General Hamilton,' Bill explained. 'The general gave me your address, so I thought I'd drop by and say hello. I hope everything was all right getting through customs?' he added, looking at Patricia.

'Oh yes, that was no problem. There's a guy I know, and he gave me a helping hand—'

Anne couldn't stand listening to them any longer. She needed answers now. 'Just what is going on here?' she asked, deliberately cutting Patricia short.

'Well,' Patricia began, 'when I knew I was going to be making a trip across the pond, I telephoned to say it would be lovely to finally meet Bill in person, after hearing so much about him from you, Anne.'

Anne didn't say anything, skilfully avoiding Bill's gaze. She didn't buy it for a second.

'All good I hope?' Bill asked with a smile.

'Oh yes, absolutely!' Patricia nodded. 'Isn't that right, Anne?'

Anne coloured slightly. 'I think I'll go and put the kettle on. My tea has gone cold. Excuse me,' she said.

Bishop glanced after Anne for a moment.

'Come on in then, Lance Corporal,' Patricia said, leading the way inside. 'Time for both of us to make ourselves at home.'

'How was your flight?' Bishop asked politely, closing the door behind him. 'And it's just corporal. Military protocol.'

'A little bumpy,' Patricia said. 'But I'm used to it by now. I fly interstate on a regular basis. And, okay, noted.'

Bishop looked out for Anne for a moment, and then settled himself down at the table in the chair next to Patricia. It didn't take long for Anne to return with an extra cup for Bishop and a steaming teapot.

'It *is* good to see you, Anne,' Patricia said. 'It almost doesn't seem real.'

'Perhaps we could finish what we were discussing?' Anne said, her tone miffed.

'What was that?' Bishop asked, not happy that his arrival had annoyed Anne.

'Patricia – Doctor Richards – was about to tell me the nature of her visit.'

'Oh, well we can talk about that another time, Anne. I don't want to bore the corporal with science babble while he's trying to enjoy his tea.'

'Yes, what exactly is it that you do?' Bishop asked, pleased to move on from the obvious source of Anne's irritation. 'I'm not sure you ever got around to telling me.'

Patricia smiled and sipped at her tea, a strand of dark hair wriggling free from her bun, making its way down her pale cheek. 'I'm an astrobiologist by trade.'

'Sounds very interesting,' Bishop said, having always had a head for science. Although he had to admit he knew nothing of astrobiology.

'It can be.' Patricia sipped her tea, and smiled at him. 'Quite simply, I examine the origin, evolution and future of life in the universe. I see what contribution meteorites make to life on Earth and help prepare space missions by analysing soil from Earth's deserts. That's why I was out in Nevada for so long. At college I studied physics, mathematics, biology, and astrology. I majored in the latter two. My dad used to take me into our backyard and we would look up at the sky and the stars and imagine what was really going on up there. Amazing how much our families can influence our future life, don't you think?' She turned to Anne. 'Speaking of which, how is your father, Anne? I sent my postcard to his house as I wasn't sure where you would have settled by now.'

'He is doing well, thank you,' Anne said with a confirming nod. 'I went to see him a week ago. He wanted us to watch the Moon landing together.'

A small flicker passed across Patricia's face, but Anne didn't seem to notice, so Bishop said nothing.

'This is incredible. All this time, beneath the castle.'

Lethbridge-Stewart glanced back at Douglas, and nodded his agreement. It *was* incredible. Of course, a military presence at Edinburgh Castle was hardly a secret; indeed, it'd had always been the HQ for the Scottish military, but almost none of the Dragoon Guards currently stationed at the castle knew about the facility built within the Castle Rock, the plug of the extinct volcano upon which the castle was built. Except, perhaps, Major Lamont, who commanded the garrison stationed there.

It was just one of many secrets Lethbridge-Stewart had

been exposed to since his meeting with Air Vice-Marshal Gilmore in May. On the Scottish military front, only Lieutenant General Leask, General Officer Commanding, knew of the reasons behind Lethbridge-Stewart's presence at Edinburgh Castle; the garrison were on a need-to-know basis, and they needed to know very little, except to allow Lethbridge-Stewart, Douglas and Captain Bartlett access to the lower levels beneath the New Barracks.

The old LONGBOW facility was, Lethbridge-Stewart imagined, state of the art back in the early '40s, but much had changed since the end of the war. LONGBOW was no longer needed, and the facility was closed down. It had been built to operate in secret, and was thus the perfect place to make the HQ of the Fifth Operational Corps. Although, looking at the state of the place right now, Lethbridge-Stewart was glad they still had a couple of months before Dolerite Base (named after the rock surrounding it) was operational.

Douglas and Lethbridge-Stewart walked through the warren of corridors, dodging workers, made up of Bryden's men and specially selected men from the Corps of Royal Electrical and Mechanical Engineers, all dressed in the same nondescript blue overalls so as not to attract attention as they came and went through the rear entrance built into Castle Rock – unused for many long years, which in itself attracted a certain amount of attention from nosy locals.

'I was thinking of Sergeant Maddox,' Lethbridge-Stewart said, changing the topic. There were too many of Bryden's people about for them to talk secrets so openly. Once the base was under his direct command, then he'd be happy to talk secrets, but until then…

'She's still going strong then?'

Lethbridge-Stewart smiled. 'Can't keep women like Jean Maddox down,' he said. 'She's stationed at RAF Fylingdales. Perfect for the head of our communications staff.'

Douglas smiled. 'Good, be nice to have some well-trained officers here. I've been reading the personnel files. Still don't understand why we're getting the dregs of the British Army.'

'Perhaps I'll ask Hamilton to explain it to you again.' Lethbridge-Stewart listened to Douglas' chuckle behind him. 'We still need to find someone to head our scientific research department.'

'Surprised you agreed to such a department.'

'Agreement wasn't really a choice. Part of Hamilton's deal with Mr Bryden; he insists we should be learning from our extra-terrestrial visitors, not just blowing them up, and since he's the money behind this operation...'

Douglas let out a grim hmm. Lethbridge-Stewart agreed. He still wasn't happy about it, not only because he'd rather deal with the threat with the action it deserved, but having a scientific research department meant having civilians as part of the Corps. Bad enough that they had to rely on people like Bryden to fund the Corps. Price they paid for being under the radar, he supposed. Politics, compromise... It wouldn't end well.

'Do you have anybody in mind?' Douglas asked.

'I've looked through a list of people, talked to a few of them, but I believe Hamilton rather fancies Doctor Travers for the role.'

'That would make sense.'

Lethbridge-Stewart nodded. Yes, it would. Hamilton had manoeuvred Miss Travers into the Vault, and Lethbridge-Stewart couldn't deny that it was a great training ground. And, rather she was working for the Corps than the Vault. She was probably the most qualified scientist in the UK right now.

'I think he is still looking to go back to Tibet,' Anne said, thinking back on all the incredible tales her father used to tell her when she was a young girl. 'I imagine he still pines for his anthropology days. He doesn't like to admit he's not as young as he used to be, that his body is no longer made for gallivanting up mountains.'

'How did you two first meet?' Bill asked, clearly quite taken in by Patricia's tales. 'Over in Nevada I presume?'

'Anne came to the think-tank I was working at. She was unlike any other scientist I had ever met before. I couldn't always see the root of her methods at first, but I always knew I could trust her.'

'*Was* working at?' Anne said, honing in on the point. '*Was* working at, as in past tense?'

Patricia sipped at her cup nervously for a moment. Anne and Bill looked at her expectantly, both of them waiting for her to respond.

'It's been a long journey,' she offered finally. 'I think that might be a discussion for another time. This jet lag really is kicking in now.'

Anne wasn't quite so sure she agreed with that sentiment, but Patricia was an old friend and she wanted to make her feel welcome. Luckily Bill came to the rescue, filling the silence dutifully with small talk.

'Have you heard from the colonel recently?' he asked Anne. She said she had not. 'He's in Scotland, but seems to be out of contact. He asked me to keep tabs on Sally for him while he's away.'

'Of course, Sally!' Patricia said. 'How is she?'

'You know Sally as well?' Anne couldn't believe it. Now she knew there was something going on. Patricia was too well connected.

Patricia smiled. 'We've met once or twice.'

'How?'

'Oh, our paths crossed during a meeting I had for a position over on this side of the Atlantic. Recommended by Colonel Lethbridge-Stewart, in fact. It was decided I wasn't the right choice in the end, but it was nice to have been thought of. It's always nice to meet others in the community.'

'What was the position for?' Anne asked curiously.

'For something called the... Oh, what was it?'

'The Home-Army Fifth Operational Corps,' Bill supplied for her.

'That's it!' Patricia reached over and patted Anne's hands. 'But I think they made a better selection in the final candidate.'

Anne returned Patricia's smile, the dots joining together.

'Stiff competition,' Patricia said.

'Absolutely,' Anne returned.

Patricia's eyes lit up. 'I know what we should do!'

'What?'

'Let's have a girl's night. Just the three of us. Wouldn't that be fun, Annie?'

'Yes,' Anne agreed after a moment. Patricia's mind had a tendency to hop all over the place and it was sometimes hard to keep up. 'I think that would be a splendid idea.' She wasn't as keen on it as Patricia, but Anne was eager to get to the bottom of what was going on, and perhaps Sally would be of help. Tongues did tend to wag when girlfriends got together.

'I think I had better come, too', Bill added. 'As chaperone.' He smiled sweetly, and Anne raised her eyebrow.

'If you must,' she said, secretly glad to spend some social time with him. Not that she'd tell him, of course. 'But everyone will have to bring something. I don't think I have enough supplies in the house to feed us all.'

'I'm sure we can manage to rustle up something,' said Patricia.

A noise from the spare room. It seemed to gurgle.

'What was that?' Anne asked.

'I think I had best just go unpack,' Patricia said quickly, disappearing into the eaves of the cottage.

Anne stared after her.

'She seems very nice,' Bill said, after a moment. 'Just what you need. Someone to keep an eye on you.'

Anne continued to stare after her friend, chewing her lip nervously. 'I have a funny feeling that it may prove to be the other way around.'

— CHAPTER THREE —

Chain of Fools

Administrator Frank Bland had always been fascinated with outer space, ever since he was a child. His father had worked on the first space research flight and resulting cosmic radiation experiments, helping to design the first rocket to reach the edge of space in '46. As a boy, Frank Bland had grown up in the imposing shadows of the Holloman's Aeromedical Field Laboratory and his father's stories had always left him wondering what lay beyond the stars.

Bland's appearance befitted his name to the letter. He was tall and fair with ice-blue eyes and a bone structure that was singularly without peak or trough, giving him an oddly flat, even face. Bullied as a youngster both at home and at school, Bland had vowed to never again experience the same powerlessness as an adult that he had had to endure as a child. Bland was a corporate man with the ear of President Nixon, or Dickie as Bland called him. Everyone was afraid of Bland, and no one stepped out of line at the Laboratory now that he was in charge.

The Laboratory was based in Washington and directly partnered with *Horizon Base*. Anything non-terrestrial was sent to the Laboratory immediately for whatever various experimentations were deemed necessary, with Frank Bland at the helm of a team of scientists handpicked from around the world.

However, as the Project Horizon mission had now been completed and all those from the lunar base had now returned, Administrator Bland knew he needed to make the most of what he had if he was going to make his mark. There had to be something special about what had been brought back to Earth, something that could be harnessed and utilised to help the US nuclear programme. He knew Dickie was counting on him and there was no way Bland was going to risk a potential future position in Congress.

'I'm sorry, sir,' the Laboratory's receptionist said as Bland strolled through the building doors, banana milkshake in hand. 'But no food or drink is permitted beyond this point.' She pointed her pencil in the direction of a sign that hung above the door confirming as much.

'I think you'll find for me they make an exception,' Bland said tersely, leaning over her desk and pressing the entry button for himself.

The white doors opened and Bland strode through, the straw in his mouth, leaving the girl to stare after him.

He studied the photographs that hung on either side of the walls as he made his way down the corridor. They were various snaps of the lunar landscape. Some were of the Vallis Alpes and the Capella Craters, but there was nothing out of the ordinary to be seen. At least not to the naked eye.

'Excuse me, sir?' the girl called out behind him. 'I really must ask you to throw that away. It could cause contamination.'

Bland finished the last of his banana milkshake with a deliberately noisy slurp, tucked the straw into his top pocket, and tossed the cup into the open mouth of the waiting trashcan before pushing through a second door.

Sally and Bill were both right on time, causing Anne to smile at their military punctuality. It was so ingrained in both of them that they couldn't be late even if they tried. Sally was carrying a large dish, Bill hovering nervously behind her, holding two covered plates of his own.

'Good evening, Anne,' Sally greeted her. 'How is Patricia settling in?'

'Fine, I believe,' Anne said, glancing in the direction of the closed spare room door. 'But I'm sure she won't be staying for too long.'

'Shame. At least we can all catch up tonight. Where shall I put this? They'll need warming before we can eat.'

'Oh, follow me,' Anne said, and the two of them followed her inside as she led them towards the kitchen. 'I didn't know you could cook, Bill.'

'Mine as well I'm afraid,' Sally said. 'I wasn't sure what to bring, so I thought a selection would be best. Don't get to exercise my culinary skill as often as I like, so I might have gone a bit overboard. I must have practiced the recipe a dozen times by now,' she said, of her ratatouille. 'And I dare say it's rather become my signature dish!'

Anne surveyed the table. There were tomatoes stuffed with chicken livers, potato-cheese Charlotte and ratatouille care of Sally, while she and Patricia had rustled up an avocado and grapefruit salad between them and found a couple of bottles of dry white wine hidden away in a back cupboard which now stood among a mismatched selection of glasses waiting to be poured. It was all a bit extravagant, but in Anne's view, well deserved.

'Sally!' Patricia said, her head appearing from around the door.

'Patricia, how lovely to see you! How was the flight?'

'A little bumpy but nothing I couldn't handle. Is all this food for us?'

'Oh, it's not as much as it looks, I promise.'

'Shall we go and get comfortable?' Anne said. 'I don't think there's enough room for us all in here.'

The girls settled down in the living room while Bill hesitated by the door, as if he wasn't sure if he should be allowed entrance or not.

'So how long have you been engaged, Sally?' Patricia asked, uncorking the wine and pouring them each a large glass.

'Since March,' Sally said, unable to hide the wideness of her smile. 'We were introduced by Dougie – I mean, Walter Douglas, Alistair's second-in-command. I don't suppose you've ever come across him on your travels?'

'Congratulations! You'll set a date soon for the wedding I hope,' Patricia said, taking a seat next to her and examining Sally's ring, which was a tasteful princess cut diamond on a simple silver band. Just Lethbridge-Stewart's style. 'How is Lethbridge-Stewart? Bill says he's managed to keep in some sort of contact with him.'

'Good, I hope. He's currently up in Scotland somewhere, with Dougie as it happens. They're maintaining radio silence, thus making it kind of hard to get in touch with him.'

'I'm sure he's absolutely fine,' Patricia reassured her. 'Lethbridge-Stewart seemed like a capable man.'

'You are kind, Patricia,' Sally said. 'But like you say, I'm sure I have nothing to worry about. He will be back at Chelsea Barracks in no time.' She got to her feet, smoothing down her dress. 'Are we ready to go then?' Sally reached for her handbag. 'I heard there are some nice little pubs in Driffield, I thought we might go and take a look at them? I quite fancy a roaring fireplace, even at this time of year.'

'Actually I was hoping we could stay here. A girl's night in, as it were. What do you think?' Patricia said.

Anne and Sally exchanged glances.

'Well, I don't mind,' Sally said, going to sit down again. 'There's certainly enough food to eat here.'

'Good,' Patricia said, her face washed with relief.

There was a silence between them for a moment, then Sally said brightly, 'How about you, Patricia, do you have someone special in your life?'

'Well, it's funny you should ask that,' Patricia began cautiously. 'There is someone who has come into my life recently and changed it in the most unexpected way.'

'Oh how lovely!' Sally reached across to squeeze Patricia's hand. 'You must tell us all the details immediately.'

'Actually,' Patricia continued. 'I think it might be easier if I show you.'

'Show you?' Bill said from his position in the doorway. 'How can you show us?'

'Just wait and see,' Patricia said with a smile. 'Back in a tick!'

'How odd,' Sally said once Patricia had left them. 'Surely she can't have stashed him away in her suitcase?'

'I wouldn't put anything past Patricia,' Anne said dryly. 'I have a feeling something strange is about to happen.'

'She probably just wants to show us his photograph,' Bill said logically. 'I don't know why you must always think something strange is going on, Anne. I'm sure there is a perfectly reasonable explanation.'

Anne was about to reply when they heard Patricia's returning footsteps. The three of them turned in unison to look at her standing in the doorway. She wasn't alone.

'Everyone,' she began a little breathlessly. 'I have someone I would like you to meet.'

The trio stared at her unable to speak.

Patricia stood before them holding a mass of swaddling cloth, a young infant squawking from within the folds.

As the door swung closed behind him all eyes turned to Bland. The various scientists scuttled out of his way; they did not want to be the subject of his scrutinising gaze. And wisely so. Bland allowed himself a secret smile. He was in charge and there was nothing he enjoyed more than being in charge. He carried on down the line.

He retrieved the straw from his pocket and tapped it against the specimen case. 'This one is empty,' he observed, bending down to peer into the vacant specimen case.

The man at his side gulped visibly. 'Is it?' he asked weakly.

'Yes,' Bland mused. 'Quite empty. Where is the occupant?'

'Oh, yes I see. I think that one hasn't been filled yet.'

The other scientists exchanged nervous looks. Bland fixed his entire attention on the meek scientist in front of him.

'Nonsense,' he scoffed. 'The station is on indefinite

hiatus. Everyone who was there is now here, unless…'

He didn't have to explain. They all knew that all those who hadn't been brought home were now most certainly dead.

'So,' Bland continued, bending his tall frame down to glare into the specimen case again, tapping it with his straw. 'Where can he have got to?'

The scientist looked at him blankly. 'I cannot say, Administrator.'

'That is… unfortunate,' Bland drawled. He began to wander around the room waving his long arms expansively. They all watched on, in tense silence. 'This laboratory is to follow the same principles as NASA – research, construction, communication.' He hesitated after the last word for affect, and then continued. 'Communication. So is someone going to speak up and tell me what the hell is going on here?'

The scientists exchanged unhappy glances again. Then one man stepped forward. He was older, his dark hair peppered with grey, spectacles on a chain around his neck, while his laboratory goggles rested on his head. 'Perhaps I can explain?' he began.

Bland crossed his arms and fixed him with an unflinching gaze. 'I think you better had.'

'My name is Doctor Jhaveri. I am the senior researcher here. I'm afraid that the specimens were no longer viable. There was nothing we could do.'

'No longer viable?' Bland repeated, his eyes wide and animated. 'Go on. Explain it to me.'

Jhaveri pressed his hands together nervously. 'They expired,' he said slowly. 'We were forced to dispose of them.'

Bland narrowed his icy blue eyes, bringing his cheekbones up dangerously high. 'So where are they now?' he asked.

Jhaveri and the gathered scientists exchanged looks. 'We burned them,' he offered finally.

The muscle in Bland's cheek pinged. 'On whose authority?' he asked. If there was one thing he could not tolerate, it was insubordination.

'On mine. As senior researcher it was my decision to make. Not one I take lightly I might add.' Doctor Jhaveri looked at him steadily.

Bland sucked his teeth. 'You need to watch your step, Doctor,' he warned him. 'There is only one man in charge of this laboratory, and rest assured it is not you.'

Bland stalked out of the laboratory.

Prior to his appointment as administrator, Bland had been a political animal. He was a professional liar and when someone fibbed to his face he took it very personally indeed. There was no way these aliens had died. Someone had taken them or, worse, set them free.

'Administrator Bland?'

He looked back. The timid man approaching him was one of the scientists, though Bland couldn't remember his name. He was small and round with a baldhead that shone with nervous sweat.

'Yes, what is it?' Bland asked ungraciously. 'I have to be somewhere else.'

The man looked behind him anxiously. 'There's something I have to tell you, Administrator. What Doctor Jhaveri said is not the whole truth.'

Bland stared at him intently. 'You have my attention

now. What is the whole truth?'

The man began to shake slightly, his voice trembling as he spoke. 'The aliens didn't all die, not all of them. There was one that was definitely still alive the last time I came into the lab. A baby.'

'Go on.'

The man swallowed. 'Not everyone agreed with the work we are trying to do here, Administrator, especially not Doctor Jhaveri. It's his fault the baby is missing.'

'Missing? What do you mean the baby is missing?'

'I saw him give the baby to a woman.'

'A woman? What woman? There are no women back here except for the receptionists, and they would never set foot inside the laboratories.'

'Yes, I understand, Administrator. But there was one. She used to work here. I guess he figured it would be less conspicuous to have a woman make off with a baby rather than a guy.'

'What are you saying?'

'Someone stole the baby.'

Anne got to her feet first. Without a word to the others, she walked towards the door until she was standing next to Patricia. Anne looked down at the sleeping baby. He was so small; it was hardly believable that he really was a living-breathing creature. He couldn't have been more than a few months old, but already his hair was thick and dark.

'Is he yours? she asked. She didn't want to pry too much into Patricia's private life, but Pat was her close friend and Anne was sure she wouldn't object.

Sally on the other hand most certainly did. 'Anne!' she

scolded, but Anne ignored her.

'It's alright,' Patricia said. 'I don't mind you asking. He isn't mine. At least, not biologically,' she admitted. 'But he is mine to take care of. That's why I need your help. All of you.'

'But what can we do?' Anne said. 'I'm sorry to disappoint you, Patricia, but I really know nothing about babies.'

'No, it's not that,' Patricia said with a laugh. 'You see this is no ordinary baby.'

'What do you mean he's no ordinary baby?' Anne echoed, staring down at the crumpled sleeping face in Patricia's arms. 'He looks just like every other baby I've ever seen.'

'Well let me assure you he is not,' Patricia said. They stared at her expectantly. Finally, Patricia spoke again. 'He's an alien.'

Anne blinked at her. During their times in Nevada they had often discussed alien technology and the positive and negative affects it could have on humanity, but never had Patricia gone so far as to mention actual physical alien contact.

'An alien?' Anne reiterated. 'But how can he be? Where did he come from?'

'I did tell you I thought it may take some time to explain,' Patricia said, sitting back down. 'But I'm very happy to answer all questions. It might be advisable to bring us another bottle of this really great wine.'

No one moved. Three sets of eyes were trained on the baby, which looked no different than a human baby. Sally got to her feet and moved closer.

'Is he the only one?' she asked, peering at him.

Patricia shook her head. 'No. There are many others like him. Those that survived the initial colonisation were brought back to the base. Plenty of them died of course, the journey was too much for them and they just sort of... faded away. It was most peculiar. Anyway, some of those that did not survive left their offspring behind. The creature – his real mother – she asked me to take care of him.'

'Colonisation?' Bill asked.

'What base?' Anne asked.

'She asked you?' Sally asked.

Patricia looked at each of them, but only answered Sally for now. 'Yes. Well, not in so many words. Their dialect is different than anything I have ever come across before. But I could feel her asking me, as if it emanated from her. She knew she was going to die and that there was no one else to help. The journey was quite a stress for them. It seems like they had never left the lunar surface before the Americans and Russians arrived.'

'They come from the Moon?' Anne asked.

'Wait,' said Sally, waving Anne down. Her eyes never left the baby. 'The journey?'

'Oh yes.' Patricia sighed. 'Not all aliens want to go whizzing about in UFOs, you know. Their creatures – people – were indigenous inhabitants of the lunar surface. They would have stayed there undiscovered and undisturbed for centuries, had we not intervened in the name of man's expansion into the universe.'

Bill shook his head, and looked at Anne. 'This is incredible. Aliens on our doorstep. The colonel will have a field day.'

Anne nodded, and turned back to Patricia. 'What are

they called?'

'We don't know what they call themselves, but they were thought to have originated as a species from the lighter toned regions known as the Terrae Highlands, so the base nicknamed them the Terrae.'

'The Terrae?'

'Yes.'

'Sounds rather too much like the terror to me,' Sally said, shivering visibly.

'Yes, I think that was part of the idea. They wanted us to fear them, to look at them as creatures, not sentient beings. But as soon as we housed them in the labs I could tell they were altogether different.'

'How?' Anne asked, ignoring the fact that Patricia was admitting to having worked on the US lunar base. That was a discussion for another time.

'They would talk to one another and communicate, but in a language none of us could decipher. When one of them died, which they all too often did, the others would grieve. It was a terrible sight and the noise they would make was utterly haunting, like a fox calling through the desert at night.'

Anne recalled the howling sound that had echoed throughout the Nevada. It chilled her to the bone.

'It was clear they were sentient beings, just as you or I,' Patricia said. 'But sadly not all those I was working with extended the same level of humanity across all creatures.'

'He looks rather pale,' Sally said peering down at him with concern. 'Is he unwell?'

'I don't think so,' Patricia said, looking at him with a smile. 'The Terrae were all fair skinned, just like the area of the Moon they originated from. I imagine it is part of their evolutionary camouflage.'

'How have they remained hidden for so long?' Bill asked.

'They are sophisticated fort builders. To the untrained eye their bridges and tunnels merely look like craters or rock formations. Until man set foot on the Moon and uncovered their habitat they were completely hidden from the naked eye. I'm sure you know that after the *Apollo 11* mission returned the astronauts were all placed in biological isolation for several days. Why do you think the government would go to all that trouble if there were no other life force on the Moon? What contamination could they be worrying about?'

'Perhaps they were being cautious,' Sally said.

Patricia shook her head. 'There have been meteorites discovered in Australia where the carbon has revealed the raw materials of the first building blocks of DNA molecules. It cannot come as that great of a surprise to even the staunchest sceptic that there is life to be found on other planets.'

'You're preaching to the converted here,' Anne said.

'How long do you think these governments have known there is life on the Moon?' Sally asked. She knew, at least in a small way, what Alistair was up to in Scotland, so she shouldn't be too surprised. The British Government and military had kept much secret for years. Still… 'It seems extraordinary that they would be able to keep such a secret.'

'No more than the secrets we've been keeping since February,' Anne pointed out, echoing Sally's thoughts.

'Since the '40s, I shouldn't wonder,' Bishop chimed in.

'The Third Reich often hinted that they were the first to set foot on the lunar surface.'

Patricia interrupted him. 'Not quite. I rather fear instead that this is all conjecture. Some thought the Nazis had a base on the Moon, and look how accurate that assumption turned out to be.'

'But don't forget, Patricia, after World War II the space race was actually given a significant boost by the capture of German rocket technology,' Sally said. 'Countries are always piggy backing on to one another to try and find the newest discovery. Docked space stations to enable product development and an outpost to maintain satellites. Once harnessed, their powers can be far reaching.'

'So the space race was never just about getting to the Moon?' Anne asked.

'Precisely,' Patricia said. 'It was always about so much more than that. It was about who would take control of it. The Americans called it Project Horizon.'

'But what were they hoping to achieve? To turn the Moon into some kind of new Earth? To create bases that could support human life?'

Patricia shook her head. The baby in her arms started to fall back to sleep. 'Actually it is quite the opposite. There has been found to be large amounts of Helium 3 on the Moon, five million tones of it, in fact. The regolith can be mined for nuclear purposes.'

A furious Bland made his way out of the Laboratory and headed straight for the vending machine in the lobby outside. He needed a sugar rush and fast. He tossed the few coins he had in his pocket into the slot and kicked the machine hard until his can of Coca-Cola rolled out nosily, hissing as he wrenched open the ring pull. Those words were still echoing over and over again in his mind.

The baby is missing. The alien baby. Someone has stolen the baby.

For a moment he couldn't decide which he found more disturbing. The fact that an alien was out on the loose somewhere or that one of his own laboratory technicians would have dared go against his orders.

He finished his can of Coke in a second gulp, threw it to one side and made his way across to the pay phone bays that lined the Laboratory parking lot. He had an untraceable call to make. No one must find out what had happened.

Someone was going to help him out of this mess.

Anne's eyes widened. She could see Bill shift his position at the door. 'Nuclear?' she repeated.

Patricia nodded. 'Yes. The Americans have been setting up nuclear reactors in the hope that they can station missiles on the Moon permanently. But they weren't the only ones to come to the same idea. The Soviets have also created their own mining operations and there has been a tense rivalry between the two nations.'

'I thought the space race was bad enough.'

'Well quite. But then it all changed.'

'Changed?' Anne asked. 'How?'

'They discovered the Moon's secret, the Terrae, and realised they would have to work together or both risk exposure.'

'Can't see how that would work,' Bill mumbled.

Anne glanced at him. Military mind-set, maybe, but he

was probably right. She brushed it aside for now, more interested in the aliens. 'Tell us more about these Terrae.'

'Well, when we first examined the Terrae it looked as if they had duplicates of each organ, but the longer they lived on Earth the other organ would die away and the tissue would be reabsorbed by the body, as if they had two systems, one for the lunar surface and one for Earth.'

Anne considered this. 'So despite the fact that they haven't been to any planets before, do you think that was their ultimate goal; that they planned to come here all along?'

'Not necessarily. We think their back-up system, if you will, was to accommodate whatever planet they came to rest on, if the situation ever arose. The Moon is only a satellite after all; I suppose evolution knew it was only a matter of time before they would need to find another home.'

Sally stood up. 'I should try and contact Alistair; he'll know what to do.'

'No,' Anne said quickly. 'We need to leave him out of this; it will only complicate matters further.'

Sally looked a little put out. Anne turned to Bill, and he nodded, although the reluctance was written all over his face.

'The Moon was already more than one planet,' Patricia said. 'Formed from the debris left over after the impact between Earth and a Mars sized body called Theia. Stop me if I'm teaching you to suck eggs.'

'What do the Americans want with them?' Anne asked.

'What they always want I suppose. To experiment, to learn and discover whatever they can from their kind. All top secret. Things would turn dire if anyone ever found out what they were doing.'

Anne thought of her work at the Vault and swallowed.

'How can we help?' asked Sally. Anne smiled and realised how much she liked Sally. They shared a same no nonsense approach, a desire to get to the crux of a matter with minimal fuss.

'I must admit I really don't know,' Patricia admitted sheepishly. 'I hadn't thought much past arriving here, to safety. I hoped perhaps you might be able to help?'

Anne looked at the child. She thought about her own mother who she had lost as a young girl. To be so far from your home and family... Anne shook her head sadly. No, she couldn't let that happen, not if there was a chance to do something about it.

'We need to keep him hidden,' she said, decision made. 'An alien baby cannot just disappear into the night without a trace. Someone is going to be looking for him. However did you even get him out of the country?'

'There's a man I know. He works in immigration,' Patricia said before pausing, a slight blush flushing across her cheeks. 'We met on my trip to Florida. He helped me, found papers for the boy that would say he's my son so that we could leave the country.'

'Are you sure you can trust him?' Anne asked, her brow furrowing.

'Absolutely!' Patricia nodded, her dark eyes flashing. 'He wants to come over here too when everything quiets down. He has promised he is going to come and join me.'

'Good,' Anne said, her mind already racing. 'At least we can be sure he won't be telling anyone.'

'He won't.'

Anne mulled things over for a moment. 'I can't imagine

the Russians and the Americans being on the same side, as Bill said it just wouldn't work.'

'They're not, only at face value and only out of absolute necessity.'

Anne nodded ruefully, and wondered for a moment what her father would say if he found out. She was sure he would share Patricia's feelings about wanting to keep this new alien life form safe and secret. He was always so excited when he came into contact with alien intelligences.

The baby in Patricia's arms gave a large yawn and then began to squirm. Sally smiled across at him. 'May I hold him?' she asked.

'Yes, of course,' Patricia replied. 'He seems to like contact with humans, and there doesn't seem to be any adverse effect noticed yet. I think he is too young to feel the loss of his mother, thank goodness.'

'What is his name?' Sally said, holding him in her arms and looking down at him kindly. His pink face screwed itself up into a yawn like any baby might.

'I don't know what his real name is, but in the lab he was listed as Baby B.'

'What happened to Baby A?' Anne asked. Patricia lowered her eyes and Anne knew better than to ask any more questions on the subject. She stood up suddenly; it was time to take charge. 'What do you want me to do?' she asked, getting down to business.

Sally rocked the baby in her arms, looking from Anne to Patricia and back again.

'I must admit, I don't know exactly myself,' Patricia began uncertainly. 'I just want to help them. It seems so wrong somehow, that we were the people who pushed them off their planet and they are the ones who are suffering. Science should be about progress, about moving forwards, not debasing ourselves back to a time we should all be ashamed of.'

'I know. Everyone thinks we are the champions of the space race, but no one knows the price we have paid for it. If they did, I think the public reaction would be quite different.' Anne looked around the room, making eye contact with each of them. 'That's why no one must know, why the government wants to keep it a secret at all costs. And there's only one option I can see.'

'What's that?' Bill asked.

'We're going to have to take him to the Vault.'

'No. If there's one place he shouldn't be, it's that place.'

'Well how else can we even start to look for his family, if we don't know what sets him apart biologically?' Anne reasoned. 'It's the only place that has the equipment I need to ascertain more about him.'

'But, Anne, think about it! What if they realise who – what – he is?' Bill continued earnestly. 'They would take him away and Patricia would never see him again.'

'Yes,' Sally said, nodding her head in agreement. 'You can't risk it.'

'What choice do we have? Look at him. There is nothing notably different to the naked eye. If we are careful, which we shall be, I can have him in and out before anyone even notices. It will be just like with the Moon landing.'

'How so?'

'People will accept what they see. Or what they think they see.'

Patricia began to smile and Anne could see relief washing

across her face. She sat down next to Patricia and took her free hand, the baby balancing comfortably on her other arm.

'Do you trust me?' Anne said.

Patricia nodded. 'More than anyone, Annie. That's why I came to you for help.'

'Good,' Anne agreed. 'You know if there was another option, I would take it, don't you?'

'I know it. But you will be careful, won't you?'

'We will be careful. I won't let you down, Patricia.'

'I know you won't, Anne. It was a risk to come here, but I knew it was one worth taking.'

'Sorry to interrupt,' Bill began, stepping forward into the room and not sounding particularly sorry about it at all. 'But do you really think you can get away with taking an alien into the Vault without anyone batting an eye? There is absolutely no chance that you will be able to get in and out without being stopped.'

'Does anyone have a better idea?' Anne asked, knowing she sounded peevish with Bill.

'If only this was a couple of months later,' Sally said.

'But it isn't. Dolerite Base is out of the question,' Bill said.

Anne nodded resolutely. She knew, just as well as Sally and Bill, why Lethbridge-Stewart was up in Scotland. Alas, his new base of operations was some weeks away from full running. 'Fine. Then the Vault it is.'

'When can we start?' Patricia said.

Anne squeezed her hand tightly. 'Tomorrow,' she said. Bill and Sally exchanged a loaded glance but they all knew there was no backing out now.

— CHAPTER FOUR —

Darkness and Light

'Is that you then, Black?'

Darren Carlin, Black to his friends (all due to a certain brand of lager), nodded as he passed Glenn Kerruish. 'Aye, that's me!'

He was on the early shift, which was still technically quite late, at least for the rest of Scotland. Most of the work was being done during the night, once the castle was closed, with very few coming and going during the day, but under the cover of darkness the real work began. Darren was unlucky enough to be one of those hired by Bryden Industries to work the early-night shift. Not that he minded, of course, after all work wasn't so easy to find at the moment; he was almost eighteen, and had left Carluke High a couple of years ago with no qualifications. He glanced down at his watch; it was almost half one in the morning, but he wasn't tired. He had been, until he'd taken a quick sniff of that new dust, Luna Haze. Now he felt wired, and it was time to hit the streets of Edinburgh, head to his dingy flat and party the night away with his flatmate and girlfriend. He had all day to sleep.

'Ye're going the wrong way,' Glenn said.

He liked Glenn, the older man had taken Darren under his wing since they'd been hired the same day, but right now his opinion didn't seem to matter. Darren wasn't sure why; indeed, Glenn's words barely registered.

It was a confusing warren beneath the castle, but usually Darren had no trouble finding his way around. His dad always said he had a great sense of direction, but that was easy to say when you lived in a small town like Carluke; right now, though, he wasn't quite sure where he was. Still, he could feel the Haze working its way into his system, so he didn't really care. All he knew was that he had to get outside and look up at the Moon.

Robert, his flatmate, told him that the dust came from the Moon itself, but Darren wasn't so sure about that. He usually believed anything Robert said, but if it had, then that meant the *Apollo* mission brought it with them. And if they had then he'd have heard about it on the radio.

He shook his head. It didn't matter. All that *did* matter was getting outside, seeing the moon while the Haze was in his system. He'd not tried it before, but Robert swore by it. He'd been the first person Darren had met when he came to Edinburgh last year, allowed him the spare room. Robert was, as the Americans said, a dude. Cool with it, too. He was twenty-one and knew everything about living in Edinburgh; all the best places to score the best drugs, where to get the cheap alcohol and fags. Darren's dad called Robert a dead end, but it was up to Darren to learn that the hard way. Well, so far, all Darren had learned was that Robert was cool, but that didn't mean Robert would let Darren have some Luna Haze for free; and so here he was working beneath Edinburgh Castle at stupid o'clock, with barely a sample of the dust to try before he paid full whack for a decent amount.

Darren turned another corner. The area before him was open, with two different corridors leading off either way. It was going to be a reception area of some kind. Already a desk was sitting there, facing the lift...

'Aye, now that's what I'm talking about,' Darren said to himself and set off for the lift.

He'd barely reached it before a voice called out to him. A London voice.

Too many of those about in this place, Darren thought. Steeling jobs from us Scots who need them more.

'Oi, what do you think you're doing?'

He recognised the man. One of those Irenes, as the lads called them. Some technical bod with the army. Craftsman thingy. Oh yeah. Tracy Ward.

'Shift's over,' Darren said.

Craftsman Ward nodded. 'Good for you,' he said. 'But you know you can't leave that way. Only the bigwigs can go via the Barracks. We take the tradesman entrance.'

'Aye, I know, but I have ta get out now.'

Ward shook his head and placed a hand on Darren's shoulder. 'Sorry, mate, but you know the rules. Tradesman, come on.'

It was a long way to the back of the instillation and Darren needed to see the Moon now. A deep panic set in. Without warning, he gave Ward an almighty shove and spun back to the lift. He pressed the button.

Behind him Ward scrambled to his feet. 'Now you've done it!'

Darren didn't care. The lift door opened and he stepped inside. He hit the 'up' button. The door closed before Ward could reach him, and Darren smiled. Soon, so very soon, he'd be able to see the Moon and discover how right Robert had been. The Moon was magical, and it was calling him.

Bland glanced at his watch; ten before eight. Almost time.

He sat opposite his wife, Nancy, who was, thankfully, still a long way from him due to their sizeable oak dining table. Things had been more silent than usual between them now that Nate, their eighteen-year-old son, had taken his place at the alma mater college of his father.

Nancy got to her feet to refill her husband's rather full glass of wine. 'Would you like any more, darling?' she asked in her Southern drawl, which he had once found charming but now seemed to be nothing other than grating.

'Is there any food to go with it?' he asked, not looking at her.

Nancy blanched visibly. 'I wanted to give Dolores the night off. Her father is very sick, darling.'

'He's not the only one,' Bland muttered darkly. 'There will be nothing left of me soon.'

'Of course, darling,' she said and disappeared into the kitchen. 'She did leaving me something on the stove to warm up. Back in a jiffy.'

Bland listened to her crashing about for a moment or two. A plume of smoke followed her efforts. It whispered its way out of the kitchen and into the dining room. Bland sniffed at the acrid smell. *It's just like being in the Lab*, he thought. His stomach clenched at the idea and he examined the time on his Omega De Ville Classic watch. It shouldn't be long now.

As if on cue, the doorbell jangled loudly.

'I'll get it, darling,' Nancy said, rushing out of the kitchen.

'No,' Bland said firmly, his eyes roving disapprovingly over her apron and disarrayed hair. 'Not looking like that. Besides, it won't be for you.'

Nancy blinked at him wordlessly, and Bland tossed his napkin onto the table and stalked towards the doubles doors. He opened one side, stepped out and closed it behind him.

'Well?' he asked the man waiting for him on the porch steps. 'Have you got any news for me?'

The man hesitated. He was an imposing figure even in the darkness, broad and dressed all in black. But in the presence of Bland, he cowered.

'Well?' Bland prompted again, his tall frame towering over him. 'I haven't got all night. Have you found the baby or not?'

'No,' the man said through gritted teeth as if he was afraid to hear the answer for himself.

Bland felt the colour rising in his cheeks.

Douglas rubbed his eyes. Another late night in Edinburgh. He stood by the One O'clock Gun, looking east across the darkened city. He had been allowed to walk its empty grounds of the castle by permission of Major Lamont. He was tired, and he missed his family. He was used to being away, came with the job, but as he looked out over Edinburgh he wondered how well they'd settle in Scotland. Penny would adapt, make new friends, but Jacob... Well, he was young, he'd soon—

'Colonel Douglas, sir!'

Douglas sighed and turned around. One of the Dragoon Guards was approaching him. A young man he didn't recognise, but then he'd hardly got the chance to talk to most of the Guards. Which wasn't like him. Another thing to get used to, Douglas realised, now he was working with a top secret unit.

'What is it?'

'Sir, Major Lamont wishes to see you. Said there's a problem that needs your attention.'

'Right you are. Thank you.'

The guardsman saluted, and continued on his rounds. Douglas watched him go, then looked towards the New Barracks. What could possibly have gone wrong now? A civilian worker being nosy, probably. They kept slipping out when their military chaperones turned their back – eager to *explore* the castle beyond the usual tourist track. Hopefully he could keep it quiet before Lethbridge-Stewart found out; this time.

He set off back towards the Barracks.

'Why not?' Bland asked, after a moment. He could see the whites of the man's eyes in the night time gloom.

'It hasn't been as easy as we thought. But we think we know who might have taken it.'

Bland took a deep breath. Okay, now they were getting somewhere.

'Do you recall a Doctor Richards?' the man asked.

'Of course not,' Bland replied flippantly. 'I take great care not to remember the name of anyone who works for me, including you.'

The man nodded and gave a smile which made Bland wonder if he was secretly pleased that he was just another faceless lackey, out of the firing line.

'Doctor Patricia Richards?' the man said.

'Oh, yes,' Bland said. 'The female. I have a vague recollection. Good friend of Doctor Jhaveri, more's the pity.'

'We think it is her.'

'Because she is a woman?' Bland asked witheringly. He could have made such a deduction if guess work was the name of the game.

The man shook his head. 'No, not because she's a woman. Because Doctor Jhaveri told her to do it.'

'Did he now?' Bland said, a smirk pulling at his lips. 'It sounds to me as if Doctor Jhaveri is getting a little above his station. So where is she now then, this Doctor Richards?'

There was a pause.

'We're not quite sure, but we're working on it.'

'Not good enough. I need to know where she is immediately. That baby could be anywhere by now.'

'I understand, Administrator. We won't let you down.'

'Fine. I trust I will hear from one of you with an update by dawn?'

'Of course,' the man said earnestly.

A dog barked in the distance and through one of his neighbour's open windows Bland could hear children playing. It all seemed rather incongruous, having such a discussion in the middle of suburbia.

'That will be all, you can go now,' Bland said.

'But I have something else for you, Administrator.'

'What is it?' Bland's patience at an end.

'A letter came to the Lab for you.'

'Give it to the secretary,' Bland said with a dismissive wave of his hand as he moved to head back inside. 'I don't need to open letters. I haven't fallen that far from grace, not yet at any rate.'

'No,' the man said, holding it out to Bland. 'I think you need to see this.'

It was shaping up, slowly. He had needed somewhere private to talk and think, and had got some of the REME squaddies to clean up his office a little. Lethbridge-Stewart smiled. *His* office. It sounded good. Of course he had an office at Chelsea Barracks, but that was only on loan really, a temporary measure to help with his cover while he secretly worked for Hamilton. But now, here in Dolerite Base, his command, he had his own office.

It was a bit bland right now, empty, but he'd change that over time. Hang up the Sword of Honour he'd received upon graduating Sandhurst; put it in pride of place behind his desk so that everybody who entered his office would see it. Lethbridge-Stewart wasn't a man given to bouts of pride, but he took a moment to accept that yes, he had done well. Very well, in fact, for a man who had once insisted he'd never join the military.

He looked down at the plans for Dolerite Base, and compared them to the old plans for LONGBOW. There were subtle changes, rooms being repurposed, modernised. Not much space for billeting the troops here, of course; plans were already afoot for stationing the troops at Stirling Castle, and others down at Salisbury. As for his key officers, they would be given rooms in the New Barracks above until they were able to permanently relocate to Scotland. It was easier for him, of course, but people like Dougie had families to consider.

Now, if only—

There was a knock at his door, and with a smile he said,

'Come in.'

The door opened quickly, and one of the civilian workers were frog marched inside, REME Craftsman Ward to one side of him, and Douglas on the other. The workman couldn't have been no more than seventeen.

'What is going on here?' Lethbridge-Stewart asked, getting to his feet. 'Who is this man?'

'Darren Carlin, sir,' Ward said. 'One of Bryden's men.'

Ward and Douglas deposited Mr Carlin in the chair opposite the desk. The young man's eyes were opening and closing rapidly, his hand stretched out as if he was reaching for something in front of him that was no longer there.

'What is the matter with him?' Lethbridge-Stewart asked with concern, walking around the desk to take a closer look at his pale face. 'This man doesn't seem to be fully compos-mentis. How has he become like this while on base?'

'He forced his way onto the castle grounds, Colonel,' Ward said.

'Wonderful. Did you smooth things out with Lamont, or do I need to talk to him?' Lethbridge-Stewart asked, looking at Douglas. 'We are supposed to be unseen while here, you know.'

'Downside of having civilian workmen on base, sir,' Douglas said.

'Quite.' Lethbridge-Stewart shook his head. Stricter measures were needed; either that or Bryden's men would have to go. Hamilton wouldn't be happy, but there you go, actions had consequences. 'So, what's this all about?' he asked.

'It seems this man has been caught with an unspecified substance,' Douglas began. 'We discovered him ingesting a power from this vial.'

He passed it across for Lethbridge-Stewart to examine for himself. The white and violet powder glinted and refracted in the light as Lethbridge-Stewart rolled the vial between his fingers.

'Do we know what it is, Douglas?' he asked. 'I don't believe I have encountered this particular powder before.'

'I'm afraid we couldn't get any sense from the man as to what it may be, or how he got hold of it,' Douglas replied. 'I suggest we send it for scientific testing to isolate the chemical structure and try and find out its origin.'

'Send it where?'

Douglas looked down for a moment. 'To Miss Travers, sir.'

Lethbridge-Stewart wasn't keen on the Vault getting their hands on a potentially lethal drug, but as long as Miss Travers ran the tests. 'Very well,' he agreed. 'Has anyone else been affected?'

'None that we have seen,' Ward said.

'Thank you,' Lethbridge-Stewart said. 'Would you give me a moment alone with him?'

'Are you sure?' Douglas asked. 'You won't get any response from him. He was found like this by one of the Guards, and he couldn't get a word of sense of him, just a rapid blinking of the eyes.'

'I would still like to give it a try,' Lethbridge-Stewart continued. 'If you wouldn't mind.'

'Very well,' Dougie relented. 'Come along then, Craftsman. I will only be outside if you need reinforcements.'

'Ward, ask around. Find out if any other civilians know of this substance.'

'Yes, sir,' Ward said, and saluted.

They left the room, leaving Lethbridge-Stewart alone with Mr Carlin. Once they were gone, Lethbridge-Stewart sat back down at his desk, leaning across towards the young man so that they were now face to face.

'Can you hear me?' he began, his voice clear and steady. Carlin didn't say anything in response but the blinking of his eyes continued with unnatural frequency. It was all rather unnerving, Lethbridge-Stewart concluded. 'Mr Carlin. Darren, can you hear me?' He clicked his fingers. 'Snap out of it, man!' The blinking continued, but there was no recognition in Mr Carlin's eyes. 'Extraordinary,' Lethbridge-Stewart murmured.

He called for Douglas, who re-entered the officer immediately.

'This man is clearly very ill, and we're not currently in a position to help him. Pass him onto the local authorities.'

'Is that wise, sir?'

'Probably not, but I don't see any other choice. And besides, he's one of Bryden's men, not ours. Not our responsibility.'

'Yes, sir.' Douglas helped the young man out of the chair. 'Come on, you, let's see what the police have to say.'

Once they were gone Lethbridge-Stewart looked around his office. No, they were still a long way from functionality, and he had made the right decision. Hopefully the substance affecting Mr Carlin would prove to be nothing more than another means of escape, no worse than what youths usually found on the streets. Still, he'd be interested in seeing Miss Travers' results.

*

It looked just like any other letter might, the usual official manila envelope. Then Bland noticed the stamp in the corner. Russian. Not direct from the country itself, but the Russian Embassy. Bland ripped it open, his eyes scanning quickly over the contents. But he need not have worried. It was merely a letter from an old friend, Vadim Kabinov, informing him of his new role as Science Attaché. Bland looked at it for a moment longer then stuffed it into his jacket pocket.

'Will that be all for tonight, Administrator?' the man asked.

But Bland didn't answer straight away. He remembered the first night he and Kabinov had met in Berlin. Bland still remembered the stories Kabinov had told him, and the memory gave Bland an idea.

'Get rid of it,' he said suddenly.

'The baby?' the man asked, his voice rising. 'But we don't know where it is!'

'Not the baby,' Bland hissed. 'The Lab. I need you to get rid of the Lab. The whole thing. It should be like it never existed at all.'

The man stared at him in horror. 'But how am I supposed to do that?'

'I'm sure you will be able to figure it out,' Bland said testily, his growling stomach now joining in their conversation aggressively. 'Do whatever you have to do. Burn it, raze it to the ground. Just make sure that there is nothing, and no one, left to find. Do I make myself clear?'

'Yes, Administrator,' the man said quietly.

'Good,' Bland said. 'I don't want to ever see you again, do you understand me?'

'Frank?'

It was Nancy. Bland had been so distracted he hadn't heard her open the door.

'Oh, I'm so sorry, I didn't realise you were with a friend, darling. Would you like to stay for dinner? We have plenty to go around,' Nancy said sweetly, her usually immaculate hair now curling around her ears.

'He doesn't need to eat,' Bland said tersely. 'It's cold. Get back inside.'

'All right, darling,' she said. 'It was very nice to meet you, whoever you are,' she ended politely, smiling across at the stranger on her porch.

'You too, Mrs Bland,' the man replied.

Bland shot him a dangerous look.

'Please don't stay out here too long, Frank,' Nancy said. 'Dinner is almost ready.'

Bland made a noise that signified he understood and closed the door quickly behind her disappearing form.

'I apologise for the interruption,' he continued. 'I trust you understand what I need you to do for me?'

The man nodded. 'But, Administrator, what happens if people ask questions?'

'Then you will answer them,' Bland said flatly. 'Good night. I look forward to reading about your work in my morning paper.'

The man gave another sharp nod of ascent and then disappeared into the night.

CHAPTER FIVE

A Day in the Life

'Are you sure this is all right?' Patricia asked, not for the first time.

She followed Anne through a vale in the Cheviot Hills and into a dark tunnel, outwardly looking disused and abandoned. The tunnel served as the entrance to the Vault, buried deep within land owned by the British Government. Very few people knew of its existence, and of those, even less knew its location. Anne was taking a risk bringing Patricia and the baby with her, but there was nowhere else safe enough for her to run the necessary tests.

'Of course,' Anne replied without hesitation. 'The Vault is one of the most secure facilities in the whole of the British Isles. There's a reason very few people know about it. Besides, he can't stay with you forever; we need to try and reunite him with the others, find a place for them too. The Moon is not sustainable for human life, who knows what our planet may be doing to him?'

Patricia glanced down at the sleeping baby in her arms. 'He seems all right to me,' she said softly. 'He's been very good and he doesn't cry at all.'

'Well let's not take any chances,' Anne said, her mind racing ahead. This was not the first alien she had come into contact with, but it was certainly the most docile. She was eager to see what she could learn as well as help to keep him out of harm's way.

'Are you positive it's safe?' Patricia asked.

'No worse than anywhere else,' Anne said. 'Just remember to stick to the story. Which isn't too far from the truth. Makes it easier to remember.'

Patricia swallowed but nodded in silent agreement.

'Follow me,' Anne instructed her. 'Remember to keep to the left.'

Patricia nodded, and they began their descent into the closely guarded Vault.

After a short while of walking in silence, Patricia spoke up. Anne was surprised it took her so long; Patricia was not quiet by nature. 'I'm not sure if I like it down here. There's something about this place that gives me the creeps.'

'Just watch your step and stay close to me, Pat. There's nothing to be afraid of. This way.'

They moved down further into the bowels of the building until they reached the reception area. It always struck Anne as odd that a place as shrouded in secrecy as the Vault should have such an area; it wasn't like the place received any uninvited guests. The surly receptionist, Peggy Orwell, looked at Anne, and twisted her mouth. Anne unclipped her pass and laid it onto the desk. Peggy glanced at it for a moment then turned back to Anne.

'Your pass only admits one,' she said. 'There are two of you. No guests are allowed in the Vault.'

'She is not my guest, she is my colleague,' Anne said patiently. 'A science colleague from an American think-tank. My seniority should be all the explanation necessary to grant her admittance.'

Peggy twisted her mouth again, this time in the other direction. 'I'm afraid I can't allow your colleague access, Miss Travers. Not without the correct identification. You can go in alone if you would like.'

'Don't be absurd,' Anne said quickly. 'If she is with me that is all the identification required. I can vouch for her credentials.'

Behind her, she could hear the alien baby begin to stir in Patricia's arms. He made a short cry rather like a yawn. Anne pushed her pass further across the desk to Peggy.

'It is very important that you let us pass,' Anne said slowly.

The baby gave another short cry as if to concur.

Peggy got to her feet and peered across the desk. 'What's that noise?'

'Nothing,' Anne said, raising her voice to cover the sound. 'Now will you kindly let us through, or I will be forced to report your insubordination to the General?'

Peggy wasn't listening. Anne's threats were falling on deaf ears. Peggy was now far more interested in seeing what Patricia was concealing.

'Is that a baby? I love babies!'

'It is no concern of yours if it's a monkey or a balloon,' Anne said testily. 'My colleague and I do not have time for further delays. Our business is most important.'

'I wish I was having babies,' Peggy continued morosely, more to herself than Patricia and Anne. 'Much better than being stuck down here with all those funny smelling liquids and odd noises.'

Patricia held tightly to the alien baby, doing her best to keep him out of reach as Peggy leaned over to get a closer look. Anne was getting annoyed.

'Now look here,' she began but another voice piped up behind them.

'She's with me.'

Anne turned at the familiar sound. Bill stood behind them. If there was one thing Anne liked about Bill, it was his fabulous sense of timing. Although what business he had at the Vault was beyond her.

'Oh,' Peggy said, Bill's voice breaking through her reverie.

'Is that any way to talk to Doctor Travers? Or her esteemed American colleague, Doctor Richards?'

Peggy blinked at him in surprise.

'Now, please let these ladies pass,' Bill continued. 'Doctor Richards is here at the behest of Mr Benn himself.'

'The prime minister?' Peggy said, staring at him blankly.

'Not really,' Bill said. 'He's the minister of technology.'

'Oh. Right, yeah. Always getting the ministers confused.'

Bill nodded slowly. 'I see.' He leaned in closer and lifted her name badge briefly, pulling at her blouse. Peggy blushed. 'Miss Orwell,' he said, smiling at her. 'Peggy, they are here on top secret government business. It is absolutely essential you let them pass without further delay.'

'I... I'm sorry, sir. No one told me.'

'That's no excuse. You must let them pass, or would you like to explain yourself to the PM personally, Peggy?'

'Yes... I mean no. I mean, yes, they can pass, but no, I don't want to explain myself to er, Mr Wilson.'

'There we go, Doctor Travers, Doctor Richards,' Bill said, smiling at Anne and Patricia. He looked back at Peggy with a wink that, Anne decided, could only be called

75

solicitous. 'Shouldn't you be getting back to work? I'll escort these ladies down the way a bit, then we can chat some more.'

Peggy blushed again and sat herself back behind her desk.

'Sandhurst training at its best,' Anne said, once they were a little distance away from the Peggy.

Bill ignored her jibe. They both knew all too well that his officer training was being undertaken at Mons College. The jibe stemmed from the fact that he was only at Sandhurst for a few weeks before Hamilton swung it for him to be trained at Mons instead. Not that there was anything wrong with Mons, as was clear by how he addressed the receptionist, but Bill had wanted to play the Sandhurst card once he made officer.

'What are you doing here, Lance Corporal?' Patricia gave him a wide smile. 'I don't think I've ever been so glad to see a friendly face.'

'I had to drop off some files to Lieutenant Johnston for General Hamilton. He has to keep the Vault sweet while the colonel is busy up there,' Bill said, nodding in the general direction of Scotland. 'Actually that's not entirely true. I dropped the files off yesterday. I followed you here. I wanted to make sure you were both here safe and sound, and it looks like it's a good job I did.'

'Of course we are,' Anne snapped. 'Patricia came to me for a reason, because she knows I can help her. I would have persuaded Miss Orwell to let us through whether you were here or not.'

'I'm sure you would have done,' Bill said, with a smile, clearly not buying Anne's assurance. 'But you don't have to do everything by yourself, Anne.'

'I'm not doing it by myself,' Anne reasoned. 'Patricia is here with me too. Now if you don't mind, I think we should get a move on before another distraction appears.'

'All right,' Bill agreed a little reluctantly. 'But you will send for me if you need my help? I'm in the area for a while yet.'

'Of course,' Anne reassured him. 'If we need anything I will call for you straight away.'

Bill smiled. Anne knew that he didn't want to just be doing administration duties, and was finally glad to be out alien protecting, if not actually alien fighting.

'Goodbye, Corporal Bishop, always good to see a friendly face,' Anne said politely.

Bill smiled, saluted at her and Patricia, and made his exit.

'You're very lucky to have friends like that,' Patricia said. 'Having people to count on is the most important thing in the world.'

Anne didn't respond. Instead she took a sharp left, leaving Patricia struggling to keep up with her.

The corridor was beginning to darken and Anne knew that soon they would lose the light. She felt along the wall for the storage cupboard and took out two pairs of night vision goggles.

'What are these for?' Patricia asked curiously.

'You'll see,' Anne said. 'Or rather you won't. Not unless you put them on now and watch your step. Keep close to me from now on.'

'All right. Which way now?' Patricia slipped the heavy goggles over her head and adjusted them onto the bridge of her nose.

'Sshh!' Anne hissed.

'What is it?'

'I'm not sure,' Anne said, her eyes scanning the pitch black corridor. 'They should pass by without noticing if we stay still. Press yourself back into the wall.'

Patricia nodded but Anne couldn't see. They both waited, hardly daring to breath as the scuffing footsteps drew ever closer. They waited for what seemed like an eternity. The footsteps passed by without slowing their pace and soon the three of them were left alone in the dark silence of the corridor once more.

'I don't know how you see at all down here,' Patricia commented as her footsteps faltered. 'I've never known any laboratory to be so dark!'

The baby was chattering happily to himself now and Anne gave an inward sigh of relief that at least he wasn't screaming the place down. It wouldn't do to alert the whole Vault.

They walked on further.

'What's down there?' Patricia asked as they passed another darkened corridor, this time with a white door at the far end.

'Don't look,' Anne advised her friend, quickening her footsteps before Patricia could have time to look too closely. That door led to the deep freeze, where several dead bodies were kept on ice. Not the nicest place to visit.

They made their way further down into the blackness of the Vault, their eyes straining, not yet accustomed to the dark and through another warren of corridors before finally stopping outside one of the laboratories.

'Are you sure we're alone?' Patricia asked, her eyes scanning the walls as if someone was watching them.

'Quite sure. Now come on, before someone comes and pokes their nose in.'

Anne opened the door to her laboratory and motioned for Patricia to come quickly inside. Once they were both over the threshold, Anne closed the door and raised the light. She refused to work in the dark no matter what the General insisted upon.

'What are we going to do now, Annie?' Patricia asked anxiously. The baby in her arms began to stir.

'First,' said Anne, striding across to one of the cabinets that were mounted on the stone walls. 'We are going to need to take some samples. I'm afraid these will need to come from inside the baby's cheek.'

Patricia nodded her understanding. She pulled the swaddling cloth back from the baby's face, which spluttered slightly with annoyance. Gently, Anne leaned over and took a swab from inside the baby's cheek. She pressed the sample together between plates of glass. She peered down at it through the electron microscope at a resolution of a hundred picometres. Her eyes scanned over the DNA strands.

'What can you see?' Patricia asked, peering over Anne's shoulder. 'Anything unusual? Besides the obvious, of course.'

'Odd,' Anne murmured. 'Most curious.'

'What is it?' Patricia pressed. 'What can you see?'

'His DNA is definitely male,' Anne began slowly, her eye still pressed to the microscope. 'But it seems amphibian, more like that of a frog than anything human, despite his outward appearance.'

'Amphibian?' Patricia repeated. 'What a coincidence.'

'What do you mean?' Anne asked, raising herself to look back at Patricia.

'Well, back in Washington when the first wave of experimentations was taking place, we discovered that the Terrae had evolved to maintain a double circulatory system.'

'Go on.'

'As I mentioned before, they had a duality of organs. Now humans, of course, have two sets of some organs – lungs, kidneys, for example. But the Terrae have a double of every single organ in their body.'

Anne looked down at the baby. He looked as human to her as any baby she had seen before, but to know all that was going on inside him was so different was thrilling.

'May I take him?' she asked.

Patricia nodded and carefully passed him into her arms. Anne gently laid the baby down. He giggled for a moment, reaching up to grab at her hair. Anne stayed focused, her mind on the science at hand. The machine made a whirring mechanical sound and then, slowly, began to move across his tiny body. Anne and Patricia watched as the red lasers scanned every cell in his body. The baby didn't seem to mind too much. He kept very still as if he somehow knew it was important, his large eyes moving from side to side as he concentrated on the light show. Finally, the mechanical noise stopped and the lights went out. Anne raced across to the other end of the machine to remove the paperwork it had produced.

'This doesn't like right, Anne,' Patricia said as she peered over her shoulder to examine the results. 'The Terrae should have two of every organ, at least at the infant stage. But looking at this scan he appears to be missing some. He doesn't have two of everything at all. I researched this aspect of the Terrae species extensively back in Washington and it was evident from the skeletal structure that it would have supported dual organs. Look,' she said, pointing to a specific point on the graph. 'There is definitely enough space in these cavities to accommodate another set of organs.'

'But what I don't understand,' Anne said, 'is why would they no longer have two? These results make him seem almost... human.'

'I don't know,' Patricia admitted. 'There must be an explanation.'

'Yes, one we need to work out.' Anne started to pace around the small laboratory.

'What is it, Annie?'

'Nothing. At least I'm not sure,' Anne added, that old twinkle appearing in her hazel eyes. 'It could be something.'

'Tell me more!'

'It is as if they have a back-up, so that if they need to adapt... You see they look like us, but what if that wasn't always the case? What if we are seeing them in their second form, not their original?'

'You mean here on Earth they take a different form?' Patricia asked.

'Precisely!' Anne nodded. 'They adapt to live in our atmosphere, but only after a certain degree of rapid evolution has taken place. The changes take place internally, but externally they seem to retain the same human appearance.'

The two were so engrossed in their findings neither of them heard the click of the door. By the time the bright friendly face peered around the side it was already too late.

'Anne?' Tim Gambrell said, his dark goggles looking unnaturally large on his small face.

Patricia hurried over to the machine, which still cradled the baby, standing in front of it to conceal him from view.

'Tim?' Anne said with surprise. 'What are you doing here?' She silently cursed herself; she must have forgotten to lock the door.

'I thought that was you.'

'Yes it's me,' Anne said. 'Where's Carl? I thought you two were supposed to be working on some secret project together.'

'We were, but then he got called away. Vault business. No one ever tells me what's going on. Anyway, never mind about that, I have something I want you to see.' Tim's round face beamed in the darkness, shining with the thought of possibilities, his voice rising and falling.

'Who's he?' Patricia hissed, once Tim had moved away from them. 'I thought you said we would be alone in here?'

'Just another overenthusiastic protégé of Leonard's; another harmless research scientist. Come on, humour him.'

'Come take a look!' Tim called back to Anne eagerly, his teeth gleaming white in the darkness.

Anne didn't know how he could always be so cheerful in the dark unrelenting oppressive nature of the Vault. Patricia hung back trying her best to conceal the baby in her arms.

'This way!' Tim said.

The two of them followed him down the corridor and into a room a few doors down from Anne's. Tim's laboratory was the polar opposite of Anne's, cluttered to the ceiling with every kind of equipment imaginable. To one side, a particle accelerator, vacuum and operant conditioning chambers. To the other, spectrophotometers and calorimeters. Patricia stared in amazement, her mouth open, as she took it all in. Anne knew this was nothing like the labs they had worked in back at the base in Nevada, and hoped that Patricia wouldn't be too nervous.

'Come over here, Anne,' Tim was saying and he beckoned her over. 'You have to see this.'

He made his way to the back wall over which was a tiny black curtain. He pulled it back sharply to reveal a small rectangular aperture that allowed them to see into an adjoining room. The three moved closer towards the small side room, but the laboratory was so tight and cramped they were forced to stand shoulder to shoulder. Patricia hid the baby under her coat as best she could.

In front of them they could see a small room illuminated by a single bulb. Inside there was a young man tied to a chair. He murmured something but they couldn't hear his words. Anne figured it must be some kind of two-way glass.

'They keep people down here?' Patricia said, shocked.

Anne coughed. 'Sometimes,' she admitted. 'I'm sure there must be a good reason for it.'

'I don't think I want to come any closer, Anne,' Patricia said. 'Reminds me of some of the things I saw back in Washington.'

'What things?'

Patricia visibly shuddered. 'Terrible things. Things I've tried so hard to forget and don't want to be reminded of.'

Anne took Patricia's arm and steered her to one side. 'All right. Why don't you stay outside with the baby? I'm sure this won't take long.'

Anne stepped forwards, but Patricia stayed at her elbow. 'I thought you wanted to stay behind?'

Patricia shook her head. 'I think I would rather stay close to you in this dreadful darkness.'

'This way, ladies,' Tim said. 'Now, observe.'

'How awful, I hate it,' Patricia said. 'This is how we got into this whole sorry mess. Keeping people trapped.'

'I must ask you both to be quiet,' Tim said.

'But he can't hear us,' Patricia pointed out.

'That's as may be. But I need to concentrate. Take a look, Anne.'

She leaned forward as instructed, and peered closer into the room. For the first time she noticed that not only was the teenager tied to the chair but that for some reason his eyes had been pinned open, the pupils scanning from side to side wildly. The close up of the eye was projected onto a screen next to them, which Tim was studying intently. It was eerily large and when Anne looked at it directly she felt a desire to turn away from it.

'What do you think to my latest subject?' Tim said.

'I have to admit I'm not quite sure. I think I will need you to explain.'

Tim smiled, his eyes concealed behind the wide impenetrable lenses of the night vision goggles. 'He has taken a new drug that has been circulating on the street. A substance we have never seen before. His name is Darren Carlin, and he was sent to us from Scotland last night.'

'Sent? By whom?'

'You know how it is here, Anne. Contacts everywhere. Even in the Scottish police.'

Anne didn't like it, but neither did she see what the big deal was. 'But why? What has that got to do with the Vault?'

Tim smiled again. 'The drug isn't native to Earth.'

'Alien?' It wasn't the first drug of alien origin she'd come across, and the last one had proven to have very dangerous side effects. 'But how would a young man like this have come into contact with extra-terrestrial material?'

'That's what we are trying to find out,' Tim said. 'If we can isolate the drug's properties, we might be able to establish where it comes from.'

'Why was he in custody anyway?' Patricia asked. 'What has he done wrong?'

'Nothing that we know of,' Tim admitted. 'Probably just another troublemaker in Edinburgh. But we've had to confine him. You see, when I say establish where the drug comes from I don't just mean who he purchased it from. We're calling it Moon Blink, due to the literal blinking sensation that it causes. It's akin to Lysergic Acid Diethylamide. Not of the ergoline family, though, but it still alters the thinking process, producing synthesia; an altered sense of time.'

'An unwilling time traveller,' Anne said to herself, remembering how she had previously used an alien drug to facilitate travel back to 1823.

'Quite.'

Tim was the only person in the Vault who knew of Anne's trip back in time, after all she had needed to take him into her confidence when securing a sample of the alien Om-Tsor to facilitate her trip.

'He doesn't look terribly well,' Patricia pointed out. 'Is it possible the drug could be fatal?'

'Doesn't seem to be as far as we can tell,' Tim said, checking the readings from the instruments next to him. 'Well, certainly not in the doses we have tested. It's rather curious but it seems that Moon Blink only stays in the system for the cycle of the Moon, roughly twenty-eight days. Then it leaves the system and the subject returns to normal, and—'

'Hang on,' Anne said, stopping him. 'How do you know this cycle? He's not the first subject you've had here, is he?'

Tim swallowed. At least he had the gumption to look guilty about it. 'I must admit there are some parts of working at the Vault that give cause to hold one's nose, as it were,' he began. 'But you cannot ignore the fact that this is an alien substance. Just like Om-Tsor, it's an extra-terrestrial drug that has found its way onto our streets. And who knows what havoc it may cause if we don't find out what damage it can do and try to keep it under control. We both know the damage Om-Tsor caused at Wembley back in April.'

Anne nodded, but inside she wasn't so sure. Nothing was orthodox at the Vault.

At her side, Patricia tensed.

'What is it?' Anne asked.

'I've seen all this before,' Patricia said.

'Seen what before? Him?' Anne pointed at Darren Carlin, refusing to simply think of him as a subject. She wouldn't let the Vault desensitise her.

'No, not him. That!' Patricia pointed at the image of the eye. 'That strange movement, the rapid blinking, and the dilated pupils that then change shape—'

'Hold on.' Anne turned on Tim, dots joining in her mind. 'What did you say the drug is called?'

'We call it Moon Blink. I suspect it had a different name on the streets, though.'

Just then Darren began to writhe and wrestle against the binding of the chair.

'Ah, he seems to be coming loose. One moment please.' Tim opened the door into the room. It was propped open for a moment and Anne and Patricia looked inside and watched as Tim tightened the teenager's binds.

'I don't like it, Anne,' Patricia said as soon as Tim was out of earshot. 'What is he trying to prove?'

'I think he's trying to understand what is making people take the drug, and then studying the side effects. As he mentioned, it's not the first alien drug we've seen here.'

'Anne! You can't be justifying any of this?'

Anne shook her head. 'Of course I'm not. But I know Tim, he's not a bad man. And like he said, there are things in the Vault that sometimes means we have to—'

Tim raced back into the room, locking the door behind him.

'What's going on?' Anne asked him. 'What is making him react that way?'

'I don't know,' Tim said, pressing his face against the glass. 'At least not yet.' He raced to his equipment, his eyes scanning over the screens and dials to see what adjustments needed to be made. 'He's going off the scale!' he cried in panic. 'Look!'

The dial was beginning to spin wildly, and the readings increased rapidly.

'What's happening, Anne?' Patricia asked.

Anne turned and saw that the baby was peering over the blanket, his eyes wide as he looked through the glass door panel. He made a little noise of delight as if he had just seen something familiar.

'What was that sound?' Tim said.

'Nothing,' Anne said quickly, stepping in between Patricia and the door. 'I didn't hear anything. Did you, Patricia?'

Patricia shook her head. 'No,' she said. 'Perhaps it's coming from inside the room?'

Tim shook his head, dismissed the sound, and turned his attention back to his experiment, just in time to see Darren struggling desperately against his bindings, his eyes opening and closing rapidly as he looked out towards them.

'What's going on?' Tim said, urgently racing to check the dials and gauges of his machines. 'I've never seen any reaction like this. The last test subject didn't display anything remotely like this.' Patricia and Anne shared a worried glance at the excitement in Tim's voice. 'This is so sudden, and with no perceivable cause as far as I can tell.'

'Oh no,' Anne murmured. 'It's the baby!' As soon as the words left her mouth, she clamped her hand over it. But it was too late, the words were out there.

'A baby?' Tim said, his face perplexed. 'What baby?'

Anne looked at Patricia apologetically. The damage was done; it was too late to keep on concealing him now.

'This one,' Patricia said, opening the cloth.

Tim stared at the little boy. 'Is that a real baby?' he asked incredulously. 'In the Vault?'

'Yes,' Anne said, as if he was silly to even ask such a question.

'I don't think we're supposed to bring children down here,' Tim said slowly.

'Oh, do be serious, Tim,' Anne scolded him. 'He's not here as an experiment! What do you think we are, monsters?'

'I kind of think you might be,' Patricia said, glaring at Tim and then looking across at Darren.

'What? No, this is just...' Tim was lost for words, a rare thing in Anne's experience. He shrugged helplessly. 'I'm just surprised, that's all.'

'What will happen to that kid now?' Patricia asked with concern. Her eyes were still on Darren, now slumped motionlessly in the chair.

Anne understood Patricia's concerns. If they could do that to a teenage boy, what would they do to a baby boy?

'He will be taken to the recovery room. Our desire is to test out the effect of the alien drug inside the human body,' Tim explained. 'We don't want him to come to any harm. He will rest and then we will try again tomorrow.' He stepped closer to the glass, his attention no longer on the baby. 'There's something I'm missing, but I just can't seem to quite put my little finger on it.'

'Well, I think we've seen enough of this. Come one.' Anne bundled the three of them out of the laboratory as quickly as possible.

'That was weird,' Patricia said. 'What do you think was the matter with him? Poor guy.'

'Maybe he just doesn't like children?' Tim offered with a smile, trying to make a joke, but Anne shot him a look. His eyes fell to his shoes.

'Thank you for your help, Tim, really *very* good work,' she said acidly. 'I will see you tomorrow.'

Without another word Tim returned to his lab and closed the door behind him.

'Sorry about that,' Anne said to Patricia. 'It's this place. It just gets inside you, corrupts you.' She sighed. 'Come on. Let's get out of here.'

After a good bit of distance was put between them and Tim's lab, Patricia spoke up. Her tone was one of anger, peppered with a bit of disappointment.

'Seriously, Annie, what the hell was that? Why would some guy go so crazy over seeing a baby? Do you think maybe he lost a kid himself or something?'

'No,' Anne said, speeding up her pace as they neared the exit of the Vault and the promise of daylight beyond. 'I think he knew. He knew exactly what he was looking at.'

'Knew what?' Patricia asked breathlessly, trying to keep pace with her friend.

Anne sucked in her cheeks, then gave a low sigh before responding. 'I think he could tell that this baby isn't human.'

Behind her, Patricia stumbled and her face fell.

'Come on!' Anne urged. 'We need to get out of her!'

Patricia was staring at her dumbly, her eyes wide with fear. Almost as wide as Darren's had been. 'But how could he possibly be able to tell that?' she asked, her voice so low it was almost a whisper.

'I can't know yet for sure,' Anne admitted. 'But if we've learned anything, then it's that there is clearly a connection between the Moon Blink compound and the Terrae.'

Patricia nodded, still feeling a little out of her depth.

'Now we have to figure how to use it to our advantage,' Anne said, her voice lowering as they neared the reception area. 'If the boy could tell the baby was an alien, maybe we can use it to find the others. Now come on.'

— CHAPTER SIX —

My Generation

Another long day of administration work was over and Captain Bartlett had the late night shift, which meant, for Lethbridge-Stewart and Dougie, a well-deserved pint was needed. They were both tired, of course, what with so little sleep after their previous late-night shift, but all the work deserved some kind of immediate reward. It was a rare thing for them to be alone without any further duties and, more importantly, without the women about. And so they found a pub not too far from their hotel, located at 100 Rose Street it was aptly called *The Auld Hundred*; a lovely traditional pub, founded in the 1800s, and every bit the kind of pub Lethbridge-Stewart tended to favour. He could see it becoming his local once he moved to Edinburgh, in fact. As he returned to their table in the corner, the first round being his, Lethbridge-Stewart smiled and nodded, joining in with the general ribald atmosphere. It was nice to be surrounded by the Scottish brogue again, reminding him of many happy times visiting his great-grandfather as a child.

He placed the pints on the table and accepted a lit cigar off Dougie.

'Like being back home, eh?' Dougie said.

'Well, of a sort. I never lived in Scotland, of course, but my father's family remained here even when he moved down to England before meeting my mother.' Lethbridge-Stewart savoured the taste of the cigar, and looked around the pub. 'My father had pretty much lost his accent by the time I was old enough to recognise such a thing, and it obviously didn't rub off on me.'

'You don't sound Cornish, either.'

Lethbridge-Stewart smiled. 'No, although I did as a child, but education and service in the military put paid to that.'

'I remember,' Dougie said. 'It was all but gone when met.'

Lethbridge-Stewart nodded. They'd known each other a long time, and it was nice to be serving together once more. Other than a brief spell in London in March, this was the first time they'd really served together since the Korean War.

'Anyway, my dad's dad, my namesake, never quite lost his accent. And as for *his* father...'

'Och aye te noo?' Dougie said, sounding like an actor on stage who had never learned to master accents.

Lethbridge-Stewart cleared his throat, and smiled good naturedly as a stocky Scotsman who looked their way at Dougie's destruction of the Scottish accent. The man shrugged and turned back to his mates. 'Quite,' Lethbridge-Stewart said.

He watched the small group of men for a while longer. They were loud, but no threat. Lethbridge-Stewart turned his attention back to Dougie, but his eyes stopped on a lone figure at the far end of the bar. He sat there, giving the term nondescript a new meaning. If Lethbridge-Stewart hadn't been looking out for trouble he doubted he would have even noticed the man, so good a job was he doing of blending in.

The man looked up from his glass of – water? Gin? Lethbridge-Stewart wasn't sure, whatever it was it was as plain as the man. He had dark eyes, lifeless Lethbridge-Stewart would have said if asked to describe them, yet the man's face seemed gentle. Totally unassuming. As if it was saying *don't notice me, I'm not here, not worth seeing.*

Lethbridge-Stewart chewed on the cigar for a moment longer, before turning his attention back to Dougie, the man at the bar forgotten about.

Dougie accepted the cigar back and took a few tugs. 'You know, Alistair, I can't say I'm convinced by all this.'

'All what?'

'Aliens,' Dougie said, lowering his voice. 'I know I was there at Fang Rock, and I've read all the files you've given me. But... It's a bit much to take in, don't you think?'

'It is. But experience will change that.' Lethbridge-Stewart supped his pint of McEwan's ale. 'I sometimes wish I could unsee what I've seen, but ever since London... Well, I'm sure you'll be face-to-face with the unexplainable soon enough.'

'No doubt. I was reading some of the LONGBOW files last night, in particular Operation George in 1939. A dragon? An actual alien.'

'Any stranger than giant alien jellyfish?' Lethbridge-Stewart asked, raising an eyebrow.

Dougie conceded the point. 'Or Project Ironside that Churchill mentioned in a report from '41.' He shrugged. 'I guess they come in all shapes and sizes, aliens. Another one?' he added, finishing off his pint.

Charlie Redfern hesitated outside the front door of his

house. Technically it was his house; he had his own key and paid rent every month, well most months at least. It was definitely his house. But somehow the creaky old building still didn't feel like his home. He had moved away from his hometown to start a new life in London and his elderly maiden aunt had been only too happy to have him stay with her. That was until he told her he wanted to be a journalist. After that she eyed him with suspicion and shuffled quickly out of the room whenever Charlie raced home with the day's papers.

The girl standing behind him on the porch step looked nervous, too, turning around so that her eyes could dart along the street and down again as if she was afraid someone might be following them. Charlie had only known her for a few hours but already he could tell that she was going to be the story that changed everything. She was going to put him on the map. The trouble was, it was the kind of story that Charlie wasn't even sure he could make other people believe – it was almost too fantastical. Still, the girl was in trouble. She had come to him for help on the advice of a mutual friend and Charlie was nothing if not honourable. He would help her as much as he could. Then he would write his story.

Once in the hallway, Charlie looked around to see if he could spot any trace of his aunt. There was no sign of her except the tell-tale sound coming from the kitchen. Her humming.

'Quickly,' he said to the pale, frightened girl behind him. 'Follow me. Up the stairs, first door on the right.'

The girl nodded and together the two of them crept up the old staircase, which creaked and groaned, threatening to give them away at any moment. Finally, they reached the attic room. Charlie went in first, the girl following closely behind. He hurriedly scooped up armfuls of clothes and papers that were scattered haphazardly across the room, trying to make things a little more presentable.

It was the first time his little room had received any guests, and certainly never a girl.

After he finished, he reached out and selected the 8-track cassette, feeding it into the tape machine and pressing play. There was a moment of silence, then crackling which turned into sound.

'Do you like music?' he asked her. He really didn't know anything about her, he realised, not even her name.

The girl smiled. 'Yes,' she said. 'I like it.'

Charlie gave an awkward grin and then hurriedly went to lock the door behind them. The last thing he needed was for his aunt to come bustling in and interrupt his interview. The room felt stuffy, so he went to open the window. He turned up the volume on the tape machine and the music streamed out across the street. He could hear someone from next-door banging against the wall, but he was so used to their complaints that he barely registered them anymore. He liked his music loud; it helped him to think.

The girl wandered over to the window and peeped through the curtains tentatively.

'Don't do that!' Charlie cautioned her.

'Why not?'

'You never know who might be watching.'

The girl moved away from the window and settled herself on the edge of the bed.

Charlie swallowed. She had appeared out of nowhere

just as he was parking his car around the corner, he never had quite enough petrol to make it all the way home. At first he had thought she was just lost, perhaps just wanting directions, but then he had realised there was something else going on. For a start, she knew his name. Charlie had thought she might be working for a paper; a fellow reporter. But she didn't seem to understand what he meant when he had made further enquires. All she would tell him was that they had a mutual friend who had told her to seek him out. She had said she was in great danger and he was the only one who would be able to help her get home.

To a lesser man it would all have sounded like the ravings of a mad woman, but Charlie prided himself on being able to investigate any situation that presented itself to a satisfactory conclusion. He had offered to help her on the proviso that she told him her whole story with no omissions. She had agreed and now the two of them sat in his attic room, her on the bed cross-legged while he positioned himself some distance away by the wardrobe.

Charlie needed to get to the bottom of this. He couldn't stay distracted by this strange and pretty girl. He reached across and fished inside his battered satchel and took out his trusty notebook and pen.

'Now,' he said. 'Do you remember what I asked you? I said that it is very important you tell me why you came to me. Otherwise I won't be able to help you. Do you understand?'

The girl smiled widely at him, her long hair falling around her shoulders. 'Yes, I understand. I will help you and then you will help me. You *will* help me, won't you?'

'Yes. What did you say your name was?'

'Selene.'

'Selene,' Charlie echoed. 'That's a nice name. Unusual.'

'Yes. Thank you.'

There was a moment of silence between them again. For the first time Charlie noticed how wide her eyes were and the odd way they stared out at him, like an owl entranced.

'Why do they call you Charlie?' she asked, her wide eyes staring at him.

'I don't know. My real name is Charles, of course, but I prefer Charlie. But that's me, just plain old Charlie.'

'Charlie,' the girl repeated. 'I like that name. What kind are you, Charlie?'

'A journalist.' Charlie sniffed. 'Or at least I'm trying to be.'

He heard voices chattering through the thin wall. Charlie got up and turned the volume up on his cassette player. The neighbours would probably come and bang on the wall again, but at least they wouldn't have the chance to hear what he and Selene were saying.

'How did you find me?' he asked her.

Selene reached into the pocket of her skirt and passed him a photograph. It was a man of Indian descent in a lab coat; just the head and shoulders, as if was taken from an identification badge of some sort. Doctor Jhaveri; Charlie had interviewed him back when he was running his university's paper a few years before.

'He was a good man,' Selene said. 'He said we must all come to Britain. That once we were here would be among friends. Are you my friend, Charlie?'

'I would like to be.' The blush spread to the corner of his temples. Charlie coughed and began his questioning again.

'So where exactly did you say you came from again?'

'Somewhere far, far away. Out there.' She pointed towards the window, the curtains still closed.

'Right,' Charlie said. He wondered what this girl had been taking. She certainly was beginning to seem more than a little touched. 'But how did you come to meet Doctor Jhaveri?'

Selene's pale face went whiter still. Her long hair cast a shadow so that half of it was hidden in darkness. Her voice was softer and Charlie had to strain his ears to catch all of what she was saying. 'There was a cage. We were there, all of us. Trapped. It was terrible.'

'So there are more of you?' Charlie asked, scribbling furiously.

The girl laughed suddenly. It was a curious sound that didn't seem to come from her mouth at all, but instead all around her. 'Of course!' she said. 'There are many of us. Oh.' Her face fell again, her mood changing rapidly. 'But they are not here. There are only a few left here. We must all return home. That's why Doctor Jhaveri said that you would help me. I could tell you the truth but you wouldn't believe me.'

Charlie felt terrible for the girl but there was another sensation too. He could smell that this had all the hallmarks of a really great story. 'Tell me more about the cage. Where was it, can you remember?'

The girl stared out into the distance as if she was trying to recall the memory. 'There was a room. It was white and there was an odd smell. They called it Project Horizon.'

'How is Penny with all this?' Lethbridge-Stewart asked.

'She knows the cost of being married to a career officer,' Dougie said. 'Her only concern was Jake. Being taken out of school.'

'Of course.' Lethbridge-Stewart had forgotten about Dougie's son in all the rush of reassignment. 'Well, he's only seven, young enough to adapt.'

'That's what I said. A bit of Scottish education won't hurt the lad, and besides, a few years and he'll be boarding at Brendon anyway.' Dougie smiled over his pint. 'Be glad you don't have children. Just you and Sally. Makes moving easier.'

Lethbridge-Stewart raised his eyebrows. 'Does it? It's a long way to commute. For her, that is.' He went on to explain that as she was still stationed in Fugglestone it made little sense in her moving to Edinburgh, too. 'She'll be here for the occasional weekend, but…'

'Wrong time to become engaged,' Dougie said with a nod. 'Well, like Penny, she knows the price. More so, really, being in the Forces too.'

'That's what I would have thought. But I don't think Sally does realise.' Lethbridge-Stewart leaned forward and lowered his voice, not really wanting the locals to hear him moan about his misses. 'Only last month she went to Hamilton while I was at that safe house. Protocol and discipline be damned.'

'I bet Hamilton loved that!'

'He wasn't best impressed, no. I haven't said anything, of course, but it does make me wonder.'

Dougie raised his glass. 'Here's to civilian wives and children,' he said.

With a rueful smile, Lethbridge-Stewart clinked glasses,

thinking that Dougie had the better deal in all this. Their toast was disturbed by a commotion near the bar.

A youth with messy shoulder length air, no more than nineteen, was disturbing the man who had been sitting quietly at the bar. The youth was pointing, clearly agitated, his eyes blinking rapidly.

'What are ye?' he asked the man. He stepped backwards, his voice louder. 'Wha' the hell is wit' ye? Those eyes are no' normal.'

The man at the bar looked around, worry all over his face. The punters around them watched, talking among themselves. The barman attempted to calm the youth down, telling him that they needed no drugs in this bar. But the youth wasn't listening, instead he continued to point and shout at the poor man.

Lethbridge-Stewart had enough. He wasn't the police, of course, but he had enough authority to put this to bed. He stood up and made his way through the small crowd, and grabbed hold of the youth's arm.

'Come on, lad, time to call it a night.'

The youth looked at him like he was mad. 'Do you no' see it?'

The smell of alcohol hung heavily on the youth, but it wasn't that which was causing his agitation. Lethbridge-Stewart recognised the glazed look in his eyes, the rapid blinking. The same as that Darren Carlin fellow.

Charlie scribbled down on his notepad. Project Horizon? Sounded like something official, probably top secret.

'That's brilliant,' he said encouragingly. 'Can you remember anything else? Tell me more about Project

Horizon.'

Selene's brow furrowed, revealing another line of circular indentations. 'No,' she said. 'I don't want to.'

'But we agreed!' Charlie said. 'I would help you in return for your story.'

Selene went quiet again, her eyes staring into space as if she could see something he couldn't.

'Far away,' she offered, finally. 'It wasn't here. Doctor Jhaveri was there but then he went away. I heard voices; someone said that he wasn't coming back. Then there was a woman. She helped us to escape; those that were left. Then there was sunlight and dust and then I came through the skies to this place. I should have gone home then but I was trying to find the others. Now I have left it too late and I had no choice but to come here to you. To the safe place.'

'The safe place?' Charlie repeated. 'For what? What do you need to do?'

Selene was about to reply when the doorknob moved violently from side to side. His aunt.

'Charles?' she called through the door. 'What's going on in there?'

Selene sprang to her feet, her eyes wide with fear. She raced across to the window, putting her shoulder against the closed latch.

'What are you doing?' Charlie said. 'Selene! Don't do that, you'll hurt yourself!'

'Charles!' persisted the voice of his aunt. 'Open up at once! I've told you never to the lock this door!'

'Who is that?' Selene asked, her voice shaking.

'No one,' Charlie said dismissively. 'It's just my aunt, she owns this place, so technically she's my landlady too.'

He swallowed, then added, 'Ignore her. She'll soon get bored and go away. She's not enlightened, man. She doesn't hear the music in the, er, music.'

It looked as if Selene wasn't hearing the music either. She shoved her shoulder against the window once more, obviously desperate to get out.

'Stop!' Charlie said, his hands hovering over her shoulders, too afraid to actually touch her. 'Please!'

'Are they coming to take me back?' Selene asked, her eyes widening. 'Not the cage! Don't let them take me back to the cage!'

'Charles!'

The door began to rattle violently again.

'No one is going to take you anywhere, I promise,' Charlie said. 'But I need you to step back from the window, Selene.'

She watched him cautiously.

'Charles!' came the raspy voice once more.

'Coming, Aunt May!' Charlie hollered then looked back to Selene. 'I have to open the door now. Please just sit still. No one is coming to take you anywhere, I promise. But I need to make her go away.'

Selene looked at him with her owl-like gaze and Charlie hoped to goodness that she had understood. He unlocked the door and opened it just wide enough for his aunt and landlady to peer around the side.

'What are you up to?' she asked him. 'You know I don't like you to have the door locked. What if there was a fire?'

She elbowed her way past him and made her way into the small attic room. She was swathed in a red dressing gown with her hair rolled up into two large curlers at the front like an antenna. The whole effect was rather startling and made her look like some undiscovered species of beetle. She tried to walk closer towards the bed but Charlie stood between them, blocking her path.

'Why is there a girl in here, Charles? With the door closed too?' she asked, narrowing her eyes.

'We are just going over my notes. There's an article I'm going to submit to a local paper. A prestigious one,' he added.

This stopped her for a moment. She contemplated what he had told her. 'Oh really? On what?' she persisted, her eyes narrowing with suspicion.

'Astronomy,' Selene said without hesitation. 'We've been looking at the stars.'

Aunt May pursed her lips and turned her attention back to Charlie. 'Well, just you mind that stars are all you are looking at,' she cautioned him, her old eyes narrowing as she struggled to see Selene clearly. 'This is not to happen again, do you understand me? Not in my house! What do you think your mother would say?'

'Thank you, Aunt May,' Charlie said. 'It won't happen again, I promise.'

The door closed behind her. Charlie waited until he could hear her footsteps receding down the stairs before he turned the lock again.

'Why does she speak to you like that?' Selene said, her long eyelashes opening and closing slowly.

'She's my aunt. Don't all families behave that way?'

'Perhaps on Earth.'

Charlie watched her again. She looked just like any other girl. Well maybe not quite any other girl. She was pretty in her own unique way, with long dark hair that finished way past her shoulders and clear lilywhite skin that seemed to shine and gleam, but in certain lights he caught sight of slight indentations across her cheeks and the bridge of her nose.

Suddenly, she leaped across and cowered against him.

Charlie felt his face getting hot with embarrassment, but the girl didn't seem to notice. She just continued to stare out of the window at the night sky, lost in her own world. She sprang to her feet.

'Are you feeling ill?' Charlie asked politely.

'No,' the girl replied. 'I am just not used to having to be afraid. Where I am from there is no fear. We have no need of it.'

A place with no fear. Charlie wondered where such a place could exist.

Gently, but firmly, Lethbridge-Stewart guided the youth out of the pub.

The youth was still pointing. 'You have ta have seen it!'

'Go home,' Lethbridge-Stewart said firmly. 'Sleep it off.'

The youth attempted to push his way past, but with a gentle shove from Lethbridge-Stewart, he staggered backwards off the pavement. 'He's no right, I tell ye! He's a bloody alien.'

Lethbridge-Stewart wanted to humour the young man, but he was already on the alert after all that business with Mr Carlin. He hadn't thought to contact Miss Travers, to see if she had run her tests on that Luna Haze stuff. Perhaps he should contact the police, find out where Mr Carlin was?

'Okay, son,' Lethbridge-Stewart said, stepping forward with his arms out to show he meant no harm. 'What's all this about? Alien?'

The young man eyed Lethbridge-Stewart with suspicion. 'Ye're on the level, are ye?'

'I am indeed. But that chap in the pub... Looked no different to you or me.'

The youth shook his head. 'Aye, but only if ye've no' had some Luna Haze. It makes you see things clearly. Like the Moon.' He looked up at the night sky, his eyes widening in wonder. 'Tha's a thing of beauty. All purple, like it's alive.'

Lethbridge-Stewart looked up too. The grey orb, low in the dark sky, just looked like the Moon to him, the place both the Americans and... He looked back to the youth and narrowed his eyes. Unless he was mistaken he'd heard that both lunar expeditions had been cancelled rather abruptly over a week ago. Had they brought something back?

'Listen to me, how could you tell that chap was alien?'

'I cannae tell ye, ye have ta see if for yeself.'

'And just how do I do that?'

The youth reached into his pocket and pulled out a small clear packet which contained a whitish-purple dust. The same substance that had been sent to Miss Travers. 'With this!' the young man said, his eyes blinking even more than before.

Selene got to her feet and made her way back towards the window. 'Why is Theia so bright tonight?' she asked.

'Theia?' Charlie moved next to her.

'It's what *we*... I call the Moon.'

'Oh.' Charlie pulled the curtain back. 'It hasn't even risen yet.'

'No,' the girl agreed. 'But I can see it now.'

Charlie followed her gaze but to him the sky remained impenetrable and grey, with dark clouds hanging heavily. Selene leaned in closer, her long dark hair splayed out across her shoulders as they looked out at the sky. Charlie hadn't felt the weight of a girl's head on his shoulder before. He coughed and moved away from her. He opened a small ceramic tin on the windowsill.

'Try this,' he said passing across the tin of dried leaves and accompanying cigarette papers.

Selene looked down at it and then shook her head. 'No thank you.'

'Do you need something to eat instead?'

The strange girl shook her head again, her eyes still watching the sky as if she could see something he couldn't.

'But aren't you hungry?' Charlie said. 'You haven't had a bite since we met.'

Selene's wide eyes scanned around the room. 'It isn't the same for me. Do you think Theia will rise soon?' she asked dreamily.

'Not quite yet,' he said, still wondering at that name. 'But the sky is getting darker.'

He wasn't sure what she was waiting for. He sprinkled the crushed leaves into the cigarette paper, then putting it between his lips he sparked a match. There was a puff of smoke and then an herbal scent filled the space between them.

'Do you think it's going to be a full Moon?' he asked her, his mind thinking back to stories he had read as a young boy. Strange goings on always seemed to coincide with a full Moon. She shook her head.

Then something odd happened. She began to cry, tears

falling down her pale cheeks.

'The time is close and I must leave! But first there is something else I need you to have.'

She reached into the heavy fabric of her cardigan and pulled out a padded envelope. Charlie looked at it as he inhaled, wondering what on earth could be inside it.

'These are from Doctor Jhaveri,' Selene said. 'He gave them to me for you. He said that you would know what to do with them.'

Charlie stubbed out the cigarette in the ashtray on the bedside table. He opened the envelope cautiously. There seemed to be several photographs, some of them laminated, tucked inside. He reached in to try to free them but instead sent the whole lot floating down across the floor. Selene rushed to help him pick up the scattered photographs from the carpet.

'Who are they?' Charlie asked, turning over each, one by one, and spreading them in a line up across the floor. They looked official, like the kind of photographs that might be taken for the purpose of an identification badge. They were men all dressed in white lab coats. A couple were bald, one bespectacled, all wearing a sombre expression. He recognised the headshot of Doctor Jhaveri at once. Then he saw something that surprised him. Among the handful of photographs there was a photograph of a woman. She too was dressed in the stark whiteness of a lab coat, which contrasted against her dark hair and eyes.

'I don't know them all,' Selene said. 'But Doctor Jhaveri said that they were all friends. That they would be the ones to help us.'

'Hang on a moment,' Charlie said. 'This woman looks

familiar.'

'Oh?'

'Yes. This woman was a colleague of Doctor Jhaveri, I think,' Charlie said, holding the photograph up to get a better look. 'Yes. I definitely remember seeing her face on some of the slides at his lecture. Wait—'

Something else had caught Charlie's eye. Right at the bottom of the pile, almost concealed behind another photograph, he saw a second picture of a woman in a white lab coat. She was dark too but her hair was shorter than the first woman's. This photograph looked older too, and a little faded as if it had been taken prior to the others. The woman's hazel eyes looked out at him with startling clarity.

'Yes!' Charlie said triumphantly. 'I think I've seen her, too.'

'Too?'

'Yes! Her name is—'

He didn't get a chance to finish. Selene had wandered across to the open window and was now staring out of it dreamily. Suddenly, she jumped onto the windowsill.

'What are you doing?' Charlie said, watching her in horror.

'Come on,' she beckoned. 'This way!'

'No way!' he said. 'You can't get down that way.'

'I don't want to go down,' Selene said. 'Up is where I want to go.'

Carefully, Charlie took her arm and pulled her away from the ledge. 'Not like this,' he cautioned her. 'It isn't safe, Selene. You wanted me to help you, remember?'

'Yes,' Selene said. She gave one last longing look out of the window and then allowed Charlie to lead her back into the room. Charlie felt a wave of relief and hastily went to close the window so that now it was only ajar. When he turned back, he saw that Selene had slipped a necklace from around her neck. She took the vial charm in her hand and carefully began to open the lid. Charlie watched as she shook it gently, sprinkling a fine purple white powder into her hand.

'Come closer,' she said.

Charlie scooted along the bed towards her until they were face to face. She pressed her lips together and blew the strange purple cloud into his face.

Lethbridge-Stewart watched as the youth finally staggered away, still muttering to himself about aliens, angry that Lethbridge-Stewart had confiscated the dust off him. Lethbridge-Stewart shook his head.

He turned back to the pub, intent on finishing his pint and talking to the man at the bar. He'd try a more peaceful approach. If this chap was an alien, then...

The door opened and the man emerged, followed very closely by Dougie.

'What's going on now?' Lethbridge-Stewart asked.

'Please, I need to be left alone,' said the man.

Dougie looked over at Lethbridge-Stewart with a shrug. 'Landlord doesn't want him in there. Gets enough trouble on weekends, apparently.'

Lethbridge-Stewart couldn't blame the landlord for that. It was the middle of the week, and you didn't go to the pub expecting noise and disturbance. Just a nice social drink with mates. Still... What the youth had said.

'Why did that chap react to you like he did?' Lethbridge-

Stewart asked.

The man sighed and looked down at the pavement. 'You don't understand,' he said, in an accent Lethbridge-Stewart couldn't place. 'I can't stay out…' His voice trailed off. Slowly he lifted his eyes, his eyes resting on the Moon, mesmerized.

Lethbridge-Stewart glanced around, but the youth was gone, thankfully. So much for a quiet drink. He stepped towards the man. 'Are you quite all right, old chap?'

The man didn't move. He started to mutter, the words barely audible.

Dougie shook his head. 'Anywhere we can help you to?'

'Home. I need to go home, but…' The man let out a gasp. 'I *have* to go home.'

Lethbridge-Stewart had seen some sights in the last few months, but watching an odd little man disintegrate into a sparkling purple dust had to be the most extraordinary. He continued to watch. The dust floated in the night air, drifting upwards as if caught on the light breeze. With a strange flittering sound, the dust faded.

Lethbridge-Stewart raised an eyebrow, and turned to Dougie, who was standing there, looking up at the night sky.

'Home,' he said, his voice conveying his incredulity. 'The Moon?'

Well, Lethbridge-Stewart reflected, that would explain a lot. He had heard rumours about the oddness surrounding the return of *Apollo 11*. He patted Dougie on the shoulder. 'What is it you said about aliens?'

Charlie staggered backwards, coughing and rasping, his eyes

stinging from the unexpected power that was now all in his eyes. When he next opened them he gasped with surprise.

Selene was standing in front of him as before but she had been transformed. Her eyes began to open and close rapidly at such a speed that no human ocular nerve would be able to process. Her whole body shone and gleamed and the indentations he had seen in her face now seemed deeper and more definite, like miniature craters all across the surface of her skin.

Charlie kept on staring and Selene smiled at him. Charlie thought she was the most beautiful girl he had ever seen.

'You look so different,' he managed at last.

'No. I'm not different. Only now you can see me. Before you couldn't. That's all.'

Charlie blinked and the power seeped further into his vision. Now Selene was transforming again, but this time it was as if her body was dissipating so that he could look right through her. It was the most incredible sight Charlie had ever seen.

'But you do look different! I can see right through you. You have two of everything – even your heart!'

She turned to look back and his eyes met hers, which were now terrifying, wide and blinking. 'I wish things could be different,' she said quietly. Charlie said nothing, his eyes still too entranced by her. 'I wish that you could come with me but it is not possible,' Selene finished sadly. Then her mood lifted and her eyes began to shine. 'It's time to go to Theia. My kind must return again to the lunar surface or be trapped here forever. I want to go back to the Moon.'

'Let me try to come with you,' Charlie pleaded, suddenly alive with purpose. 'There's nothing for me here, man. I want to see stars and...'

'You are good,' Selene said. 'Some of your species have shown us great kindness. But a greater evil is coming and I must leave you now forever. It is too late for me. I have been separated from my kind for too long. Goodbye.'

She leaned close to him and her lips brushed against his cheek. Then right in front of Charlie's startled eyes she began to disintegrate. All of the cells in her body started to vibrate and separate one by one as if she were a mirage in the desert and he could only just about make out her outline. He stood and watched in amazement and she smiled at him one last time and then, through the tiny gap left in the window, her ashes were swept up by the evening breeze and disappeared up into the sky.

'Wait!' Charlie called after her, his faculties suddenly returning. 'Selene! You can't leave! Come back! You never told me where the cage was or where I can find the others.'

But it was too late. She was gone and nothing came back to him except a wisp of his warm breath meeting the cold air.

Reluctantly, he closed the window a little louder than he had intended, making the glass shake in the frame for a moment. He had been so close to finding a great story and now it was gone and out of reach.

Bishop knew he was pushing his luck, but things were running away with themselves. He still wasn't sure taking the baby to the Vault had been the best move, but he understood Anne's reasoning. It still bothered him, and continued to do so the whole time it took his motorbike to make it back to London. He should have just returned home, but he couldn't get the face of the baby out of his mind.

He thought of his nephew, and imagined how he'd feel should Dean go missing. Samantha would be beside herself, of course, but Patricia's baby had no mother to fret over his disappearance. But the baby did have a family – at least, Bishop assumed he did.

And so motivated, knowing that the only man he trusted to really help them was Lethbridge-Stewart, he returned to Chelsea Barracks. He rushed his way to the colonel's office, or, more accurately, the ante-office. There had to be something there, some note, that included a contact number. Bishop didn't remember the colonel giving him such a number, but there was a chance that Lethbridge-Stewart left a number there for Bishop, after all Bishop was already on assignment for Hamilton when Lethbridge-Stewart left London.

After fifteen minutes of looking, Bishop sank back in his chair. Normally he'd put in some calls, but not many people were aware of the mobilisation of the Fifth, so who could he call? Colonel Douglas was in Edinburgh with Lethbridge-Stewart, Sally had no contact details.

There was only one thing for it. He'd have to go direct to…

The phone rang. For a moment Bishop stared at it. He wasn't supposed to be there; he was supposed to be home. Who could be calling this time of the evening?

Tentatively he reached for the trimphone and lifted the receiver. 'Hello, Colonel Lethbridge-Stewart's office.'

'Corporal Bishop, I think we need to talk.' It was General Hamilton.

CHAPTER SEVEN

Making Headlines

Lethbridge-Stewart stood beside his little silver Mercedes, Edinburgh Castle before him. It had been a long week, and Lethbridge-Stewart wasn't looking forward to returning to London. There was still much to do in Dolerite Base, weeks of work ahead of them, and he didn't feel great about leaving Douglas in charge of it all. Not that he was alone; he had Captain Bartlett with him, and Major Lamont was still on hand too. Unfortunately, Lethbridge-Stewart had meetings to attend, documents to read – the less exciting administrative side of setting up an operation like the Fifth. He still hadn't met Peyton Bryden, the money behind the refurbishments, and from what Hamilton said, he wasn't especially looking forward to the experience. He wondered how long he could put if off for.

Lethbridge-Stewart turned to Douglas, who was, unlike him, dressed in uniform. Lamont wouldn't let him into the New Barracks (as it was still called despite being built in 1796) during the day out of uniform. Their cover needed to be maintained, after all, and uniformed men passing through the Barracks was nothing unusual to tourists. There was, of course, the tradesmen entrance behind the castle, but that was only open to the workers and REME presently, all of them in plain overalls. It was, therefore, simply more sensible for Douglas to remain in uniform and add to the official military presence at the castle.

'I hand over control of Dolerite Base, such as it is, to you, Colonel Douglas.'

Douglas saluted Lethbridge-Stewart. 'I'll try and not let it get in too much of a state.'

'Good luck with that.' Formalities done with, the two old friends shook hands and Lethbridge-Stewart opened the car door. 'I wonder what trouble Bishop and Miss Travers have got into this time?' he mused, sitting in the driver's seat. He'd made a brief call to Sally last night, just to let her know he'd be back the next day, and she had told him that Miss Travers needed his help. She wouldn't explain what she meant, only Miss Travers was helping a scientist friend of hers from America, and that Bishop had been doing his best, but his resources were limited.

'Still no joy?'

'No, I put a call in to Hamilton before leaving the hotel, and he said he's looking into things. Although one suspects he already knows.'

'Phones have ears,' Dougie said with a nod.

'Quite so.'

'Did you tell him about our alien encounter last night?'

'Yes, and he hasn't heard anything like it. Although,' Lethbridge-Stewart added, his voice lowered. Dougie crouched down to listen. 'Have you heard of Moon Blink?'

'Can't say I have.'

'I made some enquiries, chasing up that substance we sent on to the Vault. That's what they're calling the dust – Moon Blink. Turns out Miss Travers wasn't on hand to run tests, but one of her colleagues did.'

'That makes sense, considering the reactions to it that we've seen.'

'Yes, and I spoke to Hamilton about it, but he couldn't tell me much, but he's heard rumour that it's somehow connected to what happened on the American lunar base.'

'And you think that has something to do with last night?'

Lethbridge-Stewart thought back to the youth's reaction to the alien. The incessant blinking. 'I don't believe in coincidence, and I'd lay money on it having something to do with Miss Travers and whatever is going on with her.'

Dougie nodded. 'Yes, this American friend of hers.'

'Quite. Apparently Bishop has been given a few days off training, so one suspects he's with Miss Travers now.'

The look on Dougie's face showed his ignorance, and Lethbridge-Stewart didn't feel inclined to enlighten him. Lethbridge-Stewart didn't know for sure, of course, but he knew that Bishop and Miss Travers had drawn close over the last few months, especially since Fang Rock. He was far from an expert on such things, was often oblivious to the affections of the fairer sex, even as a hormonal teenager his first kiss came as something of a surprise, but he had his suspicions. His thoughts turned to Sally. Office romances – rarely the best option. He'd need to keep an eye on Bishop, especially if Hamilton got his way and volunteered Miss Travers to the Fifth.

'What about the dust you confiscated?' Dougie asked.

'In the glove compartment here. Where it'll stay until I can personally have Miss Travers run some tests. I doubt the Vault will share their findings, and I have no intention of them having another sample of it.'

Dougie nodded. 'I imagine she has other contacts, knows

somewhere safe to test it.'

'That's my hope.' A beat. 'Right then, best be off. Long drive ahead of me.' Lethbridge-Stewart waved goodbye and the car started off down the Royal Mile.

It had been Anne's suggestion to return to London. Visiting the Vault had not been without risk, and although she trusted Tim, she was less sure of Peggy Orwell. All it would take was for the wrong word to be said and there'd soon be a knock at her door. The best course of action was, therefore, to head south and put as much distance between them and the Vault.

Her father was away, although he hadn't left Anne with any clue as to where he was off to this time. Only a disgruntled Sasquatch remained at the house, with a note to say that her father would be back soon and that there was enough cat food to last until his unspecified return. Anne felt a pang of worry for her father at first, but her current situation was too pressing to keep her ruminating on the issue for long. In fact, she was beginning to realise that they weren't going to be able to handle this alone. She needed outside reinforcements and fast.

Anne replaced the phone receiver on its cradle. She hoped her message reached the right person, since she didn't know how else to reach them directly anymore. All she could do now was sit and wait. Cautiously, she lifted the telephone to her ear again and dialled a second number. It rang only a couple of times before Bill's familiar tones came through. She quickly filled him in on their change of location, requesting that he come and be with Patricia while she was out, hopefully following her new lead. Bill agreed without hesitation and Anne breathed a sigh of relief. At least she could always rely on Bill.

'So what do you think we do next, Annie?' Patricia began anxiously, once Anne had joined her in the kitchen. 'I mean, our day at the Vault was certainly very illuminating, but I still don't think it has brought us any closer to finding out what we should do with the baby, or how we can reunite him with his kind.'

Anne nodded but she wasn't fully listening, stirring her tea even though it had now gone cold. Her mind was somewhere else. She just couldn't forget the look on that boy's face back at the Vault.

'The Terrae are few in number now,' Patricia continued. 'If they remain here too long and we cannot get the baby back to them, it is quite possible we will be the cause of their extinction.'

'I'm sure it won't come to that,' Anne reassured her. 'We are doing everything we can.'

Patricia nodded but she didn't seem quite so convinced. 'I just keep thinking back to the Laboratory in Washington. Oh, Annie, it was run by a terrible man. He never seemed to show any real interest in astrological advancement at all. He was just interested in climbing the career ladder rather than getting to the stars. When Project Horizon began, those that returned would just bring rocks and lunar specimens for us to examine. But when they started to bring back members of the Terrae, it was just awful. They looked just like us, Annie, and they were so afraid and alone. I didn't know who I felt sorrier for; those who died or those who remained locked up in cages day after day. That was when we knew things had to change. The administrator was so cruel, he seemed to enjoy their pain as if they were our enemy to be tortured.' She paused, to take a breath. Anne watched her. 'That's what really scares me. What if the baby is the last one left, the only one who has survived? What if there's no one else out there to claim him, then what will we do? We can hardly fly him back to the Moon ourselves!'

'Don't get upset, Pat,' Anne said, standing and squeezing Patricia's shoulder. 'Whatever we discover, we will find a way to help him. Besides, it sounds to me like a lot may have escaped, and if they have then they're bound to be looking for each other. If they are out there, we will find a way to bring him to them.'

'Thanks, Anne,' Patricia said.

What Anne really wanted to do was talk to Lethbridge-Stewart, but she didn't voice that desire. She didn't want Patricia to feel that she and Bill were not up to the task of keeping her and the baby safe.

'I may have to go out for a while this afternoon. You'll be all right here with the baby won't you?' Anne asked, filling up the teapot and replacing it on the stove.

Patricia paled. 'Out? Where? You can't leave me here on my own. What if—?'

'Bill will be here with you,' Anne said quickly. 'I telephoned him to be sure, and he told me he's been given some time off. Rather conveniently,' she added quietly, with a frown.

A sound, a quick snap of metal on metal, echoed down the passage way, followed by a heavy thud.

'What was that?' Patricia asked, the noise making her jump.

'Just the morning paper I suspect,' Anne reassured her.

She made her way from the kitchen to the front door where the daily rag was lying on the door mat, Sasquatch sniffing at it with interest. Anne picked it up and brushed away the cat hairs.

'Here we are,' she said, depositing the newspaper onto the kitchen table. 'Nothing to worry about. Let me refresh your cup; it must be as cold as mine.' Anne reached for the cup, but Patricia didn't notice. Something had caught her attention.

She snatched the paper off the table and flicked through the pages rapidly.

'What's is it?' No reply. 'Pat?' The teapot began to whistle softly on the stove. But still Patricia's attention wasn't pulled from the newspaper. 'Is something the matter? You look like you've seen a ghost.'

'I think I might have done,' Patricia said, her eyes not leaving the page.

'Talk to me, Patricia,' Anne said, sitting down and reaching for her friend's hand. 'What is going on?'

Patricia didn't answer for a moment, her eyes drinking in the article in front of her, then silently she turned the paper so that Anne could see too. Patricia's hand was shaking. Anne looked up at her nervously, not sure if she wanted to read what was in front of her.

'What is it?' she asked hesitantly.

'Page seven,' Patricia said, her eyes steady, but her voice trembled like her hand. 'Looks like they tried to bury the story.'

Anne's eyes scanned down the page. There had been an accident in a Washington laboratory, an explosion that had destroyed years of work and taken the life of one of their most esteemed scientists.

'How terrible,' Anne said. Patricia shook her head. 'Not terrible?' Anne pressed.

'No,' Patricia sighed. 'It isn't that. I know him, Anne.' She pointed at a small photo on the page. 'Or at least, I did know him. When he was alive.'

Anne looked at the black and white face of the scientist. She stared and swallowed. She knew him, too. Gautam Jhaveri, an old friend of hers.

'He's the colleague I was telling you about,' Patricia said. 'The one who was head hunted before me. He was also one of those helping the Terrae to escape.'

Anne felt her blood run cold. She had only spoken to him a few months ago. 'I knew him too,' she said quietly. 'He is – was – an advocate of looking past Earth-bound science to exploring what was beyond.' She turned her eyes back to the article. 'He used to call me Annie,' she added quietly, remembering the kindly doctor and how he had always made so much time for her. He had never made her feel any different or inferior because of her sex, and she had learned so much from him. To think that he was now gone forever was a horrible thought that Anne desperately tried to push from her mind. 'How could an accident like this happen?' she wondered.

Patricia shook her head, leaning forwards and lowering her voice. 'This was no accident, Anne. He was murdered, I'm sure of it.'

'How can you be sure of something like that?'

'How can I not?' Patricia said, her voice rising. Her dark eyes were flashing with emotion now, her dark hair against her reddening cheeks.

'Let's not panic,' Anne said reasonably, keen to keep control of the situation. 'First things first. Do you think someone else knows what's going on?'

'They must do by now. Oh, Anne, this is terrible!'

'I know, but we must keep a hold of ourselves. We are the only ones who can help Baby B.'

Patricia's smile was fleeting. 'But you don't understand. Jhaveri was the one who gave me the baby in the first place, he was the one who told me I needed to come here and find a safe place to hide. He must have known we knew each other... Perhaps I mentioned you in passing?' She shook her head. 'I don't know, but he must have known I'd come to you.'

'Yes,' Anne agreed. Gautam was always well-connected, and the last chat she had with him must have tipped him off. Wouldn't have taken him long to discover where Anne was working.

'But now he's dead and I don't know what to do,' Patricia said.

'That's why we have to stay focused on the baby and keep him safe.'

Tears pricked at Patricia's dark eyes once more. She glanced at the baby, who was sitting in his pram next to the kitchen table, smiling up at them guilelessly, completely oblivious to any danger he might be in. Suddenly, Patricia got to her feet.

'I should go, Anne,' she said, her eyes darting around her anxiously. 'This is my fault. I can't risk putting you or Bill in more danger.'

'No,' Anne said firmly. 'Sit down, Patricia. There is still one... man... who may be able to help us,' she said slowly, choosing her words carefully. 'In fact, he is the one I'm hoping to meet with today.'

'Who is it?'

Anne hesitated. 'I can't tell you who, not yet in any case,' she admitted. 'All I can say is that you're just going to have to trust me. It is something I'm going to have to do alone. That's why I called for Bill.'

'But, Anne, I'm scared. I don't want to be here by myself.'

'Don't be afraid, Pat. Nothing bad is going to happen to you or the baby, I promise. Beside, you won't be by yourself. Bill will be here with you soon.'

'Is he good at taking care of babies?'

'He always seems to baby-sit me, and he's always going on about his nephew. If he can manage his sister's four-year-old, I'm sure a baby will be no problem. Even an alien one.'

It took a moment, but Patricia smiled again, and as ever it was infectious. Anne smiled too. It was good to see Patricia happy, even just for a moment.

Sasquatch gave a loud yowl as there came a sound at the door again.

'That's probably him now,' Anne said encouragingly. 'Why don't you get another cup from the cupboard, while I go let him in?'

Anne made her way back down the hallway. Bill was standing outside, still in his civilian clothes. He cut a fine trendy figure, in his teal polar-neck sweater and brown Levy Bros gabardine sports jacket, his fair brown hair parted on the left side. He held a small red motorbike helmet in one hand. Anne smiled up at him; there was something to be said for friends that could be relied upon.

'Thank you for coming so quickly, Bill,' Anne said. 'I

didn't like the thought of leaving Patricia by herself.'

'I understand,' Bill said, stepping inside. As he closed the door he stopped for a moment and glanced behind him.

Anne felt her stomach tighten. 'What is it?'

'Nothing,' Bill said, closing the door. 'I thought I heard a car rather close behind me as I was pulling up, but I must have been mistaken.' He looked down as Sasquatch rubbed himself against his leg. 'Oh, I didn't realise you had a cat.'

'He's my father's,' Anne said distractedly, wondering if someone had indeed been following Bill. 'A stowaway from one of his recent trips.'

The telephone in the hallway rang.

'Take him through to the kitchen will you?' Anne said. 'Patricia is waiting there for you, too. And there's tea, a fresh pot.'

'All right.' Bill picked up the wriggling Sasquatch in his arms and made his way towards the kitchen. As soon as he was out of earshot, Anne raced to answer the telephone.

She headed in the direction of Notting Hill Gate. The walk wouldn't take more than twenty minutes, she reasoned. She didn't get far before she found herself preoccupied with a new, more immediate problem.

It seemed that Bill had been right. Someone had followed him to her house, and now it would appear was also following her.

Anne caught a glimpse of him in car windows as she walked. He was a young man with long hair and long trousers that shuffled noisily along the pavement. It was clear he was trying to stay back but it was impossible to do so inconspicuously and still match Anne's stride. She took

124

a left off Princedale Road and onto Holland Park Avenue, then hesitated for a moment, waiting to see if the young man was still behind her.

She headed along the parade of shops, stopping to examine her reflection in the window of a bookshop. A few people passed alongside her, girlfriends with linked arms and matching Mary Quant shift dresses, a small boy eagerly running away from a rather harassed looking nanny. Then she saw him again. He was on the other side of the road now.

Anne began to retrace her steps. She crossed over the road, headed around the corner and waited. She could hear shuffling footsteps, the slight dragging of his bellbottom trousers along the pavement.

'Can I help you?' Anne asked, turning to face him suddenly as he rounded the corner.

The young man staggered back in surprise, then all his words came tumbling out at once. 'Yes! I mean, I hope so. You see, I—'

'All right,' Anne said sharply, cutting him off. 'But first you are going to have to tell me what business you have in following me about.'

'I'm terribly sorry, I didn't mean to scare you. My name is Charlie.' He produced an ID badge from his breast pocket. Anne's eyes darted over the picture and name. His hair was just as long, flopping loosely over one eye, his face half smiling with impish good looks. His name was printed just below. Charlie Redfern: Investigative Journalist. 'I wondered if I could take a moment of your time?' he asked.

Anne looked at him for a moment. He seemed like a nice kid, a bit on the hippy side but certainly nothing untoward in his manner. But her mind was already on other matters, and she was keen to get to her next destination without further delay.

'I'm sorry,' she apologised. 'But I have an urgent appointment to keep. Good day.'

She began to walk away but the young man continued to follow her.

'Wait!' he said. 'Please! I think I might know something you're going to want to hear.'

'What's that then?' Anne asked, not slowing her pace.

Charlie darted to the other side to try and keep up with her. 'I know your friend.'

Right, Anne thought. *Here we go. A real Chorley in the making.*

'Which one? I have many friends,' she said, playing the ignorant card.

'The one in your house. The American one,' Charlie added, his voice lowered a little.

Well, so much for playing stupid. 'I would be very much surprised if you had ever met before, let alone know who she is.'

'Oh we haven't met,' Charlie said with a grin. 'But I know who she is, all right! She's rather famous in some circles; scientific fields. Do you think she would speak with me?'

'Sounds like you should have been following her instead of me,' Anne said, wondering what on earth this journalist could really be after. In her experience it was never anything good.

Charlie shook his head, his long hair moving against his cheekbone. 'Oh no, I couldn't do that. I wouldn't want to alarm her.'

'But you're perfectly fine with alarming me?' Anne queried, stopping so that she could turn to face him again.

Charlie halted suddenly and his face went rather pink. 'I know who you are, Miss Travers, and I know you're not given to being alarmed, but... I know there are others looking for her too, and I was afraid they might follow me and I wouldn't want to accidentally lead them towards her.'

Anne watched him closely. He was certainly a rather curious young man, but there was something undeniably earnest in his pursuit of her. She took the next turning into a side street where they could talk privately. Almost.

'Go on,' Anne said. 'Who are these other people who are looking for her?'

Charlie swallowed, heaving his heavy bag across his shoulder as if it carried the weight of all his troubles. 'I interviewed a man some years ago now, who said he had worked with you and Doctor Richards over in America, although not at the same time. A Doctor Jhaveri.'

Anne waited for him to continue. He seemed to be very well-informed. Alarmingly so.

'He told me that something big was coming. He told me that it would come and find you and Doctor Richards.'

'This sounds more like a riddle to me. Are you sure you're a journalist and not just some sort of imitation medium?'

'I'm telling you the truth, Doctor Travers! That's all that concerns me. I know something is going on here and I want to uncover the real story. People deserve to know the truth; however ugly it might be.'

'Careless talk costs lives,' Anne said, wondering if he was

too young to recall the phrase.

'That's not all. I met a girl. She told me something, something so incredible that I knew she just had to be telling the truth.'

'How?'

Charlie hesitated for a moment. Anne watched him nervously, not sure she wanted to hear what he had to say next.

'She gave me something. A substance.'

Anne caught her breath unintentionally. A *substance*? She barely allowed herself to believe it could be the mysterious Moon Blink. 'Do you still have any of it?' she asked, as levelly as she could.

Charlie shook his head. 'No. But I could describe its effects in detail to anyone who was willing to listen. That's how I knew for sure she wasn't lying. When I looked at her...' His voice trailed off. 'Anyway, I suppose that doesn't matter now, she's gone and there's no way to reach her. But she told me there were others in great danger. She trusted me to help them and gave me your names. You worked with Doctor Jhaveri, I know you must be connected to the great mystery somehow.'

The grey skies overhead began to break and a gentle flurry of rain started to fall.

Anne pulled up the hood of her pea coat. Charlie shook his head, his long hair already sticking to his face slightly.

'I have a car nearby,' he said. 'Maybe I can give you a lift some place? Wherever you want to go.'

'I can walk.'

'But didn't you say you have an urgent appointment? I could get you there in double the time, and finish telling you my story on the way. What do you say, Doctor Travers?'

Anne could feel the water making its way inside her hood and snake down the back of her neck. Charlie was looking at her with wide pleading eyes, the rain soaking through his thin coat and fluffing up his hair. He seemed harmless enough. Besides, if he tried to get clever it would give her the perfect opportunity to practise the self-defence skills Bill had taught her.

'Yes,' she relented finally. 'I will accept a lift. Thank you.'

'Great!' Charlie said, hoisting his back up onto his shoulder again. 'She's not far from here.'

They made their way across the road and then down into Princes Place, which wasn't that far from St James's Gardens. Then, much to her own surprise, Anne found herself bunched up in the passenger seat of Charlie's cramped green Morris Mini Cooper. Outside the downpour dappled against the window screen. The sky behind it was darkening too and Anne wondered if it was a bad omen. Luckily she wasn't one for unfounded suspicions. The boy next to her was scrabbling inside a rather battered satchel.

'Ah, here we are,' he said from the driver's seat, as he brandished his car keys, complete with a *Butch Cassidy and the Sundance Kid* key ring. 'Where is it you need to go? This old girl will get you there in one piece, no sweat.'

'Holland Park,' Anne said steadily, wondering if she was making a horrible mistake.

'Anywhere in particular?'

'No, just the park. It's not far from here, so it shouldn't take very long.'

'Holland Park, okay. I'll drop you by the entrance to

Holland Walk,' Charlie said. 'Coming right up.'

He twisted the key and started the ignition. The car coughed and spluttered as if it was being woken from a long sleep and objected to the fact. Anne felt for her seat belt.

'But first thing's first,' she continued as she strapped herself in. 'Who is looking for Patricia, and what do they want with her?'

So far this intrepid young journalist had made no mention of the baby. She was sure that if he knew about the baby, his instincts for the story would not have been able to prevent Charlie from asking about it. Anne certainly wasn't going to change that.

'The girl, Selene, told me that they were being kept somewhere by a man running something called Project Horizon. I don't know much about him. It seems, from what I can find out, that he is the head of the entire operation. I'm sure it won't be long before he figures out where Doctor Richards has been hiding, and comes looking for her!'

'I see,' Anne said, her mind moving quickly. 'I mean, I don't. Why does that necessitate that he would be looking for Patricia?'

'Because Doctor Richards, Patricia, is the only one of his former staff that has left a paper trail. Not much of one, and she was quite clever, but... Well, I managed to find her, you think someone in charge of something as big as Project Horizon won't be able to? I bet she knows more that she is letting on,' Charlie finished knowingly. Then his eyes brightened. 'That is, unless you know anything else?'

'Please keep your eyes on the road.'

'Oh yes, sorry. It's just not every day you get hold of a story like this!'

'So... Who was this Selene?'

Charlie chewed his lip, jerking his head back to try and move the hair from his eyes. 'I'm not quite sure to be honest. She said Doctor Jhaveri sent her to me for help. He knew that I would tell her story and find out the truth, I suppose. When we met, he said he could tell by my writing that I had integrity, and that was a rare quality nowadays, or something like that. He was the one who called me Charlie – I used to go by Charles, you know, more professional. But I don't know. After that Charlie kind of stuck. Funny.'

'Hmm,' Anne said noncommittally, thinking about her own encounters with the late Gautam. 'How exactly did you know Doctor Jhaveri? You interviewed him, you said. A few years back, when you were obviously too young to be working for the tabloids.'

'Of course. He came over to give a lecture, and I was covering it for my university paper. It was a real scoop to have such an eminent scientist give an interview to our little rag. He was a really gracious, wonderful guy.'

Anne watched Charlie's face closely. From the animated way he spoke about Gautam she deduced it was unlikely he had learned of the doctor's fate.

Soon they were pulling up alongside the entrance to Holland Walk, just as the rain clouds started to clear and patches of blue could be seen breaking through the grey. Nice that the weather was on her side today.

'Thank you very much for the lift,' Anne said. She stepped out of the car and closed the door behind her.

Charlie wound down the window. 'So when should I pick you up?'

'Pick me up? I don't see any need for us to meet again,

Mr Redfern.'

Anne noticed that Charlie's eyes got that wild, panicked look again. 'You don't understand! Please, Doctor Travers. I want to help. Someone needs to speak out and talk about what is really going on over there.'

'The best thing you can do is stay silent.'

She turned and began to walk away, but Charlie's voice called back to her from the open car window. 'If I managed to find Patricia, how hard do you think it will be when others come looking for her? Which they will, Doctor Travers. Of that I am sure.'

Anne stopped, then turned. She looked at him. Usually all her instincts would be going off and telling her to walk away in the other direction and not look back. But there was something about his open shining face that made her trust him; at least for now.

'What paper did you say you worked for?'

'I'm freelance, for now. But I'm hoping this story will be my big break.'

'I see,' Anne said. Charlie swallowed. She could tell he knew she had seen right through him. 'This is a dangerous game you are playing, Charlie,' she warned him. 'I would read the news as well as write it before you go digging around next time.'

'Here,' Charlie said. 'Take my card.'

It looked rather homemade, but there was a charm about it that made her tuck it away for safekeeping. She didn't want to tell him that she had already memorised the number plate of his car and would be able to track him down again if necessary.

'When can I see you again?' he asked her eagerly. 'I'm

in this now, too, don't forget.'

'I will be in touch if needs be,' Anne said. It seemed to satisfy the boy, who beamed back at her. As his car took off, Anne's mind was still whirring with Charlie's words. She had tried to reassure Patricia as best she could, but it seemed that things were bigger and scarier than either of them could have possibly anticipated.

CHAPTER EIGHT

Ruby

The skies had cleared by time Anne left Charlie and his new information behind her. His car had just about coughed and stuttered its way to her destination and now Anne found herself waiting alone on a park bench as instructed, after a quiet walk along Holland Avenue and past the secondary school.

She looked around her to see if she could spot any sign of the man she was to be meeting, but it was past lunchtime and the park was beginning to empty out. Adults returning to their jobs in Notting Hill or down Kensington High Street, while pupils returned to the school.

She spied a man coming from the other direction, presumably from Abbotsbury Road. His black bowler hat was pulled down low over his eyes, a briefcase in one hand with a long black umbrella in the other. Anne stood up to get a better look but the man soon passed her and she realised with a heavy heart he wasn't who she was waiting for. She sat back down again and watched as two haughty peacocks made their way in short staccato strides across the green grass before disappearing into the shrubbery.

Alone for the first time in days, Anne wondered how Bill and Patricia were doing back at the house without her. She was sure they would be safe there. She hoped Bill would be able to track down Lethbridge-Stewart. It would be a risk getting him involved, but Anne knew that she could trust him, and right now she knew they needed all the friends they could get. Besides, if he had any hesitations or objections she was certain that if anyone could talk him around it would be her.

She sat in contemplative silence for a few moments more, debating whether or not it was worth staying. Perhaps the whole thing had just been a ruse to lead her away from the house after all? Perhaps Bill and Patricia were in trouble right at that very moment, and here she was sitting on a park bench with no idea?

Her racing thoughts were halted by a voice at her side.

'Hello,' the newcomer said brightly. 'May I take this seat?'

Anne turned, expecting to see the wizened face of the man she had been waiting for. Instead she was met by a pair of flashing green eyes belonging to a young woman, of about twenty.

'Of course,' Anne said. She moved her handbag out of the way and watched, curiously, as the woman sat down next to her on the bench.

She slipped off her coat, lying it down on the damp wood so as not to get her clothes wet. Underneath the woman was wearing a fashionable green shift dress with lace appliqué sleeves. On her feet she wore white kitten heeled pumps slightly muddied by the rain, and her short hair was neatly combed with tiny flicks at the bottom just past her ears.

Anne glanced around her, wondering where her contact was.

'Now,' the girl said, taking a moment to rearrange her

hair under her ears, and settle her handbag onto her lap. 'What is it I can help you with this afternoon, Doctor Travers?'

Anne stared at her in surprise. 'I think there might have been some miscommunication,' she said. 'I am waiting for someone. He asked me to meet him here. A Mr Rupert Slant?'

'Oh, there's no mistake. I must say how lovely to see you again, Doctor Travers.'

The woman held out her hand for Anne to shake. Anne looked down at the woman's painted fingernails. She withdrew her hand and smiled at Anne.

'I didn't imagine our paths would cross again so soon.'

Anne studied her closely, but there was nothing familiar about her that she could see. 'Have we met before? I don't remember you.'

The girl smiled. 'Allow me to jog your memory, Doctor Travers. My name is Ruby Slant, niece of Rupert Slant to all those who ask after my poor uncle, now deceased.'

Anne gripped the side of the bench. This couldn't be true; he couldn't be dead not when she needed him most!

'Deceased?' Anne asked, her voice shaking slightly. 'When did this happen? Why didn't anyone inform me of his death?'

Ruby smoothed down the back of her bob with her hand before she spoke again. 'Such a change to have lovely soft hair, don't you think?' She chuckled, running her fingers through her carefully arranged hair-do.

Anne stared at Ruby in bewilderment. 'Yes,' she replied uncertainly, eager to stay on topic. 'But I am so sad to hear of Mr Slant's passing. May I ask what was the cause? When did it happen? I would have thought, as he was our family solicitor, we would have been informed to pay our respects.'

Ruby waved her hand in the air nonchalantly as if they were still discussing her hair-do and not the recent demise of her uncle. 'Life and death are not quite as distinct as everyone would like to make out. You of all people should know that, after what you experienced on Fang Rock.'

Anne looked at her quizzically. 'Your uncle told you...' She stopped. 'Wait, how can he have a niece? He wasn't even...'

Ruby's eyes were twinkling with mischief, and Anne realised how stupid she was being.

'Rupert?' she asked, tentatively.

'Indeed. I am – was – no, I suppose still am Rupert Slant. Only now I am Ruby. I must say it makes a refreshing change to see life from the other side of the table, so to speak. What do you think of my new face?'

'It is certainly a big change,' Anne offered finally.

Ruby chuckled, an odd masculine sound. But, Anne supposed, when you've lived as a man for so long, it must have been hard to change so much.

'I know what you're thinking, Anne,' Ruby said. 'But you would be amazed what the men say when they think the woman making the tea has no idea what any of the long words mean. I've learned far more being dizzy Ruby niece of the great Rupert than I ever did as Slant Senior. There's nothing *only* about being a girl.'

Anne nodded dumbly.

'But anyway,' Ruby continued. 'You didn't come and meet me here to discuss my latest exterior alterations, I'm sure. What can I help you with? More family escapades?'

'Not quite,' Anne said. 'At least, not with my family this time. Besides, you're the only alien I know – friendly alien, I should say.'

Ruby smiled. Anne could tell that she appreciated her directness. 'I can't imagine Dominic Vaar would be much help, not that he's currently in a position to do so, anyway. I believe Sebastian Collins has him quite busy. Continue,' she said.

Anne took a breath. 'What do you know about the Terrae?'

As they rolled back into Washington, Administrator Bland instructed his driver to drop him off just around the corner from his destination. For a moment Bland wondered if he was making a horrible mistake. All his life he had been taught to hold a deep mistrust of the Ruskies but there had always been one Russian with whom he had shared a common bond. Vadim Kabinov had been his brother in the pursuit of space travel and exploration. Since the commencement of Project Horizon, Bland had kept his distance from Kabinov, but now things were changing rapidly. It was time to reconnect once more.

He made his way towards the embassy entrance, walking past the roses that bloomed outside, past the guards and made his way towards the room of the Science Attaché. Kabinov's credentials were without question. Still, Bland felt a faint thrill at being suddenly on Russian soil. It was almost like trespassing.

Inside, the interior was all dark wood panelling and shiny wooden floors flanked by heavy red curtains. A young blonde showed him the way to Kabinov's office, before knocking on the door and then making her exit. Bland waited outside the door for the familiar voice to summon him inside.

'Enter,' said Kabinov.

Bland pushed against the door, which was very heavy, and made his way inside. The room was dark and it took him a few moments to get his bearings. There was a large ornate fireplace at one end, large vases of blue and white china on one side, elaborate gold candelabras on the other. The same dark wood lined the floors and walls and the red curtains he had seen downstairs hung inside this office too. By the window, daylight from outside hitting him perfectly, stood his friend.

Kabinov was bald and had possibly shrunk since the last time they had met. He squinted up at Bland through his large, round spectacles that had recently become all the fashion. Bland wasn't so sure he liked having his long face reflected back at him quite so closely.

'How lovely to see you, old friend,' Kabinov said smoothly, his Russian accent still in evidence despite his well-practiced American twang. 'How many summers have passed since I saw you last? I presume you are here as a result of having received my letter to inform you of my new commission? So tell me, is this visit to be a purely social one? I do hope so, I am very bored by business these days.'

'I'm afraid it may prove to be a bit of both,' Bland said as he strode into the palatial office. 'I see becoming the new Science Attaché has brought you the benefit of a corner office.'

'Oh, I'm not interested in what's going on outside. It is what is going on further up into the sky that holds my attention. Now, what is it that you have come to see me about? I prefer to begin with business, that way we can move past it as quickly and painlessly as possible.'

Bland smiled. He had almost forgotten what pleasant company Kabinov could be. 'I see life is treating you rather well.'

'What can I say? Appetite comes with eating,' Kabinov said, his eyes twinkling greedily behind his thick spectacles.

Bland paced the room, stopping to glance at a painting hung on the wall. It depicted an idyllic, if slightly faded, pastoral scene that looked as if it could have come from a flea market, but Bland deduced that it must be worth a fair few million roubles.

'My home village,' Kabinov explained, catching his eye. 'I am not a man for looking back, but I find the past will often try and keep chase.'

Bland nodded, even though he wasn't quite sure what Kabinov meant. He would often talk in riddles, his vernacular peppered with folk tales and superstitions from the old country. Bland moved across to the window to admire the view of Mount Alto.

'She is designed by Michael Posokhin. He also designed the State Kremlin Palace back in Moscow,' Kabinov continued. 'What a privilege it is to spend my days ensconced in such a wonderful building.'

'I can imagine,' Bland said.

Kabinov moved awkwardly around the large sweeping office. He opened up a dark wooden bureau close to his desk and took out two small tumblers and a decanter.

'Can I offer you a drink?' Kabinov swirled the clear liquid in the miniature tumbler. 'Zelyonaya Marka vodka, my favourite. Simplicity makes for the best taste experience, wouldn't you agree, Administrator?'

Bland looked at the glass and debated its merits. He would much rather have gone for his usual; banana milk shake, two scoops extra cream, but he was a long way from home now.

'No thanks,' he said. 'I think I'll pass on anything from the old country.'

'Now, now,' Kabinov chided him. 'You must have a drink with me. Just the one. I insist upon it.'

'Well, if you insist,' Bland replied.

Kabinov smiled smugly. He was a man used to getting his own way. 'Budem zdorovy, or as you might say, cheers.'

They clinked glasses, Kabinov downing his in one shot. Bland sipped at his tentatively. The vodka tasted like fire.

'Where did we two first meet?' he asked, as his eyes watched the people walking on the sidewalk below like ants. It could be any one of them, he thought suddenly, quickly pushing the disturbing idea to the back of his mind.

'Berlin,' Kabinov replied without hesitation, behind him. 'A certain bar as I recall. I am surprised you have so easily forgotten, Administrator Bland.'

Bland cleared his throat, which was still burning from the vodka. 'I have a lot on my mind these days.' He sighed. 'Can I take a seat?'

He didn't wait for Kabinov's permission and settled himself back into the sumptuous leather sofa. Kabinov remained on his feet, his shorter height suddenly towering over the seated Bland.

'Tell me, do you remember your childhood, Administrator?'

'Sure. Apple pie and Sunday school,' Bland quipped.

'Good. I remember mine. It was cold and dark, not unlike the world we are about to enter. Everything is about to change.'

'Yes, and we've got to be ready.'

Kabinov wandered around the room, letting the warmth of the vodka take effect. 'I bet I can guess the reason for your visit today, Administrator.'

'I heard your people like to tell fortunes,' Bland shot back glibly.

Kabinov licked his teeth as if he tasted something unpleasant. 'My nation has always been at the forefront of lunar exploration. Communism paved the way to the stars.'

'You forget about Apollo 9, our lunar module.'

'Ah, but the Soyuz 5 predates your Apollo, I'm afraid. It seems the messenger of the gods fell short on that occasion. Our soviet lunar programme was the first to reach the Moon, decades ago.'

'Unmanned,' Bland added pointedly.

'But we also had the first human in space too. How easily you Americans forget the great Yuri Gagarin,' Kabinov said, removing his glasses and closing his eyes with reverence.

'And Alan Shepard. It seems we are equals, no matter how hard we try to remain rivals.'

'You Americans, so arrogant. You think you can see it all, but you see so little. As my mother always used to say, "There is no shame in not knowing something but there is shame in not finding out." You must beware, Administrator Bland. You think you have learned all there is to know from your lunar base, but trust me when I say that you have only just scratched the surface. The Moon always shows her same side, the dark volcanic Maria.'

'Sounds like the sort of a girl I almost married if my mother hadn't interfered and chosen my current far more suitable wife.'

'This is no time for jokes. I don't know why you Americans always need to joke so much, such a fuss about everything.'

'Well our launches aren't so closely tied to our missile programme.'

'Are you certain about that, Administrator Bland?'

Bland shifted in his seat, the leather starting to feel uncomfortable. 'What are those?' he asked, gesturing to the bowl on the table.

'Pirozhki. My wife and daughters make them for me every morning. Delicious little parcels of rice, mushroom and meats. Would you like to try one?'

Bland got to his feet and popped one in his mouth, taking a second in his hand. 'These are good,' he said, making a start on the second.

'I'll have the recipe sent your office. Now, shall we get back to the real reason for your visit?

Bland nodded, his mouth still full, pastry flaking at the edges of his lips.

'Do you recall the mass of lunar rocks returned by the Apollo 8 mission last year?' Kabinov continued.

'Of course,' Bland said. '380 kilograms, in fact. All the Apollo missions brought back samples. 2,415 in total, all collected and analysed at my lab and measured by radiometric dating.'

'And what did they discover, these labs of yours?'

Kabinov asked, sipping at his vodka elegantly.

Bland stretched out his jaw. He could tell Kabinov was testing him and he didn't like it one bit. He reached out and took another pirozhki before continuing. 'That these basaltic samples from the lunar Mari were three-point-six billion years old, many caused by eruptions one-point-two billion years ago. They are almost all depleted in volatiles and lacking in hydrated minerals.'

'Ah. What else can we learn from this?'

'Well, chemical compounds with low boiling points are associated with the Moon's crust – nitrogen, CO_2, H_2, methane, etcetera. The crust itself contains O_2 chemical bound in the rocks. When water is added to the crystal structure of a mineral it creates a new mineral called a hydrate – a process known as retrograde metamorprism.'

'Very good. I see you know your science, Administrator.'

Bland got to his feet, once again towering over the seated Kabinov. 'Why don't we stop all this dancing around? You know why I'm really here and it's not to sample your excellent Russian delicacies.'

'Why don't you enlighten me?'

Bland wiped his fingers on his tie, then settled back into the luxurious leather couch as he considered his approach. Kabinov looked like a man who held all the cards, but as he was about to learn, Bland held a few of his own.

CHAPTER NINE

The Games We Play

A nne waited, watching Ruby's response carefully. The other woman smiled. 'Ah, the Terrae. Is that why you wanted to speak with me?'

Anne nodded. Ruby had chosen a public place for their meeting and now that they were getting down to business, Anne was glad that it was practically deserted.

'I fear a friend of mine may be in grave danger and I was hoping you might be able to offer some advice,' Anne continued.

'You need my help? How do you suppose I can be of any assistance in this matter?'

'We are not the only ones who know they are here. The Russians and the Americans have realised that several of them have escaped. My friend and I have become implicated in the situation.'

'My, my,' Ruby said. 'I didn't take you for one to get embroiled in such a potential scandal.'

'Neither did I,' Anne said. 'But here we are.'

'The Terrae are a fascinating race,' Ruby mused. 'Not unlike my own people in many ways. When my people controlled the majority of Mutter's Spiral we found them to be both peace-loving and remarkably resourceful, their ability to blend in with their surroundings is second to none.

They were only a young race on the planet Theia back then. They have a dual set of organs, you know, a sort of get out of jail free card if you like. But the Terrae seem to be everywhere nowadays. Can't move for them. Quite a source of amusement actually, for someone like me. Always pleasant to meet another species so good at assimilating into a foreign society. Not unlike my own people in many ways.'

'How long have they been here?' Anne asked, not feeling the same amusement as Ruby.

'Oh, not long,' Ruby said, fiddling with her handbag clasp. 'Only since the Soviets and Americans started mining on the Moon. For some reason the human race cannot resist taking a prisoner or two for experimentation. They certainly got more than they bargained for this time! But then again, the human race never learns their lessons. They just can't help but poke their nose where it doesn't belong. Exploration and scientific endeavour is one thing, but they cannot resist taking it too far.' She stopped and patted Anne's knee with a smile. 'My apologies. I hope you know I did not mean to include you in my previous summation. Do you like my new handbag? Pierre Cardin, of course. It is rather fun to accessorise.'

'Yes,' Anne said uncertainly, still trying to take in all that Ruby had said.

'Actually, I have something in here that might help you.' Ruby opened the clasp of her handbag. 'Oh, come on,' she scolded herself as she rooted inside its contents. 'I know you're in here somewhere!'

Anne watched her with interest, still wondering what she was looking for. Finally, Ruby raised her head.

'Found it! Now be careful,' Ruby warned Anne. 'It's very

delicate and it's the only one of its kind I have left. I used one to try and confirm someone I suspected to be a member of the Terrae, but I was mistaken. What a waste. Anyhow here it is. Isn't it wonderful?'

Ruby passed her the vial of powder. 'One never knows when a member of their species may appear and as such I like to be prepared. I always find it helps enormously when one can see to whom they are speaking; wouldn't you agree?'

Anne nodded, her eyes trained on the small vial. It seemed somehow so incongruous to see it balanced between Ruby's pretty painted fingernails as they sat on the bench in the middle of the afternoon.

'Luna Haze it's being called up in Scotland,' Ruby said. 'And the "word on the street", as I believe to understand it, is that whoever chooses to ingest this dust experiences a high. With a very useful, in our case, side effect. But I fear my words are falling on deaf ears. It is clear you have seen this before.'

Anne swallowed. This was it. The missing element she and Patricia needed.

'We want him back,' Bland said at last, before adding, 'We want him back quietly and without any fuss. Certainly no press.'

'Want who back?' Kabinov asked, accentuating every word.

Bland felt his face colour. 'So you're saying you didn't take him?'

'Take him? I'm afraid not. What interest would we have in creating such a scandal? If we had wanted one I'm sure our own government could have rearranged to bring one back themselves. But do not look so downhearted my friend. Adversity is a good teacher, although I hasten to add I cannot intervene directly, I am more than willing to dispense you some pearls of wisdom. I would advise we recover what is lost as quickly and quietly as possible,' Kabinov finished.

Bland chose to ignore the use of we. 'There is something else,' he said. 'We also noticed the loss of a certain compound. At first we assumed it must have been an abnormality, an anomaly if you will, but it looks like something altogether more sinister may be to blame.'

'Oh?' Kabinov said, raising his eyebrow.

Bland cleared his throat. 'We believe a small group has been sampling the compound for their own means. It seems it has a rather odd effect on the brain.'

Kabinov smiled, his eyes large behind his thick spectacles like a frog. 'I see. Tell me more.'

'They are often targets of vandalism; some were even reported missing, presumed stolen,' Bland added.

'Exactly, now you begin to see,' Kabinov said with quiet triumph.

'See what?' Bland asked testily,

'See that there is more to catching these aliens than first meets the eye!' Kabinov smiled. 'I understand from my own people that these aliens have proved rather challenging to control. Indeed, I have heard rumours, Administrator Bland, that of the many that were brought back to the United States, some have their liberty. Indeed, it was your own people that helped them to escape!'

'I would have thought you above idle gossip,' Bland said, feeling his face grow hot.

'There is no need to feel embarrassed with me,' Kabinov

said. 'We are old friends after all. Let me make things simpler. I know this rumour is fact. Do not ask me how I know; only rest assured that the resources of the embassy and my government are at my disposal. So, where are they?'

'That is why I'm here! That is what I'm trying to find out,' Bland spat, his temper suddenly rising.

'Do not excite yourself, my old friend. I have something that may prove useful.'

With that, Kabinov got to his feet and walked deliberately across to the painting that Bland had been admiring earlier. He lifted the frame, revealing a black safe underneath. With a few deft clicks of the knob the door sprang open and Kabinov retrieved a parcel from inside. Bland watched as he made his way over to the desk. From the package he removed a string of negatives, along with a magnifying eyeglass.

'Take a look at this,' Kabinov said. 'I think you might find it to be of interest.'

Bland got to his feet and joined him at the desk. Kabinov passed him the negative and the magnifier. Bland noted that the negatives were time and date-stamped from the Russian base.

'What can you see?' Kabinov prompted him.

Bland studied it for a moment longer, and then removed the magnifying glass. 'That it is some kind of a compound,' he said, turning to Kabinov. 'Similar to my missing compound, although not exactly the same make up.'

Kabinov replaced his glasses and steepled his fingers together. 'It is, in part, comprised of $CaAl2Si2O8$. A calcium rich mineral found in the Moon's crust, as you well know, since that is the compound you are missing. But as you can see from this negative, this sample is somewhat different. Its chemical name is anorthite, but I believe it is known, by certain people in England, as Moon Blink.'

'And? What's that got to do recovering my missing aliens?' Bland asked.

Kabinov gave him a knowing smile. 'It seems that the compound has an unexpected capability.'

'Oh really? What's that?'

'With it the user can detect the difference between species. In short, it is the only means we have of tracking down those set free, before the press gets hold of them.'

Bland's mind was racing to catch up. He frowned, not happy that Kabinov was clearly ahead of him in this. 'Hold up, do you mean it can detect the difference?'

'Just what I say, Administrator. Ingest just a small amount of this powder and it will allow you to spot the aliens; anytime, anywhere.'

'That's great,' Bland said. 'So, go on then. Where is it?'

'I beg your pardon?'

'Where is it?' Bland pressed. 'You can't just have taken pictures of something that powerful! Where's the real stuff? If you're going to help me, then I need the real thing.'

'I believe we are getting ahead of ourselves here. This is a very last minute call on which I promised to give advice but nothing more. You cannot expect my country to use their resources to fix your error of judgment.'

Bland snorted. The Soviets were always so smug, always thinking they were better than everyone else when the Americans ran laps around them time and time again.

'At least they look the same,' Bland said, giving a morose laugh. 'Could be worse. That should buy us some time. Plus, they die, you know. The older ones.'

'There is no "us" in this situation, Administrator Bland,' Kabinov said sternly. 'This was your mistake and yours alone. You did not keep enough control over your people and they betrayed you. Now, no one must know you came to see me today. We are on opposite sides and it must remain that way.'

'Fine,' Bland said. 'Well thanks for the drink, old friend – and for your assistance. I won't be bothering you again.'

Kabinov blinked at him. 'But we are not done here.'

'Oh, I think we are,' Bland said, hoping to have the last word but Kabinov had other ideas.

'Not so fast, Administrator.' Kabinov took the package and replaced it in the safe behind the painting. 'That's not all. It seems our two nations are not the only ones involved.'

Bland's eyes bulged. Not the president, he prayed silently. Please don't let Dickie know. 'What are you talking about?' he asked, his hands unconsciously making fists at his sides.

'As I intimated earlier, the problem has already extended past the borders of the United States. My people have informed me that there have been reports of sightings in England. Concrete reports.'

'Of the aliens?' Bland asked, feeling himself beginning to lose his composure.

Kabinov grinned at his wickedly. 'No, not the aliens, my old friend. One of your scientists, a Doctor Patricia Richards.'

Bland felt his half-empty stomach give an internal squeeze of panic. He had come to Kabinov for advice, but Kabinov was already one step ahead. *How could he know about Richards? Did that mean he knew about Doctor Jhaveri, too?*

'I don't remember her name,' Bland said dismissively.

'Perhaps this is why none of your people show any loyalty,' Kabinov shot back. 'It helps with controlling your people if you can recall who they are. I'm particularly surprised you cannot recall the only female scientist who was such a prominent member of the team working in your alien laboratory. You forget how long our countries have been spying on one another, Administrator Bland. I'm sure you know a vast amount about our space programme that would bring colour to my cheeks and strike fear into my heart.'

This is true, Bland thought. The realisation began to make him feel a little more at ease.

'Anyhow, I have close friends who work at Dulles International Airport,' Kabinov continued. 'When Doctor Richards passed through customs on her way to England last weekend, she was not alone. She had someone with her.'

'Who?' pressed Bland.

'A little *babushka*,' Kabinov said with almost childlike glee. 'Except Doctor Richards isn't married, neither is she likely to be any time soon. Which makes one wonder whose *babushka* can it possibly be.'

Bland didn't reply, but they both knew what Kabinov was getting at.

'Now you can thank me for my help,' Kabinov said triumphantly. 'I think this calls for another drink, don't you?'

'Thank you for your time, but I really should be getting back.'

'Don't be in such a rush, Administrator. We cannot only discuss business. Have one more drink, my old friend. For old time's sake.'

'Fine,' Bland relented, his mind already busy racing with thoughts of Doctor Patricia Richards. 'One more drink.'

Anne hesitated, still not entirely sure how much information to impart. In some ways she had known Ruby longer than anybody else in her life. They had helped each other in 1823, and yet they only met two months ago. But if it wasn't for Ruby, then Anne wouldn't be here now. Literally. Had Ruby, then Rupert, not set in motion the chain of events that led Anne to Fang Rock, then Anne would never have been born in the first place.

'I believe I have seen its effect rather than the substance itself,' she offered finally.

'At the Vault I presume?' Ruby prompted.

Anne hesitated, then gave a nod.

'Don't be so weary, Anne. Shape shifting has its advantages, you know. I don't look like Ruby all the time,' Ruby added with a wink.

Anne wasn't sure what to say, so instead she stayed on script. 'Yes, well… As I understand it, Moon Blink, or Luna Haze, or other variations thereof, stays in the system for the cycle of the Moon but has no noticeable adverse effect on the user, except for a rapid blinking of the eyes.'

'But you know what it does, I presume?' Ruby said, her heavy pastel globe earrings swinging as she cocked her head. 'If you have already witnessed these experimentations.'

'Not quite,' Anne admitted. 'Tim was unable to do anything more than assess its effect on the body. Its effects on the mind still remain somewhat of a mystery, though Tim did liken the experience of the user to taking LSD.'

'Ah,' Ruby said.

A tight smile pulled at the corner of Ruby's lip, Anne could see she had amused her.

'What have been your findings?' Anne asked.

'Oh, I haven't had the chance to explore it in so much detail. But tell me, are you sure you didn't notice anything else?'

Anne looked at her steadily. Ruby had made no mention of the alien baby and, despite the fact that Anne trusted her to a degree, she didn't trust Ruby enough to reveal the presence of Baby B. 'Unfortunately the experiment was cut short and I was unable to witness anything further,' she said, carefully.

'I see,' Ruby said steadily. Anne wondered if she was going to press the issue further, but instead Ruby changed the subject. 'There may be more you have to tell me, but for the time being I feel there is knowledge I must impart to you.'

'Tell me,' Anne said eagerly.

'Listen carefully. There is one very important element that cannot be ignored.'

'What is it?'

Ruby linked her fingers and leaned towards Anne conspiratorially. 'Using this dust,' she shook the vial, 'allows people to see the Terrae for what they are. Now, you have the same translation matrix in you as my people, so it is only you who will possess the skill to be able to communicate with them in their own tongue. Remember that, Anne, it may prove useful.'

Anne nodded, placing the vial for safe keeping in her own handbag. 'Thank you for all your assistance, but I should be getting back.' She got to her feet. 'My friends are waiting for me and I really don't want to keep them any longer.'

'Absolutely,' Ruby said. 'Please don't let me keep you. I hope you have enjoyed our meeting as much as I, and that it will prove useful to you in the future.'

'Yes,' Anne assured her. 'You've been most helpful, Rup...' She stopped herself and smiled. 'Ruby.'

Ruby's eyes twinkled with amusement.

Anne gave a punctuating cough. 'Well I have seen many things in my life, travelled all across the world, but this is the first time I've met anybody who has swapped sex. It will take some getting used to. Will we meet again?'

'Of course.'

'I'm not sure if you quite understand. Will we meet again?'

'Ah,' Ruby said. 'I think I get your meaning. Well, I might stay as Ruby for a while longer. It has been a most illuminating experience.'

'Then I must go.'

'Remember,' Ruby called after her. 'You are their only line of communication, Anne. The Terrae need you. I wish you good luck. All of you.'

As soon as he left the embassy, Bland took a sharp left in the opposite direction to the waiting car and made for the first alleyway that opened up from the sidewalk.

He scrabbled around in his pocket until he found a few spare coins, then deposited them into the waiting mouth of the payphone. He punched in the numbers and waited for an answer at the other end of the line.

'Book me on the next flight to England.'

'England?'

'Have you gone deaf? I need to get a plane charted out there at once.'

'Yes, sir.'

'And I need you to get something else for me, too.'

'Pack some cheese doodles, sir?'

'No, not tonight. I need you to find out everything you can about one of my scientists. A Doctor Patricia Richards. She was part of my original team, the one that had to be disbanded.'

'Yes, sir. Right away, sir.'

'Call me at the lab, I'll be heading back there now.'

He needed to get some of this Moon Blink. He wasn't about to let Kabinov get one over on him. If anyone was going to see them, it was going to be him; Frank Bland.

The payphone began to ring, the sound loud and jarring in the cramped alleyway. Bland grabbed the receiver and pressed it to his ear.

'Hello?' he said suspiciously, not sure the call was intended for him.

The voice at the other end was the same as before. 'I have some more information for you, sir.'

'About Doctor Richards?'

The voice on the other end of the line breathed ominously into the receiver. 'As good as, sir. I can have someone meet you at Northolt airfield and take you to a friend of hers who will be able to tell you everything you need to know.'

'Good, very good,' Bland said, sweat starting to collect

between his brows. It was coming together. Maybe he could finally get ahead of this thing after all. He would be able to make it go away quietly, just as he had gotten rid of Doctor Jhaveri.

'Will that be all, sir?'

'Yes, for now. Thanks,' Bland said. He hung up the receiver and walked back into the sunshine of the street.

A respectable looking woman walked past him. He smiled at her cordially and she returned the gesture. Bland looked out after her and smiled secretly to himself. *They had no idea*, he thought. Quickly, he began to make his way back to the waiting car.

—CHAPTER TEN—

En Route

Lethbridge-Stewart was only a couple of hours out of London, but after driving for over six hours he decided he needed a short break, not least to relax his eyes and eat some food. He knew that there'd be little rest for him when he returned to London. He had thought about going straight home, but he had spoken to Hamilton just after he arrived in Northampton, and the general had told Lethbridge-Stewart to meet him at Chelsea Barracks.

Now he sat in his car, parked beside a little café in Northampton. Many other cars were stationed along the street, with people coming and going. Mostly women, getting in their shopping and doing whatever it was that women did while the men were at work. A few very small children with their mothers, but it was mostly quiet due to it being a school day. Lethbridge-Stewart was glad for that, he needed some time to think quietly, and he couldn't do that with the incessant sound of children playing on the street.

He bit into the sandwich he'd bought from the café, and chewed it with little satisfaction. The beef was dry, and the bread a few days old. Still, it would do for now. He placed the unfinished sandwich on the dashboard and opened the glove compartment.

He lifted up the small plastic bag, looking at the purplish dust within against the sunlight. He was reminded of the last time he'd encountered a drug of alien origin. Although that had proven useful, if not essential, in sending Miss Travers back in time, he still remembered the effects it had on his nephew. It had put Owain in bed for a time. He wondered how much damage this Luna Haze would have on a man. That chap from last night didn't look too great, and neither did Darren Carlin.

He looked around at the people in the streets. Fighting aliens, keeping the UK safe, seemed like an easy and uncomplicated mission back in March. But what do you do when the aliens look like normal people? They'd met a shape shifting alien on Fang Rock, and it had replicated poor Jim Saunders perfectly. It even copied Lethbridge-Stewart at one point! But this time around...

The alien last night didn't seem intent on causing any harm. It had simply been in the pub having a quiet drink. Not the kind of behaviour one would expect from an invading alien. All it wanted, so it said, was to get home. To the Moon.

Lethbridge-Stewart shook his head. Of course there would be friendly aliens out there, he now realised. He supposed he must have known that on some level, but with one exception, so far every alien he'd met had been involved in some kind of nefarious scheme inimical to humanity on one level or another.

He regarded the dust once more. Any of the people on the street could have been another alien, but he'd never know unless he ingested some of the dust.

No, he decided firmly, drugs were of no interest to him.

Alien or otherwise. He replaced the bag in the glove compartment.

It was time to get back to London. Find out just what Miss Travers had got herself caught up in this time.

Bill had arrived shortly after Anne's departure and, despite being grateful for his company, Patricia was beginning to find the urge to be alone with her own thoughts more and more pressing. Now she sat in Anne's childhood bedroom looking down at the alien baby in her arms. He had only come into her life for such a short time but already she knew she would do whatever it took to protect him. He had awoken a maternal instinct in her that she never knew existed, and it was more terrifying and wonderful than anything she had ever experienced before. Aside, of course, from what she had witnessed at the Laboratory in Washington. Nothing could match the terror of that.

Her mind wandered again. She thought about the article in the newspaper, and it made her blood run cold. Things were clearly becoming more precarious. The death of Doctor Jhaveri was clearly no accident, she was sure of that. But what if she was their next target?

'Everything all right in there, Patricia?' Bill called up the stairs to her.

Patricia hesitated for a moment, wondering what to do next. The baby was so helpless and she was beginning to worry that the closer she stayed to him the more she was putting him in danger, instead of keeping him out of harm's way. She turned towards the door as she heard Bill's footfall on the stairs.

'Patricia?' he called through the closed door. 'You've

been in there alone a while now. Can I come in?'

She battled with her thoughts for a moment longer, then relented and went to let him in.

Bill looked at her with a concerned expression. Patricia felt a wave of guilt wash over her. It wasn't fair on Bill, or Anne either, putting them in such a dangerous position. They had been so good to her, and now she needed to protect them all. There was only one way left she could think of.

Patricia stepped back into the room, picked up the baby from the bed, and passed him across to Bill.

'Will you take him for me for a while? I'm starting to get a headache. I think I need to get some fresh air.'

'Yes, of course,' Bill said, bouncing the little boy in his arms, an act which made the baby giggle. 'But I could come with you. I'm sure the munchkin here could do with some fresh air. Why not go all together?'

'No,' Patricia said, a little too quickly.

Bill looked at her sceptically, and Patricia knew that this was going to be more challenging that she had first thought. She was suddenly glad that Anne wasn't home to try and stop her too.

'Why not?' Bill pressed. 'Were you going anywhere in particular? I don't mind being the one to look after the baby if you'd like. I often watch my nephew for my sister.'

'As I say, just some fresh air,' Patricia insisted. 'It's a beautiful day outside.'

'But you're not from around here,' Bill pointed out. 'You don't know where you're going. I wouldn't like you getting lost and not being able to find your way back. Besides, Anne would never forgive me if anything were to happen to you.'

He smiled at her but Patricia didn't see the humour. She remained stony faced.

'No,' she insisted again. 'I want to have a few moments by myself, that's all. You've no need to worry about me, Bill.'

She was doing her best to reassure him, but she could tell that Bill was not convinced.

'Anne wouldn't like it, and quite frankly I don't like it either,' he said as the baby squirmed, his little arms reaching out for Patricia. 'I think there is something else going on here that you aren't telling me.'

'Don't be silly. Of course there isn't, Bill!' Patricia said, trying her hardest to be cheerful. 'All I need is some time for myself. I feel like I will go mad if I stay cooped in this house any longer. And anyway, Anne has gone on some mysterious meeting neither of us know anything about, so why shouldn't I have a few moments alone? I think you are beginning to get rather paranoid.'

This seemed to strike a chord with Bill and Patricia waited breathlessly.

'Perhaps you're right,' he relented. 'I suppose the situation could make one feel rather on edge, jumping at shadows. If you would like some fresh air, I can watch the baby for you. But don't take too long. I wouldn't want Anne coming back and you not being home. I don't think she would be very impressed with me if that were the case.'

'Oh thank you, Bill!' Patricia said. 'I promise I will be back before you miss me.'

She took a slow walk out of the park, and with every swing of her handbag Anne felt weight of the tiny vial inside, and the portent it held. She took a path alongside Holland Walk, trees and bushes either side of her. Although the rain had not lasted long, the ground beneath her was soft, with droplets of water glistening on the leaves of the trees. On the other side of the trees was a wall that ran parallel to Holland Walk, from which she could just about make out the roof of Holland Park School peering out.

The school had produced some notable pupils over the years, and even now Melissa Benn, the MP's daughter, was there. Thoughts of the school made her mind return to Baby B. What if they never found any of the Terrae? She tried to imagine how things would turn out – Patricia would, no doubt, insist on taking care of the baby, raising it. Could they get away with putting an alien child through school?

She really wished Lethbridge-Stewart was here. The colonel moved in different circles to her, plus his best friend was a father. Surely they knew…

She stopped and turned. A rustling came from the bushes close by. The path she was on was deserted. It was probably just a peacock, Anne reasoned, and shrugged. She continued on her way towards the gates.

Then the sound came again, louder than before, as if something heavy was causing large branches to crack under foot. This time, Anne caught a quick flash of movement coming from the foliage. Her curiosity awakened, she hurriedly made her way towards the noise. She didn't expect to see a familiar face hiding there.

'Charlie?' she said, and stared down at the young man crouching in the Holland Park undergrowth. For a moment, he pretended that he hadn't heard her, but the precariousness of his position made it impossible for him to ignore her for long.

'Oh hello again, Miss Travers,' he said as nonchalantly as he could muster, brushing away the ferns that had adhered to the hair falling across his face.

'What on earth are you doing down there? I thought we had an understanding? You weren't to continue following me.'

Charlie gulped and squinted up at her. 'I'm sorry. But I couldn't help it! It's my journalistic instincts, you see. I've seen more in the past couple of days than I have in my whole life and I can't just let this story slip away from me now.'

Anne looked around her and noted they were coming to the attention of an interested old woman who had joined the path from Holland Walk.

'Is everything all right over there?' she asked, her voice cracking slightly as she raised it.

'All fine,' Anne called back, willing the old woman not to come any closer. 'It's just my nephew. He's protesting.'

She hoped this would put an end to the stranger's interest, and that the old woman would move away. She didn't. Instead she began to approach them.

'Oh, what for?' the old woman asked with interest. 'I think it's wonderful the children are getting so involved in politics nowadays.'

'Children? I'm not—'

Anne spoke over Charlie. 'He can't say. It's a silent sit in.'

The old woman knitted her brows. 'Oh.'

'He requests to be left alone,' Anne added pointedly.

The old woman looked rather crestfallen and then, after a moment's hesitation, finally began to move off. Anne gave an inward sigh of relief. Quickly, she turned her attention back to the crouching young man in the bushes.

'Come on then,' Anne said, dragging Charlie to his feet. 'We need to get out of here before you bring us any more unwanted attention.'

Charlie got up unsteadily and continued to brush himself down as he did his best to keep up with Anne's pace. 'I am sorry, Doctor Travers,' he apologised again. 'But I couldn't just leave, not after what you had said before, and what's more I've discovered more crucial information about the story.'

'There is no story,' Anne said without turning to look at him. 'Keep up. We will walk you to your car.'

'Oh you don't need to do that,' Charlie said.

'Yes I do,' Anne replied. 'I need to make sure you drive away in it, this time for good!'

Charlie went pink, but Anne could see he wasn't to be so easily deterred. He was determined to continue with his line of questioning. From inside his jacket pocket he brought out a crumpled roll of newspaper.

'You can walk me if you like, but not before I tell you what else I've found out.'

He looked to Anne for encouragement, but received only silence as she strode on ahead. He continued on anyway.

'After I dropped you off, I really did mean to leave, I promise,' he said. 'But that was before I had the chance to read through the papers. Have you read today's edition?'

Anne stopped in her tracks. She desperately wanted to feign ignorance but knew it was too late.

'Look!' he said, hurriedly scrabbling through the crinkled pages until he came to the story. 'It's the doctor I was telling you about before. Doctor Travers, he's dead!'

No doubt now it would be even harder for her to keep Charlie at arm's length.

'Yes.' Anne said, long-sufferingly. 'I'm afraid I have already seen the article. What a terrible accident.'

'Oh, you don't believe it was an accident for a second. I know you don't,' Charlie insisted. 'Anyone who knows anything about the case, knows it's murder!"

'Keep your voice down,' Anne cautioned him. 'Such flights of fancy are not befitting for a journalist of any integrity. A man is dead, Mr Redfern. I hope you fully understand the seriousness of such a situation.'

Charlie nodded solemnly. 'Absolutely I do. That's why I knew I had to come and find you at once. I had to warn you so that you could protect your friend. You didn't seem very convinced before, but maybe now you'll realise that they will surely come looking for her too.'

'Why would I be more convinced now?' Anne asked. 'I knew about the death of Doctor Jhaveri when we last spoke.'

'Oh.' Charlie was stumped.

Anne couldn't help but smile, feeling a little guilty for taking the wind out of Charlie's sails. 'That still doesn't explain why you were hiding in the bushes,' she pointed out.

'When I saw that you were alone, I was going to approach you. But then that other woman came up and I sort of lost my nerve,' he admitted. 'It seemed important so I didn't want to interrupt. Who was she anyway? She wasn't in any of the pictures of Doctor Jhaveri's team. Rather too young and pretty to be a scientist too, I suppose.'

Anne folded her arms. 'So women scientists can't be

young and pretty? Are you implying that I'm old and ugly, Mr Redfern?'

Immediately Charlie spotted his mistake. 'No, I'm saying... I mean you're... I just...'

Anne let him squirm for a moment longer, before she returned to Ruby. 'Anyway, the woman you saw me with has nothing to do with Doctor Jhaveri.'

'But she is connected somehow, isn't she?'

Anne didn't reply. The last thing she wanted was Charlie digging around trying to find out information on the other alien in her life.

'Do you think they know about me? What if more of them come to me for help, and I put them in danger?' Charlie asked suddenly.

Anne smiled at the leaps he was making. Still so young and impressionable, despite his protestations. 'I think, for now, you are quite safe. But I certainly wouldn't advise you go digging any further. Thank you for your help, Mr Redfern,' she said politely. 'But I think I can take it from here.'

With that, Anne quickened her pace until they were back on Holland Walk again, surrounded by too many passers-by to talk freely. They began down the incline towards Holland Park Avenue.

'I won't tell anyone,' Charlie said at her side as they walked. 'But I want to know the truth. I'm a journalist, I can't help it.'

'The less you are involved, the better,' Anne said. 'The last thing I need is trying to keep someone else safe. Good day.'

She walked on ahead and turned, with little surprise, to

see that Charlie was still beside her.

'I thought we were walking to my car?'

'I've changed my mind,' Anne replied. 'I don't think you need a chaperone after all. It looks like you're more resourceful than I first thought.'

But Charlie was still walking beside her. With a sinking feeling, Anne suddenly realised why. She stopped and turned to face him.

'You followed me and parked close to my house didn't you? It's you that's been watching me the whole time?'

Charlie hesitated then gave a sheepish nod.

'What am I going to do with you, Charlie?' Anne asked.

Charlie looked down at his watch. 'Buy me a late lunch?'

Anne almost walked away then, but something stopped her. 'Okay,' she relented. 'Where would you suggest?'

'There's a nice restaurant in Notting Hill.'

Anne turned around and placed her arm in Charlie's. 'Come on, then, Mr Redfern.'

They set off up Holland Park Avenue towards Notting Hill Gate. In truth Anne found herself enjoying Charlie's company. He was awkward, a little too enthused, but essentially harmless, and she knew that Bill would keep Patricia safe until she came back. If nothing else, the longer she was away, Anne reasoned, the less likely anybody would bother Patricia.

At least, she hoped that was the case.

Bland normally flew first-class, of course, but this time it was a private jet. A small thing, but fast. Faster than most. It didn't come cheap, but Bland wasn't concerned about money. He was concerned about getting to the United

Kingdom as fast as possible.

Despite what Kabinov had said, Bland knew his old friend wasn't disinterested. He could only sit in his office for so long before the temptation to get involved got the better of him. After all, it wasn't only Bland's people who had brought the compound back from the Moon. The Soviets had too, albeit a slightly different compound. But still one close enough to that which had gone missing.

Now it wasn't just the baby he wanted, but this Moon Blink too. If what Kabinov said was true, and the compound allowed people to see the aliens as they were, then…

'Your milkshake, Administrator,' said the stewardess, intruding on his thoughts.

He looked up at her with disdain, but nonetheless accepted the tall glass full of banana milkshake, made, he hoped, with fresh ice-cream. He pulled his straw out of the top pocket of his jacket and carefully placed it in the milkshake. He sipped it gently.

'Very good indeed,' he was forced to admit, and offered the stewardess a smile. She curtsied, and returned to the front of the plane.

One thing he knew he'd hate about London – the Brits simply had no idea how to make a proper milkshake.

He sipped some more of it and looked over the papers before him. He picked up the photo of Doctor Richards. He remembered her, vaguely. He had his people tracking her down in London even as his jet shot across the Atlantic. Before he landed they'd have her location pinned down. And there was also another woman that interested him, another woman scientist no less. The woman who was helping Doctor Richards.

He now studied this woman. She looked so prim and proper. Miss Anne Travers, daughter of the world-famous anthropologist Professor Edward Travers. As a young man climbing the ladder of success, Bland had once met Professor Travers. He had hated the older man immediately. And, Bland suspected, he'd hate Miss Travers equally.

Patricia had been gone now for over an hour now, and Anne still wasn't back. Bishop had sat in the kitchen alone for the first thirty minutes, save for a hissing Sasquatch who sat on the windowsill and spat at some invisible enemy outside. He decided to go through some of details of his most recent training session at Mons, but after a further half hour his mind started to fixate on the scenarios which could explain Patricia's continued absence. No longer able to simply wait around, Bishop had then decided to take the baby for a circuit of St James's Gardens, which attracted a few odd looks from passers-by; understandable since he was the only man out pushing a pram. Not the kind of thing one expected to see in the middle of the afternoon on a week day in London.

There had been no sign of Patricia out there, and he returned to the house, feeling that his initial suspicions had been right.

He was upstairs when the doorbell finally rang. He quickly checked on the baby, then went to answer it, knowing that it couldn't be Anne, as she had a key. He just hoped it was…

'Patricia,' he said with relief. 'Where've you been? You've been gone ages.'

She didn't say anything, just brushed passed him and

continued on into the kitchen. Something was wrong.

'How is the baby?' she asked.

'He's fine, asleep now. I took him for some fresh air. Do you want to go and check on him?'

'No, I wouldn't want to disturb him,' Patricia said, though Bishop could see it pained her not to go and see him. Before he could ask her any more questions, though, Patricia continued. 'Bill, I haven't been quite honest with you.'

'Okay,' Bishop said, trying his best to sound like he hadn't already worked that out. 'How about a cuppa while you tell me?'

Patricia nodded gratefully and sat at the table. Bishop set about making the tea.

'The truth is that you were right,' Patricia began. 'Something isn't quite right. When Anne and I were here this morning I read in the newspaper about the death of a colleague of mine.'

'Sorry to hear that,' Bishop said.

'Me too. But more than that, I'm afraid, Bill. This man was one of the scientists I worked with at the Laboratory in Washington. He was the one instrumental in releasing the Terrae. He was the one who gave me the baby to keep safe.'

Bishop nodded his understanding, glancing back at her to show he was paying attention. He put the sugars in the cups.

'When I left before, I had no intention of coming back,' Patricia continued. 'I was afraid that by being with the baby I wasn't keeping him safe at all, but only putting him in more danger. But then something happened and I realised that I was making a mistake.'

'What kind of mistake?' Bishop asked while he poured

the hot water.

'I think it might already be too late. I think someone already knows I'm here, and what's more is watching the house.'

'I had that very same sense before,' Bishop said. 'But perhaps we are just being paranoid and jumping at shadows. I mean, I have been here with the baby alone and there has been no sign of anyone.'

'Not yet. But that might change.'

'Do you have any evidence? Did you see anyone in particular or notice anything out of the ordinary? That damn cat has been hissing at something outside the window all afternoon, but whenever I looked I couldn't see anything.'

Patricia shook her head. 'No, nothing. I must sound crazy to you, Lance Corporal, but it feels almost like a mother's instinct.'

'No,' Bishop said, sitting down at the table. 'That doesn't sound crazy. I think it's an inborn thing for all women. Just the sight of a baby is enough to make most broody.'

Patricia smiled, and reached out a hand for his. She squeezed it gently. 'Thanks, Bill. Anne is very lucky to have you.'

Bishop just smiled back.

'All I have wanted to do since this whole mess started is to keep the baby safe. That's why I've come up with a plan.'

'A plan?' Bishop repeated. 'Shouldn't we wait until Anne gets home? I'm sure her meeting can't continue for much longer. She wouldn't want us to make any rash decisions without her here.'

Again Patricia smiled. 'Henpecked already, I see.'

'It's not that,' Bishop said, the words coming out before

he even thought of them.

'I'm just joking. Sort of.' Patricia chuckled briefly, before her expression turned serious again. 'I would like to wait for Anne, but I fear there is no time. We must act now. So here is what we need to do. You should take the baby and keep him out of sight.'

'Me?' This did not sound like a sensible plan to Bishop. He was reminded of an old military tactic – divide and conquer. 'We should stick together. Anne asked me to look after both of you.'

'Bill, listen to me. What I'm saying makes sense. We don't know who is watching us, but we can assume that they won't think to follow a lone male. If they're looking for anybody, it's me.'

She may have been right, but Bishop stood his ground.

'Have you got your motorcycle outside?' Patricia asked.

'Yes.'

'Then you need to take him. Your place must be safer; nobody will know where you live.'

'Wait just a moment. I'm not sure I can get a baby past my landlady. My digs are rather modest, to say the least.'

'That doesn't matter,' Patricia said. 'Better than a cage.'

Her words hung in the air between for a moment. Bishop shuddered at the thought of what the tiny baby must have endured so far in his short life. He began to feel himself relenting.

'What about you?' he asked.

'It's me they're after. As you said earlier, I'm not from around here. It shouldn't be too hard to get lost.'

'And draw them away?'

Patricia nodded. 'Yes, it's the only way.'

A tactical diversion. Bishop would have approved if it wasn't for the fact that Patricia was putting herself in the firing line. Clearly the baby had really got to her. He couldn't help but admire her for what she was prepared to do for a child which had nothing to do with her.

'Okay,' Bishop said.

'Thank you, Bill. And it's only until Anne gets back. Leave a note for her.'

Bishop watched as Patricia headed upstairs to wake the baby. He wasn't happy about this, but he accepted what needed to be done. The baby needed protecting, after all that's what brought Patricia to the UK in the first place. He just hoped that Anne would be back soon. Until then, all they could do was wait.

— CHAPTER ELEVEN—

On the Run

They sat in the restaurant, having chosen a two-person table by the window, looking out at the ever-busy Notting Hill Gate. The restaurant was located at the end of Pembridge Gardens, just around the corner from the Underground Station. Anne sipped her red wine, and regarded Charlie closely. The story he told her about the girl, Selene, was less incredible than it should have been – which, Anne decided, said much more about her life than Charlie's oratory skills.

She wasn't sure what to say, how much to give away. She didn't doubt for a second a word Charlie had said, though.

'So, you see, that's why you have to let me help you,' Charlie said, visibly uncomfortable with Anne's unblinking gaze. 'Doctor Jhaveri sent Selene to me exactly so I could help.'

Anne agreed, but she still couldn't allow herself to open up to a journalist. Even one as sweet as Charlie Redfern. He was too eager for a story, and despite his insistence that he only wanted to help, he had mentioned the *story* too often for Anne to ignore it. She'd had more than enough trouble with nosy journalists and reporters before.

She decided the best course of action was honesty.

'Charlie, I appreciate everything you've told me, but you have to understand. This is not a game; people's lives are at risk. If somebody is really out to exploit these…' She looked around and lowered her voice. '…aliens, then I can't risk you too. Patricia and I will be okay without you; we have our own protector.'

'But Jhaveri knew I could help you.'

'No,' Anne said, shaking her head. 'He knew you could help Selene, by putting her in touch with me.'

'But she's not here.' Charlie looked out of the window sadly. 'She's gone, but she did ask me to find help for her people.'

Anne sighed. 'Then where is she?'

'Gone home.'

'The Moon?'

Charlie nodded. 'Yes. I know it sounds incredible, but I saw her turn into dust. She drifted off into the night sky, right in front of me.'

Anne just wasn't sure. She needed to think, and seeing Charlie's deeply imploring face before her wasn't helping. 'Okay, I need to use the ladies,' she said. 'We'll talk more when the food arrives.'

She reached for her handbag, but fumbled, and it almost fell off the table. She managed to stop it, but not before the vial of Moon Blink rolled out and landed at Charlie's feet. Anne reached down to pick it up, but for once Charlie was too fast for her.

'Please give that to me,' Anne said, holding out her hand.

But Charlie was already entranced. 'I've seen this before,' he said, his eyes wide.

'I doubt it. A lot of these compounds have a similar

176

chemical make-up and many of them can look similar,' Anne said, doing her best to be dismissive. He was already too close to this, and telling him about Moon Blink would only drag him in further.

'No, I mean I've seen this exact powder before. Selene gave me some.'

Anne narrowed her eyes. 'Gave you some?'

'Yes, she asked me to take it, to see her properly. And I did.'

'You've used Moon Blink?'

'Yes,' Charlie said. 'It was like seeing through a window into another world. I saw just how alien Selene really was. You see, it is too late. I'm involved in this now too.'

'Charlie, this is…'

'You won't have to worry about me either, Miss Travers, I can look after myself. I bet I'd even be an asset to the cause.'

'Absolutely not,' Anne said resolutely. She snatched the vial off Charlie, but he refused to simply let it go. The vial fell to the floor, and the glass smashed, sending the dust everywhere.

Charlie looked at Anne horrified. 'I'm sorry, I…'

Anne stood up abruptly. Already a waitress was coming over with a dustpan and brush. Their only supply of Moon Blink was gone. Anne glared at Charlie. 'You need to forget any of this ever happened. This is a very dangerous situation, Mr Redfern, and I will not be responsible for the involvement of anyone else. Now,' she said, gathering up her coat, 'if you'll excuse me, there is someone I need to see.'

And with that she stormed out of the restaurant and

headed straight for the Underground Station. She didn't even look back to see if Charlie had followed her. The look of mortification on his face had been too pronounced. This time, she was sure, Charlie would not pursue her again.

Patricia hadn't been wrong. Getting lost had been incredibly easy. For a while she just walked, taking back streets, alleys, crossing roads at random. She no longer even knew in which direction she was heading. She thought she had initially set off north west, but that had been many twists and turns ago. She was pretty sure she'd even walked back on herself a few times.

One thing she was certain of, though, was that she was being followed. For a while she had wondered if perhaps she was being paranoid after all, but it was when she found herself on a street called Woodstock Grove that she noticed the man. She supposed that had she not been looking for it, she would never have spotted him. But the trilby with the feather in its band was rather distinctive. Now Patricia was no spy, and she'd never needed to follow someone before, but even she knew that should she ever need to do so, she'd dress in the most nondescript way possible. Never draw attention to yourself – the number one rule of any spy.

So she carried on walking, pretending to not notice him. And he followed. Giving him his due, at least he kept his distance. And the farther she walked, the farther she drew him away from Bill and the baby.

She continued up a narrow street, which ended in a large concrete block of a wall. There were people walking just behind the wall, their heads visible. Evidently the other side was higher up than the street she was on. To her left was a tall building – brown bricked. An apartment block, she assumed. There had to be a way to get off the street. Then she saw it. Not a subway, exactly, but a walled path that led up at an incline. She continued on.

She came out onto a pavement alongside a wide road. To her right was a roundabout, branching off in several directions. Three tall buildings on the far side she recognised, in particular, having passed through the Edward Woods Estate ages ago. Over an hour later and here she was, almost in a complete circle. She looked up at the large signboard. The second turning off the roundabout led to Holland Park and Notting Hill Gate it seemed, while the third turning, the one just right of her, led towards a place called Kensington High Street. She didn't know Kensington, but she recognised the name Holland Park. That was not a great distance from Anne's house.

From the corner of her eye she spotted the man coming out from the small walkway. He stopped suddenly, clearly seeing her, and failing to act otherwise. He walked off left of her, and began looking in the window of the nearest shop. She supposed she could head towards Kensington High Street, but to do so would be to give away that she knew she was being followed. So, instead, she too headed away from the roundabout, passing the man blithely.

Before her was a large green, a place called Shepherd's Bush, according to the Underground Station across the road. Cars and buses drove around the green. It was a hectic sight, reminding her somewhat of the busier areas of Washington, DC, albeit on a much smaller scale. The green was lined with trees, with a large open area at its centre. People filled the green – mothers with their children, young people walking and talking. At the far end there even seemed to be tennis courts.

She caught the man's reflection in a passing black cab. He seemed to be holding something in his hand, into which he was talking. She instinctively knew what it was. A two-way radio!

Across the road, on the corner of the green, stood a police box. She looked around. No sign of actual police though, although some distance further down the street was another police box. If she could get to it, perhaps she could ring the local police station? No, she thought, quickly changing her mind. She didn't want the man to know he had been spotted. She had to draw this out as long as possible, give Anne time to find Bill.

Thoughts of Bill and Anne led her to thoughts of the baby, and her heart ached. She had to get back to them. Thanks to the sign board she had seen earlier, she now had a sense of which direction to head in.

She wanted to ring Bill, head back to him and the baby. But first she needed to lose the man.

She cut right into the shopping centre.

She glanced at Bejams, and her stomach rumbled. Not that she could just eat frozen food, of course, but the adverts in the window made her hungry. Although walking around for a couple of hours with only tea in her belly helped. On her right was a travellator, a kind of flat escalator that enabled shoppers to take their trollies up to the car park above. She stepped on the travellator and surreptitiously looked around her. The man had stopped and was looking at the Bejam adverts.

While his back was to her, she set off at a run. It was a

bit disorientating, running up a travellator. Her mind knew the speed she was moving at, but things passed her quicker than usual due to the added movement beneath her feet. She soon reached the top of the travellator. She had considered ducking into the car park, perhaps seeing if there was a nice young man who fancied giving her a lift, but instead she decided to rush across the bridge. When she had spotted the Underground Station earlier she had noticed that there were steps nearby, leading to the bridge she was now rushing across. Holland Park had a station, too, she had seen it when travelling by taxi to Anne's house. If she could get on to a tube train, she might just be able to…

Her run turned into a trot, which turned quickly into a few faltering steps.

A man stood in front of her, blocking the steps. It could have easily been just a normal pedestrian, except he had one hand in his pocket – his bulky pocket. Patricia was pretty sure that bulk contained a gun.

She turned. Surely he wouldn't shoot her out in the public like this? The question was moot. For there in front of her was her original follower. He wasn't even four feet away. Patricia swallowed.

'Doctor Richards,' the man said, sounding like a barrow-boy. 'We'd like you to come with us. Our employer wants to have a few words with you.'

She had no choice. *Sorry, Annie,* Patricia thought. *Hope I bought you all enough time.*

Anne was still fuming over the loss of the Moon Blink by the time she returned home. Waiting for the train hadn't helped her mood, but once she stepped out of Holland Park

Station she was able to walk some of the fugue off.

She should never have indulged Charlie. She should have just headed straight home. Not that she doubted Bill's ability to protect Patricia and the baby, but she felt like her meeting with Ruby had been a waste of time now. The Moon Blink was the one thing that would have assured finding the Terrae. Now, without it, how were they supposed to know a Terrae if they bumped into one? Damn Charlie and his nosiness!

She opened the front door with a sigh.

No, it wasn't Charlie's fault. She was being unfair. Gautam had sent one of the Terrae to Charlie, so he could help. And he had, at least on some level. His story about Selene, what he had seen, confirmed what Ruby had said. The Terrae were in London, somewhere, and Moon Blink would reveal them. Now, if only there was some way to get her hands on some more Moon Blink.

The bang of the closing door echoed throughout the house.

With a sinking feeling, Anne called out. 'Hello? Pat, Bill? I'm back, and I have news.'

There was no answer. No hint of movement anywhere in the house.

Her footsteps echoed in the hollow hallway. Sasquatch looked up at her with the yellow accusatory stare that only a hungry cat could give.

'Where have they gone?' she asked him.

Naturally the cat didn't answer.

Even though she knew she wouldn't find anybody, she still searched every room in the house. Once done, she sat at the kitchen table.

They wouldn't have gone far. Bill wouldn't allow that. There was no sign of struggle, so they must have gone out of their own accord. But where?

The suddenness of the phone ring made her jump. She scrambled from the table and rushed up the hallway.

'Hello?' she said, fearing the worst.

'Miss Travers?'

She knew the voice. 'General Hamilton, is everything okay?'

'As far as I know,' said the general. 'I have been ringing for some time, I even tried Corporal Bishop's landlady.'

Anne took a deep breath. This wasn't good at all. If Hamilton couldn't contact Bill, and had been trying for a while... 'General, I think something has happened to them.'

Hamilton was quiet for a moment. 'Well, let me make some enquiries. In the meantime, please make your way to Chelsea Barracks.'

A glimmer of hope. 'Is the colonel back?'

'Not yet, but I am here and we need to talk.'

It was only after she put the phone down that it occurred to Anne that he hadn't questioned her use of 'them'. First Hamilton had told Bill to pay a visit to Anne in Kilham, and then he allowed Bill some unscheduled time off... She looked down as Sasquatch.

'Ever get the feeling that others know more than you?'

CHAPTER TWELVE

Pulling Strings

It was a deeply irritable Anne Travers that entered Lethbridge-Stewart's office. 'You summoned me?' she asked of the man behind the desk, not even waiting for the door to close.

Hamilton didn't raise his eyes for a moment. Instead he waited until he had finished the sentence he was writing, then he stood up to shake her hand.

'More important summons, I presume?' Anne said with a timed raise of her eyebrow. She had decided to play things cool, and by cool she meant icy. Hamilton clearly knew more than he was telling, and Anne was annoyed that he hadn't seen fit to inform either her or Bill. Not telling Bill she could understand, after all Bill was only a junior NCO, but Anne had been working for the general since March.

'Very good, Doctor Travers,' Hamilton said; only slightly ruffled by her remark. 'But I believe that's quite enough. I am pleased to see you made it here in good time at any rate.'

'Fortunately London has a good public transport system.' She sat down without being asked. 'What is so urgent that you needed me to come right away?'

'I called you to my office today because there is a very important matter I wish to discuss with you, and doing so over a telephone line was not an option.' The implication was clear. 'Tell me, how is your work at the Vault progressing?'

Anne narrowed her eyes; she wished he would get to the point and fast. She couldn't believe he'd called her here to give a report. This was hardly the right time, especially if he knew as much as she was sure he did.

Fine, she thought, *I'll dance to your tune for a short while.*

'Fine, I believe,' Anne said. 'Nothing new to report since we last spoke,' she added, deliberately not mentioning Patricia and the baby. Ostensibly she had been placed at the Vault by a minister at the MOD, but in reality she was there working on behalf of Hamilton. Keeping an eye on things while he and Lethbridge-Stewart set up the Fifth Operational Corps. Hamilton didn't trust the secretive General who ran the Vault, and from Anne's time there she knew it was with good reason.

Hamilton laughed a tight-lipped sound that barely made it past his throat. 'You misunderstand me, Miss Travers.'

'Doctor,' she corrected him.

'Doctor, of course, my apologies.' He clasped his hands together and leaned forward. 'I have had a call from the Americans; one of their administrators is concerned over some lunar material they have recovered. They think some of their scientists may have been smuggling certain aspects of this abroad. Have you heard anything about this, Doctor Travers?'

Anne felt her stomach begin to tighten. For a second she was torn; he was her employer, and she certainly trusted him more than anybody at the Vault. But the one she really wanted to talk to was Lethbridge-Stewart. Besides, if he wasn't willing to be straight with her about what he knew, then she saw no reason to do so herself. 'No,' she said, not breaking eye contact. 'Should I have done?'

'I see. And what about the Soviets, one Vadim Kabinov? I believe he is the new Science Attaché for the Russian Embassy based in Washington. Have you heard of him?'

Anne shook her head. 'His name doesn't ring a bell with me. Perhaps Lethbridge-Stewart could shed some light on the matter?'

'I'm afraid he's otherwise engaged in Scotland, as I suspect Corporal Bishop has told you.'

Anne bristled. 'Well, he does have a lot of time on his hands,' she said, her tone level. But Hamilton didn't bite.

Now she was doubly annoyed. She didn't like her arrangement at the Vault, although she had willingly agreed to it. On top of that she wanted to find out where Bill and Patricia were.

Although Hamilton hadn't said so exactly, his comments about the Americans confirmed what Charlie had said. They were almost certainly sending someone over to find Patricia. And the baby. Moon Blink was on the streets – but the Americans already had their own supply. If they got the baby, then there would be nothing standing between them and finding the Terrae.

Except Anne. Much good she could do on her own.

'What do you think could so suddenly have peaked the Americans interest?' Hamilton asked.

'I wouldn't know,' Anne said, pulling herself from her thoughts. 'Perhaps if you had sent me in as a spy to the Russian Embassy or back to the United States I might be able to provide some answers for you.'

'Very droll, Miss Travers. But I'm afraid the time for

joking has past. It seems this situation is growing deadly serious, and—'

A knock on the door interrupted him. He smiled and said, 'Come.'

The door opened and Anne's eyes grew wide with surprise.

'Good afternoon, General,' Colonel Lethbridge-Stewart said. He glanced at the door. 'Odd, knocking before my entering my own office.'

'Sorry, Colonel. It seemed more prudent to use your office than have Doctor Travers travel all the way to Fugglestone and attract further unwanted attention.'

'Makes perfect sense, sir.' Lethbridge-Stewart looked at Anne, and smiled. 'Good afternoon, Miss Travers.'

'Colonel,' Anne said politely. She wasn't sure she'd seen him in civilian clothes before. He looked rather handsome in his slacks and sheepskin coat. Very home-grown. 'How nice to see you. Have fun in Scotland?'

Hamilton laughed. A little too loudly, Anne considered.

'Miss Travers you really are most amusing,' Hamilton said. 'It is a wonder you chose the laboratory and didn't take to the stage.'

At that Anne simply raised an eyebrow.

'Yes, well.' Hamilton turned back to Lethbridge-Stewart. 'You can fill me on the situation with Dolerite Base later. I think Doctor Travers knows more than enough already.'

'Yes, she does have a habit of learning more than is wise, General,' Lethbridge-Stewart said, before adding, 'Have you missed me, Miss Travers?'

'Hardly noticed you were gone,' Anne replied. She didn't want to show it too much, but she was very glad to see him indeed.

'How have things been in my absence?' Lethbridge-Stewart asked.

'Fine, nothing to report,' Anne said quickly. She wanted to speak to Lethbridge-Stewart, of course, tell him what was going on, but not like this, and certainly not in front of the watchful gaze of General Hamilton. If Hamilton wanted to play at secrets, then so would she.

'Let me walk you out,' Lethbridge-Stewart offered. 'I've yet to unpack, so you can share my car home. Although,' he added, turning his attention to Hamilton, 'I notice my adjutant isn't available.'

'I granted him a few days leave,' Hamilton said, smiling at Anne.

How much do you know?

'Very kind offer, Colonel,' Hamilton said. 'I will be seeing you soon I trust, Miss Travers?'

I dare say, Anne thought, ruefully. 'Absolutely,' she said, with the most genial smile she could muster.

Once they were in the corridor beyond the ante-office, Lethbridge-Stewart leaned in slightly. 'You and I need to compare notes, Miss Travers,' he said simply.

'Oh,' Anne said innocently. 'About what?'

'I think we know one another well enough to circumvent any game playing,' Lethbridge-Stewart continued as they headed for the stairs. 'I've had word from Sally that there have been some strange goings on during my sojourn in Edinburgh, and the general intimated certain things about a substance called Moon Blink. Whatever is going on, I am keen to get to the bottom of it.'

'As am I,' Anne agreed. 'But I'm afraid it isn't going to be quite so simple as that.'

'It rarely is, Miss Travers.' They took the stairs slowly. 'Where is Bishop and your friend?'

Anne looked around to make sure nobody was listening. 'That's part of the problem. I don't know.'

'I see. Then in that case, perhaps we can grab a sandwich somewhere? I haven't really eaten since leaving Scotland, and I could do with a bit of greasy London bacon.'

'But what about Bill and Patricia?'

'Don't worry, Miss Travers. We'll find them. I'm sure Bishop is keeping your friend safe. Come on.'

They stopped off at Hyde Park, where Lethbridge-Stewart took Miss Travers to a small shack near Speakers' Corner. It was good enough for a greasy sandwich, which had 100% more taste than the beef sandwich he'd had in Northampton. Now the two of them walked through Speakers' Corner which, although not as busy as on the weekend, was busy enough for them to talk in the open without drawing unwanted attention.

He listened as Miss Travers explained about her friend's arrival, and the baby. An alien baby. Brought back from the Moon by the American mission up there. She went on to tell him about their visit to the Vault and what they had seen there.

'Well, that explains one thing,' Lethbridge-Stewart said, and sipped his steaming tea. 'That young man was working in Dolerite Base, and I had him passed on to the local police.' He shook his head. 'The reach of the Vault's paymaster is troubling.'

'I wish that was the only thing troubling about the Vault. Experimenting on innocent people; there must be laws to protect against such a thing.'

'There are, Miss Travers, there are. I'll get on to Hamilton, see what pressure he can apply.'

'He knows more than he's letting on.'

They separated to pass a young couple who seemed to be locked together by their lips. Miss Travers glanced back at them and smiled. 'Oh to be young.'

'Quite. You'd never get that back in my day.'

'Or mine,' Miss Travers agreed.

A moment of silence passed, and they both listened to the general hubbub of people preaching. The weather was turning for the better, and Lethbridge-Stewart had left his coat in his car, along with Miss Travers'. He could feel the sun on his back.

'General Hamilton always knows more than he's letting on,' he said. 'Always pulling strings. Been doing so with me ever since Sandhurst, in fact.' He glanced down at Miss Travers. 'And, one suspects, he's now pulling your strings too. You don't think it was a coincidence that we both ended up at Chelsea Barracks at the same time, do you?'

'That wily old fox,' Miss Travers said.

Lethbridge-Stewart wasn't sure if she was annoyed or impressed. Her tone was a mixture of both. He thought of her father, and decided that Miss Travers was used to such men in her life. Professor Travers was good at getting his own way too, as Lethbridge-Stewart knew from personal experience.

'As for young Mr Carlin, well, he wasn't the only odd thing I saw in Edinburgh,' Lethbridge-Stewart began, and preceded to tell Miss Travers about the alien in the pub, and the reaction of the man using the Luna Haze.

'Yes,' Miss Travers said, when he'd finished. 'My contacts tell me the same, that Moon Blink enables people to see the Terrae for what they are.' She stopped. 'I did have a vial of it, but I lost it.'

'That was careless.'

'And unintentional,' Miss Travers said, clearly not caring for Lethbridge-Stewart's comment.

'Well,' he said, his tone lighter. 'I happen to have some in my car, confiscated from that chap outside the pub last night.'

Miss Travers smiled. 'Then we can use it to find the Terrae.'

Lethbridge-Stewart wasn't too sure about that. At least not yet.

'I think it's about time I got home,' Miss Travers said, glancing at her wristwatch. 'Hopefully Bill and Patricia are back now.'

'Yes, I think I'll come with you. Bishop is a smart young man, capable officer, but it's clear Hamilton wants me to work on this. And orders are orders, even if they're unspoken.'

Miss Travers smiled at him. 'To be honest, I'll be glad for the help. I have reason to believe that the Americans have sent somebody to England to take the baby. And I doubt it's for altruistic reasons.'

'No, that wouldn't be my first guess, either,' Lethbridge-Stewart agreed, thinking about what Miss Travers had told him of Doctor Richards' escape from America. And the death of their mutual colleague, Doctor Gautam Jhaveri. It was all very well exploring space, but if human's couldn't be trusted to visit the Earth's moon without taking advantage of what they found, then what hope did the universe have if humanity ever truly reached the stars beyond? It was little wonder, Lethbridge-Stewart reflected, that aliens were drawn to Earth so much. A phrase came to mind; pre-emptive strikes.

They turned and retraced their steps through Speakers' Corner.

'Tell me all about this baby,' Lethbridge-Stewart said.

CHAPTER THIRTEEN

The Good, The Bad and The Baby

It was close to 5pm by the time Lethbridge-Stewart's silver Mercedes pulled up outside the Travers' house. Anne was out of the car before Lethbridge-Stewart even had a chance to pull the parking brake.

She climbed the steps to the front door and opened it quickly. But she didn't enter immediately; instead she stopped and listened out for the sound of the baby. There was none. Temporarily defeated, Anne's hoped returned a moment later when she heard a sound come from the kitchen. It was faint, but recognisable. A cup being placed on a saucer.

'Miss Travers,' Lethbridge-Stewart said behind her, a note of caution in his voice.

Anne stopped only a few steps into the house and turned. The colonel was pointing at her front door. She was in such a rush to see Patricia and Bill that she hadn't notice the scratch where the lock had been tampered with. Lethbridge-Stewart gave Anne a warning look, but she ignored it and made her way with soft, urgent steps towards the kitchen. She heard Lethbridge-Stewart following closely behind her.

'Patricia?' she called out hopefully, but there was no reply, only the sound of her own voice echoing back to her. 'Bill?'

It was stupid of her, she realised later, to even think that it had been Patricia. After all, Anne had left her with a key.

'There's no Patricia,' a male voice said in a smooth American accent. 'Just me I'm afraid.'

Anne stared at the strange man who was sitting comfortably at her kitchen table, his spoon hovering over a half-eaten plate of ratatouille. Lethbridge-Stewart stopped beside her. They didn't need to ask why the man was there.

'I think you have the wrong address,' Anne began, with more confidence than she felt. 'I must ask you to leave.'

'18 St James's Gardens – that's correct isn't it?'

Lethbridge-Stewart placed a hand on Anne's shoulder, protectively. 'You know it is,' he said, clearly deciding to not play the innocent card. Anne wasn't sure if that was smart or not, but she deferred to Lethbridge-Stewart's experience in such matters. 'Nonetheless, you are trespassing. Leave, or I'll have you arrested.'

'I doubt the police would come,' the man said, gesturing to the cut phone wire along the skirting board. 'And, just who are you?' he asked Lethbridge-Stewart.

'Who I am is of no concern of yours. This is your last warning. Leave now.'

'Or what?' the American wanted to know. 'You'll resort to violence?' The man tutted. 'How un-British.'

Lethbridge-Stewart made a move towards the man, who raised his spoon. 'Not so fast. Unlike you, I came prepared.'

Anne watched in horror as another man came up behind them from the living room. He moved swiftly, and before Lethbridge-Stewart could react, the man struck a blow to the back of Lethbridge-Stewart's head, sending him down in one motion.

Anne rushed to his side but it was no use; he was out cold.

'Oh dear,' the American said with mock surprise. 'I hope nothing bad will befall any of your other friends. Perhaps you had better give up now and tell me what I need to know?'

'Perhaps you underestimate me,' Anne said, slowly getting to her feet. 'I work for a military organisation that will not tolerate such threats against one of their employees.'

'Well, unless they have the place bugged I'm pretty sure that no one else is coming to save you. Why don't you take a seat, Doctor Travers? This is really quite good. What do you call it?'

'Ratatouille.'

'How foreign. All those vegetables and no meat. Almost makes me lose my appetite.' He took another large spoonful, swallowing down the lot in one go.

'How did you know where I lived?' Anne asked, genuinely curious.

'I have my sources.' The American smiled a perfect white smile. 'We all have our secrets.'

'What do you want from me?' Now that Lethbridge-Stewart was out of it, Anne decided to return to her earlier play; the innocent card. She didn't know what the American knew, except that Patricia had taken the baby from the States, and she had no intention of accidently supplying him with further information.

The American studied her with his penetrating gaze. He got up and began to wander around the small kitchen, opening and closing the cupboard doors until he found something that took his fancy.

'What do you want?' Anne repeated. 'I hardly think you

broke into my home to sample the contents of my kitchen.'

The American smirked at her contemptuously. 'You don't seem that surprised to find a stranger in your midst. Perhaps it is something of a regular occurrence for you, Doctor Travers?'

Anne wasn't about to rise to his taunts. 'Since you know my name, it would be only right that I should know yours.'

'Yes, why not? I am Frank Bland. Not that my name makes any difference to your current situation.'

'What do you want?'

Bland sighed. Anne waited to see what he would do next. Calmly, he pulled out a chair and gestured for her to take a seat. Anne complied dutifully, her eyes watching him closely all the time.

'What if I said that I have something you want?' he asked.

'What could you possibly have that would interest me?'

She could tell this had made Bland smart for a moment, but he recovered quickly. 'What if I were to tell you that we have your friend?'

Which friend? But she didn't ask. If Bill, then where was Patricia? And if Patricia, then where was the baby? Anne hoped one of them at least would keep the baby safe. She forced herself to keep her composure. She wasn't about to let Mr Bland see that he had rattled her. She could tell by the way he was looking at her so closely, that he was eager to detect her response to the news.

'Then I would say you already have everything you want from me,' Anne responded, testing him.

Bland grinned at her. 'We know you are hiding one of them. Take me to him, or things will start to take a turn for the worse.'

Anne took a deep breath. That confirmed what he was here for. 'You know I can't do that,' she said, keeping her tone as level as possible.

Bland licked the back of the spoon in a vulgar way that made Anne eye him with disgust. 'And why not?' he asked threateningly, the toe of his shoe nudging at the still unconscious Lethbridge-Stewart on the floor. 'I'm sure Doctor Richards has told you what has happened to the others who disobeyed me.'

Oh, Pat, Anne thought. At least Bill was free, and clearly the baby was still safe. She took a little solace in that.

'Believe me, Doctor Travers, the only way to keep your friend alive is to do exactly what I say.'

Anne smoothed her hair behind her ears, the action calming her. 'I already told you. I can't tell you.'

Bland pulled at his lip. 'I had heard you were stubborn, but do not mistake courage for foolishness. You and your scientist friend are little use to anyone once dead.'

'And what about him?' Anne motioned towards Lethbridge-Stewart.

Bland shrugged. 'What's one more death?'

'A lot, when one of those you kill is a high ranking military officer.'

For the first time doubt passed across Bland's face. 'Well,' he said eventually. 'That would complicate things, but it is a risk I'm prepared to take. Now,' he leaned over the table. 'Where is the baby?'

'I can't tell you where he is, because I don't know myself.' Anne met Bland's cold look. That was one truth which couldn't hurt her to share.

'What?'

Anne sighed. 'Just as I said. I have no idea where he is. He was with Doctor Richards when I left her this afternoon, and that was the last I saw of him. You say you have Patricia, so why not just ask her yourself?'

He looked at her for a moment with a wild animal expression. Anne knew it was a risky move bating him, but her heckles were rising and she wanted to see what he would do next. Perhaps if he lost some of his maddening composure he might slip up and give away some detail as to where he was holding Patricia.

'I like you, Doctor Travers, I really do. In fact, I have a fondness for the British as a whole. That's why I'm going to give you the night to think it over. I'm sure you'll change your mind by the morning.'

He finished his final bite, wiping his hand on her tea towel. He threw the spoon into the sink with a loud clang.

'Surprisingly good,' he mused wiping his mouth on his sleeve. 'Amazing how quickly I can change my mind. You see I really am a reasonable man after all. I'm sure you'll see your way to doing the same.'

Anne doubted that very much. The way Bland moved around her kitchen reminded her of some species of reptile, all undulating muscles and strange jerky head movements. She knew he was the only one who could lead her to Patricia, but every part of her wanted him to get out of her house as quickly as possible.

'How will I reach you?' Anne said, gesturing to her now severed phone line.

Bland smiled at her again. 'Don't worry,' he said. 'I know where to find you.'

He made his way to the front door, retrieving his coat.

'I would be careful what side you choose, Doctor Travers. No use throwing the baby out with the bathwater, as they say. I can always use a great scientist on my team. Remember that before you make your next move.' His aide opened the door, and Bland glanced back. 'And do warn your military friend there, I have contacts everywhere. It would be unwise to seek further assistance.'

Anne had no need to do so. Clearly Bland had no idea who Lethbridge-Stewart was, or that he'd already been assigned to the case.

Anne remained on the chair for a short while, her mind running over things. Knowing that Bill and the baby were safe – or at least free of those who wished the baby harm – was one good thing. Patricia being captive to the strange American was not.

Lethbridge-Stewart was starting to come to. Anne moved to help him to his feet.

'Be careful, Colonel,' she advised him. 'You had a nasty bump.'

'Where is he? Are you hurt, Miss Travers?' Lethbridge-Stewart struggled to his feet with Anne's arm for support.

'Yes, he's gone. His man too.'

'What did he want?'

While Lethbridge-Stewart drank the water, Anne explained what Bland had said. 'I do know that Patricia isn't really what's important here. What he is really after is the baby.'

'Who is, presumably, with Corporal Bishop.' Lethbridge-Stewart stood up. 'We must look for clues. He wouldn't have gone without leaving some indication of where we can find him.'

Anne hadn't thought of that, but it made sense. They still didn't know what had happened, but they could make an educated guess. Patricia must have used herself as a diversion, allowing Bill the time needed to get the baby to safety. Lethbridge-Stewart was right; Bill would have left some kind of note.

They searched the house, but didn't need to look far. Lethbridge-Stewart called Anne over to the small table in the hallway upon which sat the phone. He lifted the small notepad. 'What do you make of this?'

Anne took the pad off him. Two lines of numbers, mixed with letters. 'Two, nine, one, two, one, two,' she said, reading the top line. 'A code of some sort.' She shook her head. 'It's not my father's hand writing.'

'No, it's Bishop's.' Lethbridge-Stewart smiled and nodded. 'Of course, numbers that correspond with the alphabet. Two is *B*, the second letter of the alphabet.'

Anne saw it now. 'Okay, so we have *B, I, A, B...*'

'No, that's a twelve, not one and two. *L.*'

The top line said 'Bill'.

'The second line then?' Anne wondered.

'A phone number,' Lethbridge-Stewart said. He counted the number of numerals and letters. 'A London number at that.' He read the translated number out. 'Bishop's home number. He's taken the baby to his house.'

That made sense. Getting the personal details of members of the British Army would have been a hard task, even for someone clearly as resourceful as Mr Bland. Made more difficult, no doubt, because of Bill's connection to Lethbridge-Stewart and the Operational Corps.

'I take it you know where Bill lives?' Anne asked.

Lethbridge-Stewart smiled. 'Well, of course. It would be remiss of me not to know the home address of my adjutant. He currently lives in a modest abode just off Ladbroke Grove. Come on, Miss Travers,' he said, patting her companionably on the shoulder, 'it's not that far from here.'

Bland's limousine was parked on Princes Place. He sat in the back, an earphone listening in on the conversation being held in Miss Travers' hallway. As he suspected Miss Travers knew where the baby was. He hadn't had much time before she arrived, but there had been enough time to plant a bug beneath the phone.

He removed the earpiece and leaned forward to lift the receiver of the limousine phone. He dialled a number.

'Find the address for this phone number,' he said, reeling off the number Miss Travers' military friend had said. 'It belongs to some residence near Ladbroke Grove. The baby is there. No,' he said, answering a question. 'Don't follow them. I don't know who Miss Travers' friend is, but he's a colonel in the British Army. He'll spot any tail. Find the address, and get me that baby. But be careful, the baby is precious.'

Bland put the phone down. He tapped on the partition between him and the driver. It slid open.

'Yes, sir?' the chauffer said.

'Take me to the laboratory. It's about time I had a personal word with Doctor Richards. Explain to her the futility of stealing from me.'

Lethbridge-Stewart was true to his word and it wasn't long before Anne found herself standing outside Bill's West

London digs. She hammered loudly on the door until she heard the sound of running footsteps inside. The door opened and a harassed looking middle-aged woman stood in the doorway, dressed in flowery dress and apron, with her hair in curlers and slippers on her feet.

'What is the meaning of this racket?'

'Excuse the interruption, Mrs Postlethwaite, but we're here to see Corporal Bishop,' Lethbridge-Stewart said.

Mrs Postlethwaite regarded Lethbridge-Stewart coolly. Anne got the impression they had met before, and it wasn't a happy meeting. 'Well, he isn't home to you.'

'What?' Anne was stupefied. 'But he has to be.'

'And who might you be?' Mrs Postlethwaite asked.

'This is Doctor Anne Travers, a very good friend of Corporal Bishop,' Lethbridge-Stewart said.

'Oh, you're Anne! My dear, it's delightful to meet you at last. William talks about you a lot.' Mrs Postlethwaite stood aside and waved them both in. 'Come in, come in. I'll get William,' she added, throwing a look at Lethbridge-Stewart before she closed the door and set off down the hallway to the back bedroom.

'What was all that about?' Anne wondered, stepping into the living room behind Lethbridge-Stewart.

'Clearly Bishop is only home to you.'

Anne glared at his back. 'That's not what I'm talking about. And you know it.'

Lethbridge-Stewart glanced over his shoulder with a slight smile. 'I'm quite aware of that, Miss Travers. But some things are need-to-know, and in this case, you don't.'

Anne wasn't so sure about that, since the colonel was always sticking his nose into her business. Speaking of...

She wasn't sure how she felt about Bill talking about her so much. Of course, as Patricia pointed out a few days ago, she spoke much about Bill too, so it shouldn't be so much of a surprise. Anne found herself smiling at the sound of footfalls on the lino in the hallway. Lethbridge-Stewart noticed her smile, and raised an eyebrow. She looked away, forcing her face into a more neutral expression.

Just in time, as Bill entered the room, baby in arms.

'Anne,' he said, his own smile not so contained. Anne stepped forward to take the baby. Bill looked over at Lethbridge-Stewart and offered a salute. 'Sir.'

'Report, Corporal.'

Before he did, Bill closed the living room door and offered them both seats. They sat and listened as he told them what had happened at the house, about Patricia's diversion. 'I left my phone number in code, so that you'd know where to find me,' he said, looking at Anne.

'I would have called, but my phone line was cut. Luckily, the colonel was with me and knew where you lived.' Anne looked down at the baby, who didn't seem to be affected at all by what was going on around him. He was asleep again. 'What about Patricia, did you tell her where you were going?'

'Of course, but not my address. Although she did memorise my phone number. I had hoped she'd call by now.'

Anne and Lethbridge-Stewart exchanged a glance. 'I'm afraid that's unlikely. She's being held as ransom, for the baby,' Lethbridge-Stewart explained.

'Then she was right,' Bill said.

'Yes.' Lethbridge-Stewart explained about Bland's visit, and his ultimatum.

'Damn it!' Bill stood and walked over to the window. 'I knew I should never have let her go. I told her, but she wouldn't listen.'

'You should have tried harder,' Anne said, and instantly regretted it the moment Bill's body tensed. 'I'm sorry, Bill, but I asked you to protect both the baby *and* Patricia. The only way we can stay safe is if we stick together. Now they have Patricia they can use her to try and blackmail us into giving them the baby.'

'It was Doctor Richards' risk to take,' Lethbridge-Stewart pointed out. 'Now we need to decide what to do. What's more important; this baby or Doctor Richards?'

Anne had no immediate answer to give. Patricia was her friend, but the baby was an innocent in all this. She didn't know exactly what Bland wanted the baby for, but she knew it wasn't anything good.

'We must do everything we can to find her,' Bill said resolutely. 'Don't worry, Anne, we'll get her back. Patricia and the baby will both be safe.'

'I'm not sure you realise what we're quite up against,' Anne warned him. 'Mr Bland is not above resorting to violence to achieve his aims. He threatened to kill us all to get the baby.' Anne looked over at Lethbridge-Stewart and added, 'Although knowing you're British military gave him pause.'

'I doubt we can rely on that staying so for long.'

Just then the baby began to cry, his pale face turning puce as he squawked feverishly in Anne's arms.

'What's the matter with him?' Anne asked.

Bill shrugged. 'I don't know. He's fine, then he gets like this.' He offered his arms out and Anne returned the baby to him. 'He misses his mother, I'm sure.'

'Or Patricia,' Anne said, with feeling.

Bill gave a weak smile. 'Perhaps it's the same thing now.'

'Perhaps he needs wrapping up?'

Bill nodded. 'Good idea. Do you want to sort it out?'

Anne stood. 'Okay.'

'My room is at the far end of the house, just next to the kitchen.'

Anne made sure the baby was comfortable, easing his crying a little, and left the living room.

She'd been in difficult situations before. In the Underground her life had been under constant threat of Yeti attack, she'd almost been stranded in 1823 too, and that didn't even include the situations her work at the Vault sometimes put her in. But this was different. This was personal.

That people were behind everything, normal human people, made the danger more real somehow. Aliens she could understand, because their motives were unknowable. But people. She knew what motivated them. Greed, power, pride... Bland's need to protect his secrets, to secure the Terrae, was dangerous. And now, not only was Anne's life at risk, but so was her friends. Patricia, the baby, Bill... Even Lethbridge-Stewart. At least two of them had signed up for this kind of thing.

She made her way down the hallway towards Bill's bedroom. She opened the door and looked around. Unsurprisingly the room was tidy. A bed, wardrobe, bedside cabinet. Bill hadn't been here long, a few months, but he was not one to carry clutter around with him. Anne smiled. Much like her, Bill liked things to be organised, easy to find.

She placed the baby on the bed and found a towel hanging on a radiator. She wrapped the baby up tightly. She straightened up and shivered.

The bedroom was cold, the curtains fluttering in the breeze. That wouldn't do, not with a baby in the room. She went to close it, then paused.

A sound behind her alerted her to trouble. But it was too late.

An arm reached around her neck and dragged her backwards. She tried to call out, but the man applied pressure. She gasped, barely able to draw breath.

Another man climbed through the window.

She couldn't allow this. They already had Patricia – they couldn't have the baby too!

With as much strength as she could muster she stamped her foot backwards, crashing her heel into the man's shin. He yelped. Using the self-defence lessons Bill had taught her, and helped by the releasing of the pressure around her neck, Anne grabbed the man around her throat and leaned forward, twisting slightly. The man flipped over her, landing on the floor by the bed.

'Bill!' she called out.

The man clambered to his feet, but before he could attempt to move towards Anne, the bedroom door flew open. Lethbridge-Stewart and Bill raced inside.

Thinking quick, the man pushed Anne backwards with an almighty force. Lethbridge-Stewart was barely able to contain his balance beneath her unexpected weight.

The men clambered back through the window, the first one holding the baby tightly in his arms.

They had what they came for.

'Bishop, follow them,' Lethbridge-Stewart ordered. 'But keep your distance, don't let them see you. And don't put the baby in harm's way.'

Without a word, Bill leaped through the window.

'Are you all right, Miss Travers?' Lethbridge-Stewart asked. This time it was his turn to help her to her feet.

'They've got the baby,' Anne said. 'They've taken him.' Even as she spoke, she could feel the panic settling in. 'Now we'll never see Patricia again.'

Lethbridge-Stewart took her by the shoulders and led her over to the bed. He sat her down gently.

'We mustn't panic, Miss Travers,' he cautioned her. 'Bishop is in pursuit of them as we speak. He's well-trained. Don't you worry, we'll get them both back.'

Anne was barely listening. All she could think about was how she'd failed Patricia.

CHAPTER FOURTEEN

Three to the Rescue

The sky was turning from dusk to the inky black of night as the car drew up near a nondescript looking office building just off Finchley Road in South Hampstead. Lethbridge-Stewart parked the silver Mercedes next to Bill and his motorbike. Anne got out of the car, pulled the seat forward and climbed into the back. Bill took the passenger seat and closed the door.

He had followed the baby kidnappers to the building, and once sure that nobody was leaving the place, he'd found a phone and called Lethbridge-Stewart. They had agreed to let the night fall before they too left Mrs Postlethwaite's house. In the meantime, Bill would remain, keeping an eye on the building.

'Any change, Corporal?' Lethbridge-Stewart asked.

'It looks deserted,' Anne noted, before Bill could answer.

'I think that's the idea,' Bill said, looking at Anne through the windscreen mirror. 'Bland seems to have sent his masked goons off on another mission.'

'How much time do you think we have?' Anne asked.

'Not much,' Lethbridge-Stewart admitted. 'We need to hurry.'

They all got out of the car. The men went to the rear of the car and Lethbridge-Stewart opened the boot. He handed

Bill a pistol.

'Miss Travers?'

She looked down at the automatic pistol he was offering her. Anne couldn't help but feel affronted. 'I'm a scientist, Colonel. Not a soldier.'

'Suit yourself,' Lethbridge-Stewart said, and replaced the pistol in the boot. He pulled out, instead, an old Enfield revolver and checked the barrel. 'Make sure you stay close to us,' he told Anne, once he closed the boot again. 'Bland won't hesitate to kill you if you get in his way.'

Anne didn't need reminding.

They cautiously made their way towards the building.

'Look,' Anne said, once they reached the double doors of the front entrance. 'Someone has forced them open.'

'Hmm,' Lethbridge-Stewart said, leaning forward to examine it more closely. 'Looks like a crowbar or something of the sort made this indentation. We need to tread carefully.'

He stepped back from the door, pacing backwards so that he could look up at the building.

'What are you doing?' Anne asked, but Lethbridge-Stewart ignored her, his brow furrowed in concentration. 'Aren't we going inside? Bill?'

'Miss Travers, please try not to announce our presence to all and sundry.' Lethbridge-Stewart's eyes were trained on the upper floors of the building. 'There, look! I think I can see movement.'

'Where?' Anne asked.

'Just there. The sixth floor. The window next to it looks like it may be a stairwell. That could be our chance. You're a trained sniper, Corporal, used to spotting the smallest detail, what do you think?'

Bill squinted in the direction Lethbridge-Stewart indicated. 'It looks like two figures. I can't see much from this distance. One looks to be very tall and the other one...'

'The other one what?' Anne pressed. 'Is it Patricia?'

'It looks as if the other one isn't moving,' Bill said.

'We must get inside now!' Anne said. 'Who knows what he might have done to her by now.'

She raced towards the double doors, pulling them open and slipping inside. She heard Lethbridge-Stewart tut behind her. The men joined her, and Bill took point, with Lethbridge-Stewart at the back, safely sandwiching Anne between them.

Together, the three began to make their way with careful steps from the front door towards the central lobby. In the dim light, they could just about see another set of double doors leading down into a corridor.

'Doesn't seem to be anyone on the ground floor,' Bill confirmed, and they continued to make their way further inside.

Lethbridge-Stewart reached across and tried the second set of doors. They opened without resistance.

'Looks as if someone has tampered with this lock too,' he said. 'Quickly, onwards.'

Lethbridge-Stewart took the lead. Anne and Bill followed closely behind him. Like the rest of the ground floor, the corridor was dark and deserted, a reception desk at one end flanked by chairs. Near the desk was a large brown door, and opposite that the closed silver doors of a lift. Anne was just about to press the button to call the lift when Lethbridge-Stewart stopped her.

'I think it's best we take the stairs, Miss Travers,' he

advised.

Anne nodded, realising not for the first time that she wasn't trained for this kind of work. She had a feeling that such training might be needed soon. For now, though, she followed Lethbridge-Stewart through the brown door, which led to a stairwell. The cramped stairs had an odd smell, like the noxious gases from a chemical reaction.

'Up here,' Lethbridge-Stewart said. 'They should still be on the sixth floor.'

They climbed the steps carefully, pausing here and there to listen for any change of sounds. They came out on the sixth floor into another dark corridor.

'Bishop, take point,' Lethbridge-Stewart said quietly, and Bill obeyed.

They barely moved a few feet when the sound of breaking glass echoed down the corridor. The sound was quickly followed by something that made Anne's heart ache. The cry of a baby.

Bill looked back at Anne, but she refused to allow herself a response. He nodded, and glanced at Lethbridge-Stewart.

'Keep them sharp, Corporal.'

Bill set off at a jog, while Anne continued at her previous pace. She daren't jog, too, for fear of her heels making too much noise. Further along the corridor, Bill stopped and pressed himself up against the wall. He glanced back and waved them down. Anne and Lethbridge-Stewart squatted into a crouch and joined him.

Bill lifted his head and looked through the wire-mesh window set high in the door. Without any thought as to her safety, Anne stood and looked over him.

'Miss Travers!' Lethbridge-Stewart hissed behind her.

But it was too late. What Anne saw made her blood run cold.

Bland stood there, talking slowly, standing in front of a chair to which Patricia was crudely tied. But that wasn't the worst of it. Baby B was inside what looked to be an airtight container. Anne swallowed, her mouth suddenly dry.

'How much air does he have left?' Anne hissed to Bill, but Bill shook his head. He had no idea.

She steeled herself. No doubt the men were thinking up ways to best handle the situation, but Anne couldn't wait for them to run their highly trained military minds through all the variables. The baby needed saving now.

'You create a diversion, Bill,' she said, taking command. 'Colonel, go for the baby; I'll untie Patricia.'

Lethbridge-Stewart regarded her with a raised eyebrow. He shook his head slowly. 'Absolutely not.' He motioned both Bill and Anne to resume their hidden position. He stood and glanced through the window, then looked back down at them. 'You will wait right here, Miss Travers, and by that I mean *here*. Bishop and I will handle this. Things could escalate quickly, and I'd rather avoid that if I could. Running in half-cocked will end in disaster. Trust me.'

Bland's strident tones began to rise. Lethbridge-Stewart crouched down again.

'Do you think he has spotted us?' Anne asked.

Bill shook his head, and desperately signalled for her to be quiet. Anne closed her eyes. She listened in silence as Bland continued his interrogation of Patricia.

'You're not getting away that easily.' His self-satisfied manner grated on Anne's nerves. 'Just ask your colleague

Doctor Jhaveri. Oh wait, I forgot. You can't.'

He gave a horrible laugh that echoed around them.

Before she knew she was going to do so, Anne felt herself spring forwards, but Bill's reactions were better. He held her arm firmly. After taking a deep breath, and nodding at Bill's warning look, she stood slowly, careful to keep her back to the wall, and squinted through the glass.

'Now,' Bland said, settling himself down at one of the vacant laboratory benches. 'What can I do to convince you to tell me where the rest of them are being hidden? I know you have them, Doctor Richards. I can't believe you thought you could betray me and get away with it. How long do you think it will take me to find them? You're smart, but I'm smarter. I'm always one step ahead.'

'Then you can do it without my help,' Patricia shot back.

Bland evidently found that amusing. He laughed. Anne felt her cheeks flame with indignation for her friend. Bland reached into his jacket pocket and took out a pack of half-finished marshmallows. Slowly, he began to toast the marshmallow on the Bunsen burner, the flame burning blue and hot. Anne could see Patricia watching him with wild terrified eyes. She wondered what Bland was planning next and, more crucially, when Lethbridge-Stewart would give the order to make their move.

Bland chewed noisily and the smell of the burned candy filtered out under the door.

'I'm going to ask you one last time, Doctor Richards. Or perhaps I should call you Patricia? No? Very well, where are the rest of them, Patricia? Where are you hiding the rest of Terrae?'

'I don't know,' Patricia said, her resistance suddenly

giving way, her chest heaving with heavy sobs. 'I really don't know. I've already told you everything. Please don't hurt him, he's just a baby!'

'An *alien* baby,' Bland corrected her. 'An alien baby who belongs to me.'

'He doesn't belong to anyone!' Patricia fought back fiercely. 'He is alive and free. He is his own person.'

'Don't be so stupid, Patricia. Of course he belongs to me,' Bland said with contempt. 'He was the property of my laboratory until you stole him. If anyone is the criminal here, it is you, not me.'

'Children are not property,' Patricia said, the hatred dripping from every word.

Bland laughed again, spearing a second marshmallow and toasting it savagely, watching the flame dance higher as the melted sugar dripped ominously onto the wooden bench. 'All children are property of someone. A child becomes the person it is shaped into. And this baby shall be shaped by me. You seem like a nice lady, Patricia,' he said, his voice softening for a moment. 'I wonder how your friend will feel when she learns of your fate from the pages of the newspaper. That is if anyone takes any notice of the demise of a female scientist.'

Patricia bit back her response, and Bland smiled. 'I have everything I need, except the rest of the Terrae. But, you know what, I believe you. You don't know where they are. Which means you are no longer any use to me.'

'I can't wait any longer,' Anne hissed. 'We need to do something right now.'

'No, not until there is a moment when Patricia is out of danger,' Lethbridge-Stewart said. 'Mr Bland's behaviour is too erratic to predict what he may do next. We must wait a little longer.'

'But what about the baby? He's going to die in there.'

Lethbridge-Stewart looked at her. 'I'm sorry, Miss Travers, but the life of your friend is of more importance than that of an alien.'

Well, it was nice to know Lethbridge-Stewart had solved that issue. In his head at least. Anne had not.

'But he's just a baby,' she said, forcing herself to keep her voice low. 'You're as bad as Bland.'

She turned her head away from Lethbridge-Stewart sharply, to find Bill staring at her, his brow furrowed, his blue eyes looking troubled.

Bland waited until the marshmallow was engulfed in flame and then swung it slowly across the surface of the container. The baby watched with wide eyes as the red orange light moved backwards and forwards.

'Strange that they can breathe our atmosphere, isn't it, Patricia?' he said. Patricia didn't reply, dry tears clinging to her cheeks. 'Most odd. You know, nothing eats up oxygen faster than fire. Do you think I should speed things up? His fate is already inevitable.'

'I can't wait any longer!' Anne said. 'I'm going in!'

'Stand down, Doctor Travers!'

But Anne wasn't listening.

'That's an order!'

'And I've told you before, Colonel, I'm not in the military, you can't order me around.'

She rushed past Bill, well out of Lethbridge-Stewart's reach. She was momentarily surprised that Bill didn't attempt to stop her, but the moment passed and she was through the laboratory door.

'Stop!' Anne said. 'Stop this now. We have you surrounded.' Even as she said it, she hoped Lethbridge-Stewart and Bill would prove her right.

Bland watched her for a moment, and then leisurely blew out the flame. 'Doctor Travers,' he said, sauntering across the room to meet her. 'What a pleasant surprise. I wondered how long it would take for you to find us. Clearly you're as resourceful as I've been told. You're just in time for the grand finale.'

'Leave them alone,' Anne demanded.

'What? Leave this alien baby here for someone else to find? I don't think so.'

Anne wanted to look back, to see if the men were getting in position – whatever that would be. She kept her voice steady. Had to keep Bland distracted.

'Isn't that what space exploration is supposed to be all about? Expanding our horizons, not shutting them down. Alien life has so much to teach us. Don't you want to learn more instead of destroying the only chance we may ever have to understand this species?'

'You British will never get it. You're too romantic, hopelessly naïve. That's never been what this is about. Being the best, that's all that matters, being the first. These aliens may look cute now, but make no mistake, if we let them have our planet even for a second, they will take it and keep it for themselves.'

'Mr Bland, I need you step back at once,' Lethbridge-Stewart ordered, stepping through the doorway, his gun seemingly resting casually in his hand by his side. 'We have the situation under control. There is no way you can escape.'

Anne noticed that Bill wasn't there. She raced across to Patricia, but Bland was too quick for her. He grabbed the container holding the baby, brandishing it above his head. Anne froze, barely two feet from Patricia.

'Set the baby down immediately,' Lethbridge-Stewart ordered, his measured tone calm. 'No one is going to get hurt today.'

'Help him!' Patricia cried desperately from her position in the chair.

Anne made to move closer. 'Patricia, please, we have—'

'Move, and the baby dies!' Bland snapped at her.

'Let me untie her,' Anne pleaded. 'She is no use to you now. You have what you want.'

Bland shook his head savagely. 'No! Nobody move or – I drop it!'

Anne swallowed, and watched him closely. His hands were shaking, his confident demeanour slipping away. It was being replaced by something else altogether more unstable. Fear.

'Please be careful,' Anne said, trying to keep the same tone as Lethbridge-Stewart.

'Me? Careful? Ha! Maybe it's you who needs to take care!"

'What do you mean, Mr Bland?' Lethbridge-Stewart pressed. 'Is someone else in danger?'

Bland shook his head wildly, his long arms shaking with the effort of holding the container. 'Who is to say you are not one of the Terrae?'

Anne stared at him in amazement. For an undeniably intelligent man he was certainly tossing out wild accusations. But now was no time to point out the obvious.

Bland began to laugh. It was a hollow terrifying sound. 'You British think that you are so smart, but you know nothing. Always letting the Americans lead the way! Did you think you guys would be the only ones to get hold of this stuff?'

'What stuff?' Lethbridge-Stewart pressed. 'What have you taken?'

Without seeming to even notice himself, Bland put the container down on one of the nearby workbenches. Patricia and Anne exchanged a loaded glance – at least the baby was out of harm's way, for the moment at any rate.

'This!' Bland hissed with glee, taking a rolled up sweet wrapper from his other pocket. He smoothed it out and from within he pulled out a vial.

'Oh no,' Anne whispered.

'Moon Blink,' Lethbridge-Stewart said, with an abrupt nod.

Bland took a swig of the vial, his eyes widening as the drug pulsated through his veins. 'Why do you not reveal yourselves to me?' he asked.

'There are no Terrae here, Mr Bland,' Lethbridge-Stewart said.

'Colonel,' Anne said, worried. 'Even a slight pinch of it produces an extreme reaction, and the amount he has taken...'

'I can see you!' Bland said, gesticulating wildly. 'You cannot hide from me any longer!'

'I'm afraid we are not one of them,' Lethbridge-Stewart said in a placating voice. 'Now, Mr Bland, it is very important that you listen closely to what I have to say. You are acting under the influence of a highly hallucinogenic drug. There are no aliens here.'

Bland patted the specimen tank on the bench beside him. 'You!' he said, pointing an accusing finger at the wide-eyed baby. 'I see you now for what you truly are. You are mine, and I will destroy you!'

'What are we going to do now?' Anne said, looking over at Lethbridge-Stewart. 'There's no reasoning with the man now. If there ever was.'

'Indeed,' Lethbridge-Stewart agreed, his own voice low enough to not arouse Bland's attention. 'It's in hand, we just need to keep him talking. And away from the baby.'

'No!' Bland cried, his hand gripping his face in agony. 'Why do I not see them? Where have you gone?'

A figure appeared behind Lethbridge-Stewart, just catching the edge of Anne's eye. She turned her head slightly, expecting to see Bill, but before she could attempt to focus her peripheral vision, there was a flash of bright white light accompanied by a loud bang, which reverberated around the room. There was a strange smell, like something burning, and Bland crumpled to the floor.

A man stood in the door, a smoking pistol still in his hand. 'I haven't come for you,' he said, his accent a strange mix of Russian and American. 'Shoot me if you wish,' he added, looking at Lethbridge-Stewart who had raised his own gun, 'but I wouldn't advise it, comrade.'

Anne looked across to Patricia, to make sure she was all right, but instead the baby in the specimen tank caught her attention. He wasn't moving at all. She wanted to run to him, but she couldn't risk it, not with the gun trained on them.

Lethbridge-Stewart watched him closely, as the Russian made his way across the laboratory. The colonel's gun never left the man.

'*Prasti*, my old friend,' he said, as he stood over Bland's twisted, lifeless body. 'I will miss your unexpected visits. But our planet is at stake, and I must protect my country above all else. It seems we have always been embroiled in mutually assured destruction in more ways than we thought. An uncontrolled public will always pose a far greater danger than anything we have ever faced before. I am doing this for us, Frank, for the future of our nations. There will always be sacrifices, and tonight, my friend, it was you.'

Anne listened, and something Hamilton had told her returned to the forefront of her mind. This man, she was certain, was Vadim Kabinov.

His eulogy finished, Kabinov turned to Anne. 'You.'

'Yes?' Anne swallowed. There had to be something she could do, keep him distracted like the colonel had done with Bland. Obviously Bill was out there somewhere, almost certainly getting into a better position. Why else had Lethbridge-Stewart kept Bland talking? A stalling tactic. 'Just please don't hurt my friend,' she said in Russian.

Kabinov stared at her blankly for a moment, as if he suspected a trick. 'You have spent time in Russia?' he asked tonelessly, also switching to Russian.

'No, but I like to embrace different languages,' Anne explained, not looking to get chummy, and certainly not interested in revealing that she had been altered by alien science.

Kabinov cocked the pistol in Patricia's direction. 'Untie

her.'

'What did you just say?' Anne asked, not sure if she had heard him correctly.

'I don't enjoy having to repeat myself. This will be the last time I ask you.'

Anne did as she was told.

'What are you doing?' Patricia said in a hushed voice.

'Stop talking,' Kabinov ordered. 'Now, get the child.'

Anne moved forwards but Kabinov raised the pistol threateningly. 'Not you. Her.'

Patricia edged closer and opened the specimen case. She lifted out the baby carefully. Anne was relieved to hear him cry.

'Shut it up!' Kabinov cried, switching back to English. 'If I wanted to hear the sound of a screaming child I would have stayed at home.'

Patricia hushed the baby, and his cries began to lessen. Kabinov grabbed her and began to lead her towards the door.

'Dammit,' Lethbridge-Stewart hissed, his eyes roaming around. Anne watched him. She knew it. He was trying to get a lock on Bill's position. 'Now look, this has gone far enough,' he said.

Kabinov raised the pistol. 'I know your man is out there, I saw him leave. If he doesn't let me leave,' at this he raised his voice, 'I will kill them both.'

'We can't do that,' Lethbridge-Stewart said.

'You have no choice. You may think that I am outnumbered, but you would be wrong. I have men waiting outside, many men. Bland was resourceful, but not like I am. While he has been playing Hide and Go Seek, I have been busy. The whole of the Soviet Embassy's resources are at my disposal and I have used them to their full. Only a handful of these aliens still remain alive on Earth, and I already have them.'

'How?'

'As I said, by using my time wisely while Bland played his foolish game with you English. I have the Terrae. They learned I had the *babushka*, and they came to me.'

'But you didn't have the baby,' Anne pointed out.

'No, but I am very convincing. The Terrae are a loyal species, unlike humans. They would never leave one of their own in danger. Look how depleted their numbers have already become in a matter of weeks. They would rather stay here on Earth than leave a single member behind. Only those who are cowards would have returned to the Moon without him.'

'How can you be so cruel?' Anne asked.

'I am not, my dear, I am being practical. This is a situation that needs to be controlled. The good Doctor Jhaveri tried to hide them all in one place to keep them together as a family. He thought that here in the UK they would be safe from the prying eyes of the Americans and Soviets. But as you can tell, he was very much mistaken.'

'Well I hope you aren't thinking of doing anything foolish. You know that you can't escape,' Anne cautioned him. 'We have you surrounded; you won't make it out of this room. Face it. It's over.'

Kabinov smiled at them coldly, his eyes dead behind his large glasses. 'I wouldn't be so quick to claim victory if I were you. It is so American. I know you will still choose your friend's life over the fate of millions. You do not appreciate the beauty of the Communist way.' He looked around. 'If your man had a good, clean shot, he would have taken it,' he said. 'I have been watching this room for a while, there are no clear shots where I step.'

He clicked the safety off the pistol and held it to Patricia's head. Her eyes bulged with fear. Lethbridge-Stewart took a step forward, but Anne rushed between him and Kabinov.

'Miss Travers, you must not interfere,' Lethbridge-Stewart warned her. 'I know this is a difficult situation for you, but this is not your call to make.'

'It is exactly my call to make,' Anne responded, her eyes flashing from Lethbridge-Stewart to Kabinov and the pistol still perilously close to Patricia's temple.

'I think you'll find she's coming with me,' Kabinov said. 'The *babushka*, too.'

'No,' Anne said. 'Please, you can't do that. Take me instead. I speak Russian, I could be of more use to you.'

He studied her for a moment, weighing up this option in his mind. Then he shook his head. '*Nyet*,' he said. 'You have steel in you, she is...' Kabinov shrugged. 'Just an American. We are leaving now. If you want your friend to stay alive, I suggest you make no attempt to follow us.'

Anne watched them go, never having felt so helpless in her entire life. As soon as they were through and the door had closed behind them, Anne made to follow but Lethbridge-Stewart caught her by the arm.

'Let them go, Anne,' Lethbridge-Stewart cautioned her. 'We can't go after them now. It's too risky.'

'So you're just going to let him take them? You're not going to try and stop him?' Anne asked.

'Of course we're going to try.' Lethbridge-Stewart lifted

his arm and made a complicated signal with his hand.

Anne looked around. Still she couldn't see Bill. 'Where is he?'

'On the way to my car. Don't worry. We'll get them back.'

They listened intently to the engine of a car starting below.

'Come on,' Lethbridge-Stewart said, and led the way out of the room.

— CHAPTER FIFTEEN—

The Pale Moonlight

The silver Mercedes turned one last sharp corner, deeper into Hertfordshire, just in time for Bill to spot the car in front pull off the road altogether. He switched off the headlamps and the Mercedes rumbled along at a safe distance from the leading car.

'Kabinov has to know we are following him,' Anne said.

'It doesn't matter now,' Lethbridge-Stewart reassured her, catching her eyes in the rear view mirror. He sat in the cramped back seat, due to expedience sake when he and Anne had left the building in South Hampstead. She was much slower and he didn't wish to waste time when she finally reached the car. He had simply climbed in the backseat, and waited for her. 'I'm sure Kabinov knew we always would. I suspect it is all part of the game he is playing with us.'

Anne nodded, listening to the low growling of the engine for a moment. The tail lights of the leading car were still clear ahead of them.

'I recognise this area, we're not that far from Little Gaddesden,' Lethbridge-Stewart said. 'We recovered fallen meteors just outside Ringshall last month, shortly after all that business with Dominex. A huge crater had to be disguised.'

'Meteorite,' she automatically corrected him. 'They are only meteors if they survive ablation in the atmosphere.'

Bill glanced at Lethbridge-Stewart through the rear-view mirror. 'She's got you there, sir,' he said with a grin.

'Hmm,' was the only answer Lethbridge-Stewart had.

Anne wasn't bothered about meteorites right now, her only concern was Patricia and Baby B. 'What do you think he is going to do to them?'

'Don't worry, Anne,' Bill reassured her. 'I'm damned if we'll allow you to find out.'

Anne felt helpless. She trusted Bill, and appreciated his support, but she wasn't so sure about Lethbridge-Stewart. The colonel had already made it clear he was more concerned about Patricia, and Anne knew she should take some comfort from that, but she didn't. She couldn't choose between Patricia and the baby. They were equally important to her. She wasn't sure when that had happened, but she knew it was true.

She sighed and looked out of the passenger door window. There had to be something else she could do. But then again charging in head first hadn't exactly helped so far. Instead, she resolved to wait and see what Lethbridge-Stewart advised them to do next.

Kabinov's car had finally stopped near a place Lethbridge-Stewart called Hoo Wood, and Bill pulled up a little distance back. Anne watched quietly; the Moon reappeared from behind the thick covering of clouds and the landscape in front of them was illuminated for a moment.

A handful of what looked to be young men all dressed in the uniform of the Russian military stood in a clearing, with the woods behind them.

A familiar Russian voice was issuing orders nearby. Anne listened to Kabinov intently. It seemed that he had dressed both his men and the Terrae in the same clothing so that without the Moon Blink it was impossible to tell them apart.

She explained what she heard to Lethbridge-Stewart and Bill.

'What are they doing? I can hardly see a thing,' Bill said, straining his eyes to see in the dim light.

'Keep your head down!' ordered Lethbridge-Stewart. 'And for goodness sake, do not make any sudden movements.'

Anne rolled her eyes but stayed perfectly still. She didn't want to spook Kabinov and whatever crazy plan he had come up with. He had killed once that night and she wasn't about to let Patricia or the baby become his next victim.

'Come closer!' Kabinov urged the shackled group. 'You thought that you would be able to escape, but alas not from me. The Americans were foolish and no match for the organisation of my Russian forces. I knew you would all come for this last one.'

Anne watched as Kabinov took a deep expectant breath, but the Terrae didn't move or respond.

'I want you to tell me your secrets!' He chortled with glee, his spectacles glinting in the moonlight. 'The Americans wanted to see what you are made of, but I want so much more. I want to become one of you; I want to live on the Moon without the help of breathing apparatus or gravity bases. Tell me your secrets!'

The Terrae didn't move.

Bill and Lethbridge-Stewart continued to watch closely. While they were distracted, Anne opened the glove compartment. There was something in there that she would be needing soon.

Kabinov scowled and the sound of his voice echoed out through the empty field. 'Very well then! If you will not help me, then you leave me no other option.'

He placed the baby on the ground as the mixed line of troops and Terrae drew closer.

'I know you need this child to complete your circle and return home. Don't forget, I can see you for what you truly are. If one of you comes closer, I will evaporate you. Do you understand?'

Anne studied their faces closely, watching to see if any movement would give away one of the Terrae from the soldiers, but it was no good. The line of men remained stony faced.

Patricia was kneeling down by the rocks, watching on helplessly. Kabinov wasn't even looking at her anymore; his entire focus was fixed on the baby.

'I can't just sit back and watch this any longer,' Anne said, and went to open the passenger door. 'We can't let it continue like this!'

'Just one moment longer, Anne,' Bill said, pulling her back by the arm. 'Look!'

But it was too late. Anne had the door open. She shrugged Bill's hand off her and climbed out of the car.

She inched her way closer to Patricia and the circle of Terrae.

From her position on the ground Patricia had already spotted her, but Anne raised a finger to her lips, cautioning

Patricia to stay silent. Patricia nodded but Anne could see a light of relief had come into her eyes, and as Anne got closer Patricia was already opening her arms to embrace her.

'Oh, Anne!' she whispered gratefully. 'Thank goodness you are here. I knew that you would find me.'

'Of course,' Anne whispered back. 'I promised I would keep you safe.'

'I don't care what happens to me, just don't let him take them,' Patricia said. 'They managed to escape once; he will never let it happen again. I cannot imagine the horrors that await them if they get taken by the Soviets.'

Anne nodded. She could well imagine it too. 'Don't worry, I don't think that's what Kabinov wants,' she reassured her friend. 'Besides, Bill and Lethbridge-Stewart are here with me, and I have a plan.'

'What sort of a plan?'

'Let's just say I think there may be one last untried option left,' Anne said. She felt in her pocket for the packet of Moon Blink she had purloined from the glove compartment.

'What are you doing to do?' Patricia asked, anxious. She had to squint to see what she was up to. Anne held the packet in the palm of her hand. The particles inside glittered like precious stones under the light of the Moon. Patricia's face went white. 'Don't, Anne,' she pleaded. 'We don't know what it might do to you. Just look what happened to Bland back at the lab; it turned him cuckoo crazy!'

'He overdosed,' Anne said, partly trying to reassure herself. 'A small sample of this stuff should be enough to see exactly where they are in this darkness, and get them out of harm's way before Kabinov can do anything stupid.'

'You can't, Anne! I won't let you do it!'

'Don't worry. There's not much of the dust in this packet.' Anne surveyed the sea of faces in front of her. There was no other way to tell them apart; she knew there was no other choice. Besides these aliens weren't evil or cruel. Her body's chemistry might well react badly to the Moon Blink, of course, but Ruby had infected her DNA back in May and she had survived. She could survive this, Anne was sure, besides without the compound it was impossible to tell the Terrae apart from the Russians. It was a calculated risk; one she was willing to take.

'I must, Pat,' she said firmly. 'If I don't, we might as well hand Baby B over now and be done with it. This is the only thing left to do that might help him.' She opened the packet and raised it to her mouth.

Just then there came a noise close by. Someone else had joined them in the darkness.

'Who's there?' Patricia called out anxiously.

'No cause for alarm, it's only me,' Bill said in a hushed good-naturedly voice. 'How are you feeling, Patricia? They didn't hurt you, did they?'

'Not much,' Patricia said. 'I don't know what I would have done if you hadn't come to rescue me.'

'Never mind about all that now,' Anne said. 'Where's Lethbridge-Stewart?'

'He's taking the other side where Kabinov is. He thinks if he can get him alone he might be able to stop him before this goes any further.'

'But what about the Terrae? How are we going to set them free?'

The three pressed themselves closer into the rocks as

230

Kabinov resumed his self-given position of centre stage. Anne noted he had the same arrogance as Mr Bland, but something about Kabinov was far more dangerous. Whereas Bland had succumbed to the lure of the Moon Blink and lost all control, Kabinov remained self -possessed.

They watched closely and he reached inside his jacket.

'What's he looking for?' Anne strained her eyes to see. The shape of the object was unmistakable. 'Oh no!' she whispered, but Kabinov's voice rose into the air again, drowning hers out.

'Do you know what this is?' he asked the assembled crowd. 'She is a Stechkin automatic pistol. Russian made you understand. A man of flesh and bone can be taken down in a single shot. I wonder what effect she might have on an alien specimen such as yourselves?' The people before him looked at each other nervously, none daring to move. 'How about... this one? Sergey!'

His commander unshackled the maybe-Terrae standing at the end of the line.

'Do you have anything you would like to say to me?' Kabinov asked as the man was forced to his knees. There was no answer, just a dignified silence. 'Very well. Alas, sometimes we find one must be sacrificed in order to change the minds of many.'

The sound of a single shot sang through the air. There was a moment of violet light and then the male Terrae evaporated into thin air; his body transformed into glistening white and purple particles. Anne watched as the powder settled itself onto Kabinov like confetti.

'Curious,' Kabinov said without emotion, rubbing at the power that had collected on his eyelashes. 'An unexpected reaction.'

'Moon Blink,' Anne whispered to herself in the darkness. 'He's covered in Moon Blink!'

'Anne?' Patricia asked.

'It's the Terrae, somehow they're the source of the Moon Blink. The dust...' Anne swallowed. She hadn't even considered it, but... 'It's them. Their ashes. That's what the Americans and Soviets found. The ashes of dead Terrae.'

'But, that's...' Patricia shuddered. 'It's horrible.'

Bill nodded grimly. 'To us, maybe. But to the Terrae?' He shrugged. 'They're alien. Who are we to judge?'

Bill was right, but still Anne felt... She wasn't sure. Disgusted, perhaps. Disgusted that humans had defiled the Terrae graveyard. 'What's Lethbridge-Stewart waiting for?' she asked, to take her mind off the disturbing thought.

'Give him a moment,' Bill said.

Anne looked back towards Kabinov. From what she had seen, he had most definitely ingested a vast amount of Moon Blink. More even than Bland. There was no way things would end well for Kabinov.

'The baby is unguarded,' she said. 'If I made a break for it I'm sure I could reach him.'

'No, Anne,' Bill said. 'The colonel can't show his hand now, not with the baby alone. We have to wait until the right moment or the baby could get caught in the cross fire.'

'Now, who I wonder, is to be next?' Kabinov asked, giving a relaxed sigh as if he was deciding what appetizer to select from a menu. 'I have an idea.' Idly, he made his way back towards the rock. 'What about this little *babushka* here?'

'Hold it right there,' Lethbridge-Stewart called out

through the darkness; strong and clear.

'Ah,' Kabinov said, a smile pulling at his lips. 'I wondered how long it would take you to show yourselves. My men warned me that we were being followed, I expected nothing less. I trust you have been enjoying the evening's entertainment?'

'Stand down, Kabinov!' Lethbridge-Stewart warned. 'We have you surrounded, there is no escape.'

'And you even know who I am. Well done. But, you see, this is where you are wrong,' Kabinov said, reaching up to rub his eyes again. 'What time have you had to get reinforcements?' He shook his head. 'No. Now, where is your delightful accomplice? The one who speaks my mother tongue? I would be most grateful to see her again. English is such an ugly language, but alas it seems to be the most widely used, for now at any rate. But soon we will have no use for Earth. Not when there are other moons just waiting to be colonised.'

'There is nothing you can do, Kabinov,' Lethbridge-Stewart continued steadily. 'There's no way out of this now.'

'Oh, I wouldn't be so sure about that. What is it Taras Shevchenko once wrote? Oh yes. *Don't envy anyone my friend / For if you look you'll find / That there's no heaven on the earth / No more than in the sky*.' Kabinov placed the gun to his temple. 'I have always wanted to go to the Moon,' he said dreamily. 'In the old country the Moon was so large on summer nights it was as if I could climb onto her back from the lake house. Perhaps now I can.'

'What are you doing, man?'

Kabinov smiled. 'You have seen what happens when the Terrae die? They dissolve into what the British have quaintly called Moon Blink. They float on the breeze, into the air, back to the Moon.'

'You're not Terrae,' Lethbridge-Stewart pointed out.

'I am now,' Kabinov said, rubbing at the Moon Blink that had settled all over him. 'Pure, unfiltered, and I will return to the Moon. And from there…'

Anne and Patricia turned away as the sound of the single shot rang out through the silent night air.

Without their leader, Kabinov's men didn't seem so confident alone with the Terrae. Anne heard them call out to one another in Russian as they raced back to their vehicles and sped off into the night.

'The baby!' Patricia gasped.

The two of them turned to see Baby B quite happily waving his hands in the air. Patricia rose to her feet and ran across to him, taking him up in her arms. Anne and Bill watched from a distance as Patricia held him close to her. It looked to Anne as if she never wanted to let him go.

'What about him? What about the baby?' Anne turned from Patricia and the baby, towards the Terrae, who were still standing motionless just as Kabinov had ordered them. 'Why don't they come and take him?'

'I don't know,' Bill admitted.

'Then I think one of us is going to have to ask them.'

Anne closed her eyes and before Bill could stop her she emptied the packet of Moon Blink with one gulp. It fizzed for a moment on her tongue, rather like sherbets she had enjoyed as a child.

Everything else began to fade away. Bill, Patricia… Only the figures in front of her remained, their pale skin shimmering, the crevices in their faces becoming more and more defined as the Moon Blink began to absorb into her system and take hold. There was only one man in their midst now. He stepped forward, holding out his hand for Anne to take.

'I come in peace,' Anne said slowly. 'I do not wish to harm you.'

The man looked at her, his eyes blinking slowly.

'My friend and I,' she told him in the ancient language of the Terrae, 'we have been guarding this child and keeping him safe, you have our word we would do the same for you, all of you. But I need your help. Who are the parents of this child?'

'He has no parents, not in the way that you humans would understand it to be. That is not how it works for the Terrae. We are all from one world or another, whether it is yours or a different host planet. We cannot help you. The only way now is for us to disappear, become one of you. Only then shall we be truly safe.'

'But I don't understand,' Anne said. 'I thought you could not return to the Moon without one another, that if you were apart for too long you would expire?'

The Terrae smiled at her. 'You misunderstand. We cannot all return unless we are in the same place and can complete our circuit. But he was the youngest taken, a special kind. Our ancestors have enabled you to see us but it was not always that way.'

Ancestors. He meant the dead, the source of the Moon Blink. 'Where are your women?' Anne asked.

'Only one or two were taken. We feared our abduction from our home planet and advised them to remain hidden in the craters. This war is not for them to fight. Now that your friend holds Brayn Dun,' the Terrae said, gesturing towards Patricia who was rocking Baby B in her arms, 'we can return home. Our kind will leave your planet forever and you will not be disturbed.'

Lethbridge-Stewart joined her side. 'Will you translate for me, Miss Travers?'

'Of course,' Anne said. 'Anything you want me to say.'

'I hope you will not take him as the primary example of our race,' Lethbridge-Stewart said, pointing towards Kabinov's dead form. 'Or Mr Bland. There are others on Earth who wish you no harm, and have sacrificed greatly so that you may return to your home.'

Anne translated for him, surprised by his words. She wasn't sure she'd ever hear Lethbridge-Stewart be so diplomatic about an alien race. Something had changed, but was it something in him, or his orders? Anne hoped the former, but she rather suspected the latter.

The Terrae smiled knowingly, then nodded their understanding as they made soft grunting noises between them.

'Where will you go?' Anne asked.

'We shall return to the lunar surface,' the Terrae replied. 'It will be as if this never happened. The cycle of the Moon sees many changes.'

'But what about...' *What did the Terrae call him? Oh yes.* 'What about Brayn Dun?' Anne asked.

The Terrae eyed him with large sad pupils. 'He cannot return with us any longer.'

'Why?'

'He has been on Earth too long. His organs are only

singular now. He does not have the reserves to make the journey back to the lunar surface. Soon he will need sustenance and human food. His growth will accelerate for a short time, but soon it will be as if he were a normal human child. There is nothing left that we can provide for him.'

As if on cue, the baby began to mew softly, a sound that quickly escalated into a full-blown scream. Patricia bounced him and soothed him.

The Terrae pointed towards Patricia. 'We choose her,' he said softly. 'She is to be the mother of our son.'

'Your son?'

'Yes. He will be the first of our kind to be raised on Earth. Something good must come from all this evil. Those who have been lost, their lives must not have been in vain.'

'Are you sure you want him to stay on Earth?' Anne said, looking across at Patricia and the baby. Surely she couldn't have heard them correctly.

The head of the Terrae stepped forwards, his hand resting on Patricia's shoulders. 'We choose you to care for him,' he said. 'The doctor who set us free.'

'What is he saying, Anne?' Patricia asked.

'He says that they want to return the favour. Now it is their turn to learn about our kind.'

'But she must make a promise,' the leader of the Terrae said.

'What is it?' Anne said. 'We will do all that we can.'

'The boy must never know his true identity. It would be too painful, and I would not choose that fate for him. I have had no decision in much that has happened to us, but I will do all I can to protect my people, and especially our one and only son. Raise him so that he might make a difference to your planet. We will watch down on him always, just as your mother does for you.'

The Terrae began to walk away.

'Wait!' Anne called after them. 'What was that about my mother?'

But it was too late. The Moon was rising into the sky and stars were sprinkling their way across the inky horizon. Anne blinked. The Terrae were gone.

For a short while they all stood there, and then, like a switch was flicked, Lethbridge-Stewart and Bill set about discussing back up and the unenviable task of removing Kabinov's now lifeless form.

Anne's attention was drawn to the road where she could see two dim headlights approaching up ahead. She turned back to look for Lethbridge-Stewart and Bill but they were both preoccupied, and Patricia was now some way away engrossed with the baby in her arms.

As the car drew closer, Anne turned back then she began to relax. She had recognised it immediately. Leaving the other three behind her, she made her way down towards the roadway before the car could draw up any further. The driver inside saw her coming and instantly rolled to a halt.

'I wondered when I would be seeing you again,' Anne said good-naturedly as she stood by the driver's side, the window wound down.

'Hello again, Doctor Travers,' Charlie said. 'I couldn't resist following up on the story.'

Anne could see he was a little miffed that she had spotted him so quickly. 'You seem very good at following people,' she noted. 'Are you sure you wouldn't prefer a career as a private investigator?'

'I think I will stick with journalism for now,' Charlie said, doing his best to peer over her shoulder to get a good look at the scene behind her. 'I also wanted to apologise for what happened at the restaurant.'

Anne nodded. 'It's okay,' she said. 'I found another supply, and it helped me sort things out. I'm afraid you've missed all the action,' she added, following his gaze.

Charlie got out of the car and closed the door behind him. 'Then you won't mind if I take a quick look around?' he asked hopefully, giving her what he no doubt imagined was a winning smile.

'Fine,' Anne agreed, confident that there was nothing left to see. 'But not with that.'

She pointed to the camera slung around his neck. Charlie opened his mouth to protest but then shut it again. Instead he took it from around his neck and deposited it back through the open car window and onto the driver's seat.

'Come along then,' Anne said. 'Follow me.'

Charlie stayed close behind her as she led him back towards the others.

'What happened here?' he asked, his voice betraying his disappointment that he hadn't quite made it in time.

'You know I can't tell you that,' Anne said solemnly. Then as they walked, Charlie gave a gasp. 'What is it?' Anne asked, the sound making her jump. Charlie lifted his finger and pointed to her.

'Yours eyes!'

'My eyes?' Anne echoed. 'What about my eyes?'

'Your eyes!' Charlie said again. 'That must mean that they got to you too, didn't they?'

Anne turned away, blinking hard. Now that the Terrae were gone and there was no use for the Moon Blink powder any longer she had forgotten how strange she must look to a casual observer.

'Yes, I rather suppose they did,' she said softly, continuing to rub at her eyes gently.

Charlie quickened his pace so that he was now standing in front of her, halting Anne in her tracks.

'We are the lucky ones to get to see them you know, Doctor Travers,' he said breathlessly. 'I know you don't trust me completely and that's fine, but please know I've been where you are. I've had strange and amazing encounters too and all I want to do – all I ever wanted to do – was to find out the truth.'

Anne listened to him in contemplative silence. She could see Lethbridge-Stewart had spotted them now and was looking across at her curiously. Charlie continued to stare at Anne hopefully; he was willing her to give him a chance. Finally, she gave her response.

'You know what I'm going to say next, don't you, Mr Redfern?'

Charlie bit his lip and nodded, his long hair flopping across his earnest face. 'I think you're about to tell me that the story of my career is going to become so top secret and classified that it will be as if it never happened at all?'

'Quite right.'

'All right,' he said reluctantly. Then his face brightened. 'But you won't forget about me will you? I mean, in the future. I can't imagine this is the last time that we're going to be involved in something wonderful together.'

In the distance, Anne could see Patricia and the baby.

The Moon Blink in her eyes made the baby seem to glow and sparkle like a jewel.

'Good night, Mr Redfern,' she said, turning back to Charlie. 'It shouldn't take you long to get back home. There's a full Moon tonight.'

'But will I see you again soon?'

'We'll see.'

Charlie's face broke into a broad grin and he headed back towards his car.

'Who was that?' Patricia asked, joining Anne. 'He doesn't look familiar.'

'Just a new acquaintance,' Anne said dismissively. They both watched his car purr into life and then drive off into the night. 'A story for another time, Pat. More importantly, how is he doing?'

As if on cue, the baby in Patricia's arms began to stir and she quickly hushed him back to sleep again. 'I can't believe after everything, that they didn't take the baby,' Patricia said to Anne as she continued to soothe his cries, looking down at the bundle in her arms.

'They want you to care for him,' Anne said. 'Something good to come from all the bad that has taken place.'

Patricia looked uneasy.

'What is it, Patricia?'

'I just can't believe that they really chose me. Me? But I don't know the first thing about raising a baby!'

'Perhaps your sister and her husband can be of some help? Didn't you say there was someone back home waiting for you?'

'Oh yes, my man in customs,' Patricia said with a smile.

'He's a Brit in any case, so at least he's on the right side of the Atlantic. That is if we choose to stay here.' She gave a light laugh. 'You won't believe what his surname is.'

Anne was too tired to guess. 'Go on.'

'Richards.'

'Like Cliff?'

Patricia nodded. 'Like me... That will make things easier, you know, if...' She let out a giddy laugh. 'Oh, listen to me. I feel so mixed up, I don't know what to do.' She shook her head.

Lethbridge-Stewart approached them. 'Corporal Bishop is taking my car to Little Gaddesden to call in the local constabulary. They can help me take care of Kabinov. What remains of him at any rate.'

Anne nodded and then turned away. She stared back up silently at the Moon, wondering if the Terrae had already completed their journey home. She became aware of Bill hovering at her side.

'What will happen to you now?' Bill asked trying, and not succeeding, to sound less anxious than he felt.

'To me?' Anne said. 'I'm fine, it's Patricia I'm worried about.'

'I mean after taking the Moon Blink,' Bill clarified. 'We all saw what happened to Bland back at the lab. As for Kabinov, he killed himself because of the Moon Blink. You won't start to lose your marbles like that will you?'

'I should think not!' Anne bristled. 'The Moon Blink will degrade. It will lose its power by the first night of the new Moon, so there is really nothing to be concerned about.'

'Ah. Good to know,' Bill said, his face revealing the relief he felt. Then he pointed towards Patricia and the baby.

'They look natural together don't they? Sort of as if it was somehow meant to be.'

Anne nodded. 'I hope so,' she said quietly. Leaving Bill behind her, she made her way back to her friend. Patricia turned to her with a smile, Brayn Dun reaching out with podgy fists to grasp at the strands of her dark hair that had come loose.

'I'm so sorry, Patricia,' Anne said softly.

Patricia stared at her in surprise. 'Whatever for?' she said.

'You came to me for help and I failed you,' Anne replied.

'No you didn't! If anything, you and your friends have given me the most wonderful gift. Now I have the family I always wanted,' Patricia said. 'Maybe it's not quite how I imagined it would be when I used to play house as a kid, but that's because it's so much better than that. I mean, look at him.' She gazed down at him lovingly. 'He was going to end up as some experiment and now he is going to have the most wonderful life, and it's all thanks to you, Anne.'

'Come along,' Lethbridge-Stewart said rallying them both. 'I'm afraid it isn't safe for you to stay out here any longer. You must leave before the baby attracts any further unwanted attention. Bishop, take Miss Travers and Doctor Richards with you. I'm sure Mrs Postlethwaite will dote on the baby,' he added, with a touch of distaste.

Anne looked at Bill, who shook his head. 'Long story for another time,' he said quietly, so Lethbridge-Stewart couldn't hear him. 'Come on, let's get the baby somewhere warm.'

— EPILOGUE—

Sitting in the kitchen of her cosy bungalow it seemed to Anne Travers that the past week or so had been little more than a strange dream from which she had now finally awoken.

She heard footsteps crunching up the driveway and went to meet her guests at the door.

'Good morning, Miss Travers,' Lethbridge-Stewart greeted her, Bill Bishop standing behind him, both in uniform. After the last week she had almost forgotten that seeing them out of uniform was the exception, not the rule. 'How are you feeling this morning?'

'Fine,' Anne said curtly. Lethbridge-Stewart had information for her and she was anxious to hear it. 'How are Patricia and Brendon?' she asked, using the Anglicised version of his name which she had insisted upon. 'Did they get to safety? I do wish you had let me come with you.'

'It was for the best, Anne,' Bill reassured her. 'The less people who know where they are, the best chance there is to keep them safe until the dust settles on this.'

Anne looked out of the window across the wild moors. She remembered how enamoured Patricia had been that first night. She wouldn't be able to see either Patricia or Brendon for a while.

'Don't be too sad, Anne,' Bill said. 'What Patricia did was very brave. I've never known someone give up their life before to save an alien. It really is quite remarkable. And after all we've seen, it's nice to know not all aliens are bad.'

'Oh yes, I know that,' Anne said, though her tone wasn't as convincing as her words. 'It doesn't matter now. Pat and the baby are safe and that is all the matters. I have kept my promise to help Patricia and the Terrae, and that is all I can ask for.'

'I must admit I did rather enjoy the excitement of it all,' Bishop said. 'Was nice to be back in the field again.'

'I'm sure you'll be seeing more of that soon,' Lethbridge-Stewart said, not missing a beat. 'Which reminds me.' He reached into his jacket pocket and took out an envelope. 'I received something this morning that I think you shall find will affect us both. Partly why I drove all the way up here, actually.'

'What is it?' Anne asked.

'A telegram from General Hamilton.'

Her face fell for moment. It probably wouldn't be anything interesting, she reasoned to herself. More work to be done at the Vault she suspected. 'What does it say?' she asked a little half-heartedly.

Lethbridge-Stewart smiled knowingly. 'I will read it. *Dear Miss Travers. In light of current events it has been decided that your contract at the Vault has run its course. As I'm sure you are aware, your position there was only ever temporary until I could find a better use for your talents. And as a reward for the service you have provided, I hereby assign you to Dolerite Base as the Head of Scientific Research at the Home-Army Fifth Operation Corps.*'

'Reassign me?' Anne wanted to sound surprised at the

cheek of it, but she couldn't muster the will. She wasn't a soldier to be ordered about, but she was more than happy to leave the Vault. And, given the choice, she would much rather continue her research into alien technology with Lethbridge-Stewart running the show. And, of course, she would be working alongside Bill...

'What do you think?' Bill asked. 'It sounds like quite the opportunity.'

'Yes it does,' Anne said, still ruminating the prospect. 'I just can't imagine taking up any opportunity at the moment. Everything seems to be upside down somehow. I hardly know where to begin.'

'We all miss her,' Bill said. 'The baby too. It hasn't been the same without them.'

'Do you think he really will be all right?'

'He is protected by the best in the country. He will come to no harm, neither will Doctor Richards,' Lethbridge-Stewart said.

'But do you really think he will be able to survive a life here on Earth? He is an alien after all. How can he ever really fit into our world?'

'History defines a man, Miss Travers,' Lethbridge-Stewart said. 'However this little boy is raised, it will not erase the fact of where he has come from and who he has been before. We cannot escape our past or who we are, however much we may try.'

'Is that supposed to make me feel better?' Anne asked. 'If so, it isn't working.'

Bill stepped forward, smiling. 'Let me try, sir.' He took her to the window. 'Now, here we see the Moon.'

'Yes, thank you for that,' Anne quipped.

'The dark side of the Moon, reflectance – there is always light in the dark.'

'I'm not sure I follow, Bill. Are you trying to persuade me to take this job or not?'

'Of course the decision is to be entirely your own,' Lethbridge-Stewart said behind them, his tone light but stern. He knew, like she did, that she had little choice. Hamilton had drafted her; it was not a request. 'I shouldn't wish to coerce you in any way,' Lethbridge-Stewart continued, 'but listen carefully. We all have a duty and what has happened these last few days does not change facts. You are an exemplary scientist, and however long it takes for you to get back in the field that is where you belong. And our experiences together tell me that you will take up a new post, whether it is this one or another. But it would certainly be a shame to see you turn this down. You are the perfect candidate, and I for one cannot imagine another.'

Anne was taken aback. Such openness from Bill she could accept, but from Lethbridge-Stewart? Perhaps Sally was having an effect on him? Inside Anne scolded herself. She was being facetious. He was many things, and chief among them was a good man. He may rub her up the wrong way at times, but that changed nothing. Lethbridge-Stewart was honourable, and he needed her.

'I've made my decision. Shouldn't we get back to work?' Anne said quickly, not wanting to dwell on the topic any further.

'Ah yes,' Lethbridge-Stewart said, with a slight smile of thanks to Anne for not extending the moment of awkwardness. 'The contents of that telegram should tell you where to go next. The Vault is behind you now, Miss

Travers, and the Fifth Operational Corps is waiting for us. I'll expect you to report to me at Chelsea Barracks tomorrow.'

Tomorrow? Anne thought. Well, perhaps that was for the best. She would certainly be glad to see the back of the Vault for a while.

Lethbridge-Stewart and Bill wished her good evening and then made their way towards the parked car. Anne watched from the window as Bill glanced back. A wry smile creeping across her lips.

'Well, this should be interesting,' she said.

ACKNOWLEDGEMENTS

A huge thank you to the team at Candy Jar for giving me the opportunity to write *Moon Blink,* and for their support throughout the journey, especially Andy Frankham-Allen for his tireless editing know-how.

I would also like to say thank you to my husband, Jon, for letting me write during Christmas, New Year and our honeymoon!

Most importantly, I would also like to thank all the fans who continue to welcome me into the fold and share their thoughts, memories and experiences with me.

Character Profiles

(An Unofficial Guide)

Alistair Lethbridge-Stewart

Cry Havoc...

Alistair Lethbridge-Stewart was born in the Cornish village of Bledoe on February 22nd, 1929. As he grew up, young Alistair found himself resentful of the idea of military service due to, firstly, his paternal grandfather (after whom he was named) insisting Alistair should one day enter military service himself, and secondly, because his father's career in the Royal Air Force constantly kept him away during important moments in Alistair's young life. Shortly after his ninth birthday, Alistair lost his brother to a tragic accident, when James fell into Golitha Falls and drowned. This tragedy was compounded in 1945 when Alistair's father was reported missing in action. Both these events led to his mother taking him away from Bledoe for good, although during the journey to Lancashire both he and his mother totally forgot about the existence of James.

His resistance to the military continued into young adulthood, and he intended to pursue a career in teaching, but he was drafted for National Service during the Korean War. As a private in the Signals he was held as a prisoner in a temporary Chinese prison camp. He met 2nd Lieutenant Spencer Pemberton of the Parachute Infantry, and the friendship they built up during that time led Lethbridge-Stewart to a new appreciation for military service. He was breveted as a 2nd lieutenant during the war. After his National Service, he placed himself on the waiting list for Sandhurst Military Academy. His mother was initially concerned about this career change, but soon realised Alistair was doing this for his father as much as himself. In 1954 he enrolled in Sandhurst and trained to be an officer. He graduated bestowed with the Sword of Honour and Queen's Award for being the most outstanding cadet on his course. During his Sandhurst days, he was one of the 'holy trinity' that included fellow cadets Walter Douglas and Leslie Johnston. These cadets caught the eye of Brigadier Oliver Hamilton at Sandhurst, and he continued to follow Lethbridge-Stewart's career. Alistair and Douglas remained in contact, while Johnston went a different way, led by a totally different ideology to Lethbridge-Stewart and Douglas. As a 2nd lieutenant in the Scots Guards, in 1956, he met Sergeant Samson Ware, and encountered a young woman called Pearl Hammond, a barmaid on the Kentish Coast. Despite what his platoon said, nothing romantic happened between them, although he didn't dissuade his men from thinking otherwise.

While Hamilton rose in the ranks, so too did Lethbridge-Stewart, with Hamilton sponsoring him all the way. In 1968 he met Doris Bryden in Brighton, where they had a weekend fling. They kept in touch for a few weeks after, but his duties soon got in the way. Nine months later, unknown to Lethbridge-Stewart, Doris gave birth to a son she called Albert. Later that year, while stationed briefly at Aldgate, Lethbridge-Stewart was introduced to Corporal Sally

Wright of the Women's Royal Army by Douglas. The two hit it off quickly and began dating. Lethbridge-Stewart wasn't too bothered about dating someone in the Forces, since Sally was stationed at Fugglestone as adjutant to Hamilton. Their responsibilities were unlikely to clash.

This all changed, however, in February 1969 when Lethbridge-Stewart was pulled from manoeuvres in Libya to help out in London at the behest of Colonel Pemberton, now an officer in the Parachute Regiment's Special Forces Support, when it was surrounded by a strange mist. While Pemberton commanded forces in Central London, Lethbridge-Stewart handled things on the outer edge of the mist. Until Pemberton was killed while 'escorting' Professor Travers across London. Lethbridge-Stewart made his way to Goodge Street, but his team was killed in an ambush and he found himself lost in the Underground. He arrived at Goodge Street to take command, and along the way bumped into the Doctor.

They did not have the most auspicious of starts to their relationship, with Lethbridge-Stewart initially suspicious of the impish little man. But the Doctor soon proved his worth, and the seeds of their friendship were formed when Lethbridge-Stewart placed his trust, not to mention the safety of his men, in the Doctor's hands. He was highly doubtful of the Doctor's claims about a time machine, but Professor Travers seemed to believe the Doctor, so as it was expedient to do likewise, Lethbridge-Stewart accepted the Doctor's claims. After their defeat of the Great Intelligence, Lethbridge-Stewart considered the Doctor a hero, but the Doctor disappeared after he learned that reporter Harold Chorley wanted to make him a household name.

Lethbridge-Stewart was given command of the clean-up by Hamilton, and stationed himself at London Regiment Offices in Battersea. Douglas was assigned to take over from him, while Lethbridge-Stewart and Sally were due to take some much needed leave. That never happened, however, since Lethbridge-Stewart followed the trail of dead-soldier, Staff Sergeant Arnold, back to Bledoe. There he faced off against the Great Intelligence again – from the distant future – and discovered the truth about James. His brother was possessed by the future Intelligence in 1938, which then killed him and removed all memory of him from Lethbridge-Stewart and his mother. He also learned that James was born with an immortal soul, which was later reincarnated in Owain Vine, a seventeen-year-old in Bledoe – the soul would eventually be reincarnated and ascend to become the Great Intelligence. Lethbridge-Stewart reconnected with his childhood friends, Ray and Henry, and bonded with Owain; they decided to look at each other as uncle and nephew.

These events convinced Lethbridge-Stewart even more of the need for a special taskforce to deal with aliens, but Hamilton vetoed it, claiming the British Armed Forces weren't ready for such a thing yet – and no, he couldn't approach the United Nations Security Council about it, either. Hamilton agreed to look into things, while Lethbridge-Stewart looked for more concrete evidence of aliens. He was officially stationed at Chelsea Barracks, and assigned Lance Corporal Bishop, who had helped him in Bledoe. It was at this point, the end of March 1969 that he became engaged to Sally. He intended to go to Tibet, but his plane crashed en route and he ended up in an alternative version of Earth, ten years in the past. Drugged, he became convinced he was in a faux-English village in East Germany, but found that hard to tally with meeting an adult version of James. He returned to his own England, and only later, in conversation with Anne Travers, learned the truth of what had happened. Further evidence of time travel came his way on Fang Rock, when first Owain and Bishop were sent back to 1902, and then Anne was transported back to 1823. He learned about the war between the Rutan Host and the Sontaran. Hamilton sent him to meet with Vice Air Marshal Gilmore, who revealed to Lethbridge-Stewart the truth about the Doctor's involvement over the last couple of decades and of the Home-Army Fourth Operational Corps. Together they uncovered a secret bunker beneath London, owned by the Vault and run by Lieutenant Leslie Johnston. After the incident with the Dominators and Dominex, Lethbridge-Stewart and Hamilton had enough evidence to put together a secret military force, the Fifth Operational Corps, to protect the UK from alien threats. They were supported by Gilmore and Peter Grant, on behalf of the Ministry of Defence, and received private funding from industrialist Peyton Bryden.

Becoming the Brigadier...

Four years or so after his first encounter with the Intelligence, Brigadier Lethbridge-Stewart was married to Fiona, and they had a three-year-old daughter, Kate. He was assigned as the first commander of the United Kingdom branch of the newly-formed UNIT; the United Nations Intelligence Taskforce, created after Lethbridge-Stewart and Peter Grant approached the Security Council. Part of

Lethbridge-Stewart's orders were, should the Doctor return, he had to obtain his services; much was still unknown about the Doctor, but Hamilton preferred him to help UNIT than other agencies. All information about the Fifth had to be kept, deliberately, from the Doctor. Lethbridge-Stewart wasn't keen on playing dumb, after all he trusted the Doctor, but he had his orders. The Doctor was not to know that the Fifth was really behind UNIT's UK operations.

It was while UNIT were investigating the strange goings-on at International Electromatics, run by industrialist Tobias Vaughn, that the Doctor and Jamie stumbled into things. They were spotted by UNIT surveillance, and brought immediately to a reunion with Lethbridge-Stewart. It was a happy meeting, and Lethbridge-Stewart enlisted the Doctor's help, as per his orders, to prevent the invasion of the Cybermen. Following this, the Doctor left, and Lethbridge-Stewart was debriefed by Hamilton and was told to draft in a scientific advisor; Lethbridge-Stewart wanted Anne, but she was too connected with the Fifth and it was felt her involvement with UNIT would compromise the secret nature of the Fifth. After months of interviews, Lethbridge-Stewart drafted Doctor Elizabeth Shaw as UNIT's scientific advisor.

Freshly regenerated by the Time Lords and exiled to Earth, the Third Doctor was not initially accepted by Lethbridge-Stewart, who didn't believe him to be the same man. After encountering shape-shifting aliens before, it was an understandable reaction, however the Doctor clearly knew him. He gradually warmed to the new Doctor, who was somewhat brusque towards Lethbridge-Stewart, dismissing him with a wave at one point. Once the first

Nestene invasion was defeated Lethbridge-Stewart, upon orders from Hamilton, quickly asked the Doctor to stick around in case the Nestene tried again. The Doctor became UNIT's official, although unpaid, scientific advisor, with Liz serving as his assistant.

The Doctor remained for several years, even after his exile was rescinded, and over that time an extremely strong friendship developed between the two men. It took some time, however, since the easy companionship Lethbridge-Stewart and the Second Doctor enjoyed was gone, replaced by a Doctor that was less forgiving of Lethbridge-Stewart's military mind-set. One of the most notable early examples of them coming to loggerheads was over the solution of the Silurian problem at Wenley Moor. Once the Doctor and Liz had successfully beaten the Silurian plague, he wished to broker a peace between humanity and the Silurians (the original owners of the Earth), but as soon as his back was turned, Lethbridge-Stewart set off charges and destroyed the Silurian hibernation settlement beneath the moor; the Doctor considered this possibly genocide, or at the very least murder. Their relationship remained strained for a short while afterwards, but still stranded on Earth the Doctor continued in his role as scientific advisor. Things came to a head once more after Project Inferno was halted, when the Doctor decided he was leaving Earth, having seemingly got the TARDIS console working again. He made a point of saying he would not miss Lethbridge-Stewart, but when the console fetches up at a nearby rubbish tip, he returned with his tail between his legs. Lethbridge-Stewart took great pleasure in reminding the Doctor of his harsh words before agreeing to help. This pretty much encapsulated their relationship for the next few years – two men who had a grudging respect for each other, but were not quite friends.

Owing Peter Grant a favour, the Brigadier assigned his niece, Jo, to the Doctor. When the Doctor wanted rid of her, the Brigadier refused to accept the responsibility of telling her, and told him if the Doctor wished to 'sack' Miss Grant he would have to tell her himself. The arrival of Jo mellowed the Doctor and smoothed relations between him and the Brigadier. It was shortly after the incident at Devil's End that Lethbridge-Stewart's marriage failed, because of the secrets he was keeping, and Fiona left him. He was determined that he would never be married again; his work did not allow for successful relationships – first Sally had died, and then Fiona had left him. In the years that followed Lethbridge-Stewart would have a very distant relationship with his daughter.

By the time Jo made known her intentions to leave UNIT (and the Doctor) to get married, the friendship between the Doctor and the Brigadier was strong enough to keep the Doctor attached to UNIT, even though he had no reason to remain behind any more.

When the Doctor learned of the Brigadier's tryst with Doris in Brighton, he ribbed the Brigadier, who took it well, even though he was embarrassed by such private information being revealed. He became used to the Doctor's sporadic trips in the TARDIS, especially once Sarah joined him, and was more amused than annoyed when the newly regenerated Fourth Doctor departed abruptly rather than attend Buckingham Palace. Lethbridge-Stewart was there when the Doctor underwent his third regeneration; his reaction was a far cry from his protracted acceptance of the

Third Doctor. He merely raised an eyebrow and said, 'Well, here we go again'.

In the early 1980s, the Brigadier became heavily involved in the bureaucracy of UNIT business and spending an increasing amount of time away from direct command of UNIT UK. When the Doctor returned to stop the Kraal invasion, and deal with the Krynoids, UNIT was being commanded by two replacements while the Brigadier was away in Geneva. The Brigadier officially retired from military service in 1976 and took up teaching A-Level maths at Brendon Public School.

He met Tegan, a companion of the Doctor, in 1977 during the Queen's Silver Jubilee, and became involved in an adventure which saw him losing much of his memory – particularly in connection with the Doctor. He remembered his work with the Fifth, and UNIT, but nothing of the Doctor's involvement. The whole event was written off as a nervous breakdown. To help him regain his focus, he was asked by Brigadier Douglas to watch over Damon Vandervoorde, the son of a notorious London gangster, who was being placed at Brendon for protection. When the Fifth Doctor arrived at Brendon in 1983, the Brigadier totally failed to recognise him, despite the Doctor reminding him of their time at UNIT and his ability to regenerate. Eventually the Doctor jogged the Brigadier's memory, and he accompanied the Doctor on a ship stuck in a warp ellipse. There he met his younger self from 1977 and as they touched hands the Blinovitch Limitation Effect shortened out the time differential, causing the 1977-Brigadier to lose all memory of the Doctor.

Sometime later, while attending a reunion at UNIT HQ,

the Brigadier was visited by the Second Doctor. They were both time-scooped to the Death Zone on Gallifrey, where they had to find their way to the Dark Tower and Rassilon, the single greatest figure in Time Lord history. There the Brigadier encountered other incarnations of the Doctor, the Fifth, Third and First and was reacquainted with both Sarah and Tegan. He also took great pleasure in flooring the Master with a single punch, 'how nice to see you again,' no doubt taking out years of frustration at being beaten by him so many times during his UNIT days.

In the new year of 1990 he received a phone call from a young man claiming to be his son, and he reconnected with Doris, and slowly built up a relationship with their son, Albert. He was around for the birth of Albert's first son, named Conall. Family reconnections continued during the '90s when he finally made his peace with Kate, and met his first grandchild, Gordy – named after both the Brigadier and his own father. He gave up teaching and married Doris. It was during the 1990s that he helped the United Nations to implement new dating protocols to cover 1969 to 1989, after he discovered that those twenty years had been condensed into ten, with events overlapping, due to the continual visits of the Doctor in his damaged TARDIS.

In 1997 he was taken out of retirement by a call from Geneva telling him that the Doctor was back. Doris didn't want him to go, but the presence of the Doctor was the deciding factor. He had to go. He threw himself into the events at Carbury and rather enjoyed the adventure. After reading the report of Brigadier Bambera, he assumed his replacement was a man and was a little surprised to discover that *Winifred* Bambera was a woman. Although he didn't let any respect for the fairer sex get in the way. His awkwardness around women was emphasised in his initial bad handling of Ace, but they soon bonded over her love of explosives, and worked together to blow up King Arthur's spaceship. The Brigadier, an old hand at regeneration by now, was not slightly fazed by the Doctor's new appearance, recognising him immediately; 'who else would it be?' he asked with a smile. He single-handedly stood down the Destroyer, armed with only his faithful revolver and silver bullets. The Destroyer asked if the world can do no better than the Brigadier, to which he replied, 'Probably. I just do the best I can,' and pumped bullets into the Destroyer. The Doctor thought the Brigadier dead as result, and states how the Brigadier was supposed to die in bed, but the Brigadier waved it away.

Over the following years the Brigadier was made a Commander of the British Empire and became Sir Alistair. Shortly after that he took up a position as UNIT's special envoy, and was often sent overseas, especially to Peru, where he tended to get stuck quite a lot. Shortly after returning from Peru in 2008, he was debriefed by Major Kilburne and visited by a very old friend, Sarah Jane Smith. Although they hadn't seen each other in a long time, they still kept in contact and Sir Alistair often pulled strings at UNIT whenever Sarah needed help. By the time of Sarah's wedding, Sir Alistair was back in Peru and thus unable to attend, as he was when a faux funeral was arranged for the Doctor in 2010.

Tragedy finally stuck in December 2011. Illness took its toll and the Brigadier spent his final days in a nursing home, surrounded by his family. When the Eleventh Doctor made a phone call to speak to Sir Alistair early 2012, he discovered the old soldier had died peacefully in his bed, as the Seventh Doctor had previously anticipated. The nurse to whom the Doctor spoke informed him that Sir Alistair always talked of the Doctor, and kept a small glass of brandy ready for him.

Alistair Lethbridge-Stewart was survived by a wife, Doris, an ex-wife, Fiona, and two children, Albert and Kate. He also had five grandchildren; Gordon, son of Kate, a further unspecified offspring of Kate, and three children born of Albert and his wife; Conall, Nick and Marie.

The long-standing friendship between the Doctor and the Brigadier inspired Kate, who went on to be the lead scientist in UNIT (now renamed as the UNified Intelligence Taskforce). She forced the old organisation to reform with the scientists taking the lead and not the military. Kate finally met the Doctor sometime after her father's death. She explained why she changed UNIT, what her father had taught her, and how he had 'learned that from an old friend'. When they parted she told the Doctor that he really was as remarkable as her father said, and kissed him. 'A kiss from a Lethbridge-Stewart – that's new!' the Doctor said, beaming.

Just like her father, Kate continued a friendship with the Doctor, spanning several incarnations, and even met three different incarnations at the same time. The memory of her father was enough to convince the Zygons to sit down and discuss a peaceful solution to their attempted invasion of Earth in 2015. In 2016 Kate was rescued from a crashing UNIT plane by a Cyberman who was the resurrected form of her father (one of hundreds of dead people turned into

Cybermen by Missy, the latest incarnation of the Master). In a poignant moment, witnessed by Kate, the Doctor finally saluted the Brigadier, before the cybernised version of the old soldier flew away to... who knows.

Anne Travers

Her Story So Far...

Anne Travers was born October 28th 1938 to Edward and Margaret Travers.

The Goffs, Anne's maternal ancestors, were very much dominated by the male gender; eccentrics all of them, which is why both Anne and her mother pushed against such eccentricities and became very straight-laced women, a trait Alun (Anne's elder brother) also held tight to. Anne is strong, determined, focused in the more real aspects of life. Edward Travers, however, became quite enamoured with his wife's family, and soon developed their eccentricities. Anne's mother, Margaret, died when Anne and her brother Alun were very young.

There was a long history of bad blood between the Travers and the Goffs, which only healed with the marriage of Edward and Margaret. However, it was a rift that never healed entirely, and to this day the Travers and Goffs have a fractious relationship. The source of the bad blood, which goes back to the early 1800s, was a mystery to both Anne and Alun until Anne travelled back to 1823 and met her ancestors, Archibald Goff and Jacob Travers.

Anne was highly qualified and experienced in a great

many fields, including some most scientists would have deemed errant nonsense. She also had a wide range of interests. Anne studied since her mid-teens. Her formal training was initially sponsored privately by her father, but she went on to study for several years in both the Victoria University of Manchester and Cambridge University. Prejudice in the male dominated world of science in the '60s often made things difficult for them, and more than once put a wall up in Edward's own professional path. This just made Anne more determined to excel, which she did in spades, gaining qualifications and experience in many subjects, and in one or two cases advancing fields with original research of her own.

Between 1964 and 1969, Anne travelled extensively, learning everything she could about different cultures and other views of science and the world. Anne, always an original thinker with real courage in her convictions, matured into a determined but pragmatic truth-seeker, primarily interested in enriching the world via new discoveries. For a time she worked in a think-tank in America alongside Doctor Gautam Jhaveri, and built a strong friendship with fellow scientist Patricia Richards.

She became interested in the idea of a family of her own, a husband and children, and realised she may well start one when she can figure out a way of integrating her personal and professional lives in a way she considers healthy and balanced. As such she has found herself looking around her for such a suitable husband.

After the events of The Web of Fear, Anne went to work at the Vault, studying the technology left over by the Great Intelligence. She was recommended by Major General

Hamilton, who secretly wanted a pair of eyes in the Vault to find out just what was really going on there. Over time she began to doubt the good she was doing there, growing suspect of the mysterious General who ran the Vault. She was, therefore, much relieved to be called into the field by Colonel Lethbridge-Stewart to assist him at Fang Rock. This afforded her a chance to spend more time with Corporal William Bishop, a man she considers husband material, although she's not even aware of this fact herself. While at Fang Rock she discovered her ancestors played a large part in the history of the lighthouse there, both in the 1820s and in 1902. She also made friends with a shape changing alien called a Rutan, and convinced it to make amends for the accidental death it had caused. She discovered that the Rutan, now calling itself Rupert Slant, still lived in 1969 and served as her family's solicitor. Later, when Patricia Richards arrived from America with an alien baby, Anne sought out Rupert Slant's help, only to discover that Rupert was now living as Ruby. Following this adventure, Anne knew she could no longer stomach the work at the Vault, and with Hamilton's agreement, she was pulled out of the Vault and assigned to the newly formed Home-Army Fifth Operational Corps, working as the Head of Scientific Research for Colonel Lethbridge-Stewart.

Juggling work with a private life is something Anne struggles with, and she is becoming increasingly concerned about her father's ailing health. Despite his reluctance, she is adamant that he move to Scotland with her...

William Bishop

Officer material...

William Bishop, is a highly trained junior officer of the Home-Army Fifth Operational Corps. As a person he's very laid back, with a very easy-to-get-along with attitude, which serves him well when welcoming new people into his life. He has a sharp, analytical mind, with an abundance of intellectual curiosity. He's a bit of a joker, happy to tease those he becomes close to, although with that comes a fierce loyalty. He's very focused on his military career, but knows that such focus only comes with the ability to be able to balance a healthy personal and social life aside it. As such he enjoys socialising with his friends, and paying regular visits to his various family members.

His maternal grandfather was an officer in the British Army and served in North Africa during World War II, while his father was enlisted to fight in 1943. Born in August 1945, Bishop was raised in a London recovering from war, where his father continued to make his living as a market-stall holder. As such he developed a healthy respect for community and giving to those in need. He is the third of four children; Samantha and Daniel being the eldest, with Michelle being the youngest. In 1965 he became an uncle to Samantha's first born, Dean. His parents still live in South London, while his siblings are now spread all over England. He was often teased because of his ginger hair growing up, but he refused to let it bother him, taking the insults on as a badge of honour instead. Thus the insult of 'ginge' became a nickname among him and his friends. It still remains so, with his childhood friends, even though through his teenage years his hair darkened into a chestnut brown. As a child he was always interested in science fiction, and took to reading science journals during his teen years. It was a practice he continued after enlisting with the British Army in 1963.

He joined the Royal Green Jackets at the age of eighteen. After a year of service, he was trained as a sniper. He was later trained as a medic. By 1969 he was stationed near Plymouth with 5 Battalion. During March of that year he was called in to assist the pile up on the A38 Liskeard Bypass, where he was assigned to Colonel Lethbridge-Stewart and helped in combating the Robot Yeti in Bledoe. He took everything in his stride, endearing himself to Lethbridge-Stewart. The colonel considered Bishop to be good officer material and decided Bishop would make a good addition to the special team he planned on building.

He returned to his regular duties, although he maintained contact with Anne Travers following events in Bledoe. He was under no allusions as to the reasons for the contact, at least for him; it was a romantic attraction. Anne took to calling him Bill in an attempt to tease the man who was fast becoming a good friend; secretly Bishop liked it – after all he was used to the name, as it was one his sister, Samantha, had always used, and his nephew called him Uncle Billy.

Late April saw him transferred to the Scots Guards by Major General Hamilton, ostensibly to serve as Lethbridge-Stewart's adjutant at Chelsea Barracks. He was granted a promotion to lance corporal, a rank still below the standard for an adjutant in the British Army. To facilitate a full commission as officer, Hamilton put him through the Mons Officer Cadet Training School. This he was to undertake while serving with Lethbridge-Stewart. All this was a part of his training for the soon-to-be-established Home-Army Fifth Operational Corps. As a result, he was the first NCO to be read into Lethbridge-Stewart's real mission at Chelsea Barracks – to find evidence of alien threats to the UK, giving Hamilton the leverage he needed to create the Fifth.

Bishop investigated the strange goings-on at Fang Rock, after stories of a falling star reached Lethbridge-Stewart's office. It was his idea to enlist the help of Anne Travers, and the three of them travelled to Fang Rock. There they uncovered the truth and came face to face with the shape-changing alien race, the Rutan Host. He was more than happy to be astral projected back in time, encouraging Owain to join him. It was during this time that he and Owain, Lethbridge-Stewart's nephew, started up a friendship. He witnessed the arrival of the Rutan on Fang Rock in 1902, and returned to help Lethbridge-Stewart fight another Rutan in the present. He was electrocuted during the fight, and suffered severe burns. While on Fang Rock his relationship with Anne developed extensively, the two of them drawing on a mutual, although unspoken, affection.

He was removed from active-duty for a short time, while

his injuries recovered, and given administrative work at the behest of Vice Air Marshal Gilmore. He was assigned to uncover and redact all files pertaining to the previous Home-Army Operational Corps and present the information to Lethbridge-Stewart. During this time, he was approached by Corporal Sally Wright, Lethbridge-Stewart's fiancée, to help uncover the colonel's whereabouts, but Bishop was unable to help.

He was, however, able to help Anne and her friend, Doctor Patricia Richards, when Patricia arrived from America with an alien baby. He was working directly for Hamilton at this time, while Lethbridge-Stewart was in Scotland, liaising with the Vault, where Anne was working. He assisted both Anne and Patricia in uncovering the truth about the baby, and latterly worked alongside Lethbridge-Stewart to bring down Administrator Bland and his unethical experiments on the Terrae, the original inhabitants of the moon.

Taking command...

Bishop completed his training at Mons by the beginning of September 1969, and was officially promoted to the officer rank of 2nd lieutenant and stationed at Dolerite Base, beneath Edinburgh Castle.

Over time the mutual affection between him and Anne developed into a full-blown romance, with their first formal date in March 1970, a year after they first met. They continued to work together, finding a perfect balance between official duties and their personal life.

By 1989 they were married, and Owain served as

Bishop's best man. Bishop had attained the rank of lieutenant colonel, and became second in command of the Operational Corps beneath Brigadier Douglas. He attended Lethbridge-Stewart's New Year party, and informed the retired officer that Anne was resuming her world travels with her father, who Bishop called Teddy. During the intervening years tragedy struck, which saw Owain in need of serious medical care. A tragic event in which Bishop had a hand, and for which he blamed himself.

During the 1990s Anne and he had a son, who they named Samuel after Bishop's eldest sibling.

As commander of the Operational Corps in the mid-2000s, Brigadier Bishop was one of the advisory board behind the integration of the Corps into UNIT. Once full integration had been finalised, and rebranding UNIT as the UNified Intelligence Taskforce in 2007, Bishop went on to be a military advisor for the World Security Council.

Available from Candy Jar Books

LETHBRIDGE-STEWART: THE FORGOTTEN SON
by Andy Frankham-Allen

For Colonel Alistair Lethbridge-Stewart his life in the Scots Guards was straightforward enough; rising in the ranks through nineteen years of military service. But then his regiment was assigned to help combat the Yeti incursion in London, the robotic soldiers of an alien entity known as the Great Intelligence. For Lethbridge-Stewart, life would never be the same again.

Meanwhile in the small Cornish village of Bledoe a man is haunted by the memory of an accident thirty years old. The Hollow Man of Remington Manor seems to have woken once more. And in Coleshill, Buckinghamshire, Mary Gore is plagued by the voice of a small boy, calling her home.

What connects these strange events to the recent Yeti incursion, and just what has it all to do with Lethbridge-Stewart?

"A solid start to the series. The Brigadier is such an integral part of Doctor Who mythos, it seems right and proper he now has his own series." – Doctor Who Magazine

ISBN: 978-0-9931191-5-6

Also available from Candy Jar Books

LETHBRIDGE-STEWART: THE SCHIZOID EARTH
by David A McIntee

Lethbridge-Stewart was supposed to be in the mountains of the east, but things didn't quite go according to plan. On the eve of war, something appeared in the sky; a presence that blotted out the moon. Now it has returned, and no battle plan can survive first contact with this enemy.

Why do the ghosts of fallen soldiers still fight long-forgotten battles against living men? What is the secret of the rural English town of Deepdene? Lethbridge-Stewart has good reason to doubt his own sanity, but is he suffering illness or injury, or is something more sinister going on?

Plagued by nightmares of being trapped in a past that never happened, Lethbridge-Stewart must unravel the mystery of a man ten years out of his time; a man who cannot possibly still exist.

"McIntee turns in a fine Who-based thriller that harkens back to the era in which it's set while also exploring ideas and concepts more modern. It's a fast paced tale that makes for a wonderful addition to this new series." – Warped Factor

ISBN: 978-0-9933221-1-2

Also available from Candy Jar Books

LETHBRIDGE-STEWART: BEAST OF FANG ROCK
by Andy Frankham-Allen
Based on a story by Terrance Dicks

Fang Rock has always had a bad reputation. Since 1955 the lighthouse has been out of commission, shut down because of fire that gutted the entire tower. But now, finally updated and fully renovated, the island and lighthouse is once again about to be brought back into service.

Students have gathered on Fang Rock to celebrate the opening of the 'most haunted lighthouse of the British Isles', but they get more than they bargained for when the ghosts of long-dead men return, accompanied by a falling star.

What connects a shooting star, ghosts of men killed in 1902 and the beast that roamed Fang Rock in 1823? Lethbridge-Stewart and Anne Travers are about to discover the answer first hand...

"With a story of ghostly recordings much in the style of Nigel Kneale's *Stone Tape*, Anne Travers rather steals the story and becomes the key character. Overall a good tale. Worth a read." – Starburst Magazine

ISBN: 978-0-9933221-7-4

LETHBRIDGE-STEWART: MUTUALLY ASSURED DOMINATION
by Nick Walters

The Dominators, the Masters of the Ten Galaxies, have come to Earth, and brought with them their deadly robotic weapons, the Quarks!

It's the summer of '69. Flower power is at its height, and nuclear power is in its infancy. Journalist Harold Chorley is out of work, and Colonel Alistair Lethbridge-Stewart is out of sorts. Dominex Industries are on the up, promising cheap energy for all. But people have started going missing near their plant on Dartmoor. Coincidence, or are sinister forces at work?

Join Lethbridge-Stewart and uneasy ally Harold Chorley as they delve into the secrets behind Dominex, and uncover a plan that could bring about the end of the world.

ISBN: 978-0-9933221-5-0

Available from Candy Jar Books

MARK BRAKE'S SPACE, TIME, MACHINE, MONSTER

Space, Time, Machine, Monster: Doctor Who Edition takes you on a journey into the science of *Doctor Who*.

Jam-packed with aliens, time machines, spaceships and lots of monsters, this book explores the secrets of the Universe's favourite Time Lord.

And, for an extra bit of fun, we present our own *Doctor Who* Top 10s on topics such as planets, companions, favourite stories and catchphrases!

So how does a Dalek poo? Let's find out!

ISBN: 978-0-9933221-3-6